Alma Rose

Edith Forbes

Seal Press

Series and cover design by Patrick David Barber
Text design by Laura Gronewold

Library of Congress Cataloging-in-Publication Data
Forbes, Edith, 1954-
Alma Rose / Edith Forbes.
1. Lesbians—Fiction. I. Title.
PS3556.0662A46   1993   813'.54—dc20   92-42985
ISBN: 1-58005-011-5

Printed in Canada
First Djuna Books edition, September 1998

10 9 8 7 6 5 4 3 2 1

Distributed to the trade by Publishers Group West
In Canada: Publishers Group West Canada, Toronto, Ontario
In the U.K. and Europe: Airlift Book Company, Middlesex, England
In Australia: Banyan Tree Book Company, Kent Town, S. Australia

To my mother Sal, with love

Alma Rose

Prologue

BY THE TIME ALMA ROSE CAME
to Kilgore, almost the only people who still lived here were
the ones who fed off the Interstate highway. Everyone else
had left. Most of downtown was boarded up. The going businesses were clumped around the on-off ramps of the highway, like ticks with their snouts burrowed into a vein. We
had a Pizza Hut, a Motel 6, a truck stop, three gas stations,
a Royal Comfort Inn and a Country Kitchen.

Once upon a time, when roads were smaller and
rougher, and people didn't travel so far so fast, Kilgore had
been a hub. It was a very small hub, but a hub nevertheless. It sat in the middle of several hundred square miles of
red-brown rocky buttes, scrub pines, sagebrush, dust, and
here and there enough tufts of grass to support a cow, if
she didn't mind a good lot of walking. The cows supported
ranches, and the ranches supported us, the people who

3

lived and worked "in town," meaning Kilgore.

Even when Kilgore was a hub, there wasn't much to it, about eight or ten stores and a corresponding number of bars. We had more than one street, however, and that made it a real town, unlike the numerous dots that appeared on road maps but were nothing more than a stretch of thirty-five-mile-an-hour speed limit bracketing a bar and a gas station.

I could remember only dimly the years before the Interstate was built. It came through when I was eight or nine. At first, the town greeted its arrival with the excitement of the early settlers greeting the stagecoach. Here was a messenger from the glamorous modern outside world. The cafe and gas station owners envisioned the swarms of Eastern tourists who would descend with wallets bulging. The shopkeepers stocked up on curios. All of us together reveled in how easy it was to travel the sixty-five miles to Seco Springs, the county seat, which was almost a small city with its ten thousand people, two movie theaters, bowling alley, roller skating rink and full scale rodeo grounds.

For a while, the Interstate brought strangely little change. Tourists did not swarm into Kilgore. The novelty of city entertainment soon wore off. People settled back into life the way it had been before. The change, when it did come, crept up on us so slow we didn't notice at first. It began, probably, with a few lean years in the cattle market. Feeling pinched, the ranchers found it worth their while to drive the sixty-five miles to buy their feed and supplies from the bigger, cheaper companies in Seco Springs. Once they had driven all that way, they bought clothing and groceries, too. The Kilgore Ranch Supply was the first business to shut down. Then Dan's Western Wear closed, and then the supermarket, and then some others. About the same time, some corporate executives must have cruised out the Interstate for a vacation in the Rockies. When they saw those signs reading "Next Services 65 Miles," they saw dollar signs. Before we knew it, we had a half dozen huge lighted plastic signs in bright trademark colors, each on a pole higher than the last, beckoning the weary drivers off the highway. To Eastern travelers, numbed by hundreds of miles of apparently empty landscape, they must have looked like beacons of welcome to a familiar harbor.

The landscape probably did seem empty, seen at high speed from the Interstate. Unlike the old state highways, the Interstate did not trace the paths of human settlement. In this country, settlement meant water, and the old roads followed the meandering route of the occasional stream bed. The Interstate was more like a county boundary, a line on a map. The planners decided which towns were large enough to warrant an exit, and then charted a compass course between them, heedless of inhabitants or topography unless those things presented a difficulty in engineering. Kilgore was barely big enough to meet their exit criteria, but it was the only town bigger than a dot for fifty miles in either direction, so the Interstate came through.

After that first cluster of bright plastic signs arrived, the town settled into more or less a steady state. Those businesses scooped up all the people who could be pulled off the highway by the sheer distance to the next accommodation. We had no other enticements, natural or man-made, that might increase their numbers. We had no Custer Battlefield, no prehistoric cliff dwellings, no Reptile Gardens, no Wall Drug, no caverns or waterfalls, no abandoned gold mines, no cowboy museum, nothing at all that the town could splash onto a billboard as a promise of relief from the monotony that lay between Kilgore and the Mississippi River.

Only two businesses still survived in what had been downtown Kilgore. One was the Cloverleaf Donut Hole, which was run, almost single-handedly, by Marge Gorzalka. Probably she had never sat down to calculate what her hourly wage would be if she divided her small profits by the hours she worked, 4 A.M. to 3 P.M. six days a week. Probably she did not want to know. If she had ever made the calculation, she would have had to face the fact that she made less money than the high school girls working at the Pizza Hut.

She had run the Donut Hole for almost thirty years, at least as long as I could remember. Nearly everyone who worked in town would stop in there sometime during the day, for breakfast or a coffee break or lunch. Every year there were a few less people who worked in town, so every year Marge earned a little less money.

"If the only way I can make a living is to put on a paper hat and hand out pre-fab pizzas to tourists and truck drivers, I'd just as soon go and have the vet put me to sleep," she said. She said the same thing, though not always in the same words, about once a quarter, when she had to do her books. I knew Marge pretty well, since I was one of her few remaining regulars. I came in every day at one-thirty for coffee and a sandwich. The coffee and I would arrive at the counter simultaneously, and then she would say, "Afternoon, Pat. The usual?"

Most days I nodded, turkey and cheese on brown bread, and coleslaw. Sometimes I asked for ham instead, or a cheeseburger, and then Marge would smile and bustle around, as if it were a special occasion.

For the half hour while I was eating, Marge filled up the space with conversation, mostly the news she had heard from the other regulars who came in earlier in the day. She asked one ritual question, "How's business at the Mercantile?" and I answered, "Not bad." Other than that, she didn't expect any talk from me.

I was known as quiet. Over the years, that reputation had grown to be a comfortably untroublesome niche. No one expected me to say anything, so I didn't. People liked me well enough without my saying anything. If I spoke up now, it could only change their opinion for the worse.

I worked at the other surviving downtown business, the Kilgore Mercantile, which was a three syllable name for what was basically a gas station and grocery store. We kept a few shelves of clothing, hardware and sporting goods, but these mostly collected dust and created extra work at inventory time. The groceries and beer brought in the income.

Pops, my father, owned the store, so I had job security if nothing else. The two of us split the hours it was open. He worked mornings and I worked evenings. During the day we had a couple of part-time stock clerks and a cashier to help out, but after six-thirty I had the place to myself.

Though he was free to leave when I came, Pops often hung around until supper time, and sometimes all the way to closing. After Mom died, he didn't have any particular reason to go home. He was a jokester and a storyteller, and he did not like to spend time alone.

To look at, Pops was a little, wizened, balding man. He was shorter than me, and I was not unusually tall for a woman. In temperament, he was the sort who might punch a guy twice his size in a bar, but who totally fell to pieces when his wife died. Since I was the only child he had, he taught me to hunt and fish and throw a baseball, but because I was female, he didn't quite trust me to manage the business properly. "Women don't have the right sort of head to run a business," he said. He said it even now, when I was making almost all the decisions that had to be made. "Anyhow, people around here expect a man to be in charge," he would add, and this was true.

He had said the same things to my mother, for twenty years, and for twenty years she had worked as a clerk in his store. If she chafed, she did not show it. She had found solace in books, which she bought by the bushel from a discount paperback club, and from her garden, and from hours and hours playing the upright piano in the living room. She was born too early to have been raised in the belief that she could demand more for herself. She had been born late enough, however, that she wanted more for her daughter. She was determined that I would go to college.

When she was diagnosed with cancer, late in my junior year of high school, I saw a look of desperate fatality in her eyes. It sprang, not from the knowledge that she was going to die, but from an anguished conviction that she was dying before she could make sure that I was launched on a course different from her own.

All through that summer and autumn, she put herself through every kind of chemical and radiation treatment, every surgery that the doctors said might add a few weeks or months to her life. She spent the brief intervals when she had strength and lucidity hounding me to write the essays and fill out the application forms for the state university, and for several other more prestigious universities on the West Coast. She hung on through the winter with a frenzied energy that puzzled the doctors. In January, I overheard them telling my father that the cancer had spread to every major organ of her body and she could not possibly live another month.

The first college acceptance arrived in the mail on the morning of her funeral, April eighteenth.

If it had been my father's funeral, and my mother had been facing a life alone, struggling to keep the store afloat with me a thousand miles away, she would have said, "You get your hind end onto that plane. I'll manage."

My father broke down in tears and said, "Don't leave me, honey."

Part One

1

"YOU ALWAYS WERE AN ODD CHILD,
Pat." Mrs. Chase had said the same thing many times, but she said it with particular conviction then, in response to my announcement that I was not going to college after all, that I had torn up all the acceptance letters I had received.

Mrs. Chase was the history teacher at Kilgore High School. She doubled as guidance counselor, because the school was not big enough to have a full-time guidance counselor. Perhaps with training, a guidance counselor actually learns how to help adolescents through their peculiar agonies. In Mrs. Chase's case, the job became that of a sorting gate at the stockyards. The students ran through a four-year chute of classes, accumulating grades and a reputation along the way. When they got to Mrs. Chase, at the end of the chute, she swung the gate this way or that. You are smart enough for the university. You should be content with a community college. You would do well to find a job.

She knew all of us pretty well, having taught us at least one, and sometimes as many as three classes in social studies and history. Maybe her judgments were more accurate than the ones made by specialists, who saw students only by appointment. The trouble was, she didn't have time to do anything more than shunt us in the direction she thought was appropriate. Her teaching load had only been reduced by one class, and what little time she had for counseling was mostly spent on such things as conferring with the sheriff about what to do with Fred McNeil and Marty Alderman after they got drunk and shot a dozen holes in every mailbox between Kilgore and Wister, the dot on the map fifteen miles to the north.

Mrs. Chase knew me almost as well as she knew Marty and Fred, not because I shot up mailboxes, but because I was, as she said, an odd child. I was the sort who could easily become a guidance counselor's obsession. I was obviously smart, smart enough to get good grades whenever I chose, smart enough to be worth pushing towards great accomplishments. At the same time, I was annoyingly peculiar. The oddness went beyond my disinclination to talk, although that by itself was enough to make teachers feel they needed to change me. There was something else about me, too, that made adults worry. The other kids just called me weird and left it at that. Adults felt responsible. They felt they had to do something to keep me from coming to grief.

I was frequently called in to Mrs. Chase's office, ostensibly to plan my brilliant future, but in fact so that she could probe for the roots of my maladjustment.

"Why don't you ever join in? Don't you like parties?" she asked.

"Not really. I go sometimes." I did in fact talk, if someone asked me a question point blank.

"Do you have any girlfriends?"

"Not really."

"Don't you like any of the other girls?"

"Most of them giggle too much."

"Don't you like to laugh?"

"Laughing is not the same as giggling."

"Do you have a boyfriend?"

"No."

"What about Chuck?"

"Chuck is my friend, not my boyfriend."

Chuck wanted to be my boyfriend. He had kissed me once, very tentatively, and I had kissed him back, with an academic curiosity. His mouth was wet and tasted of cigarettes. Passion had not exactly run amok in my breast, and I suggested, as tactfully as I could, that we had better just stay friends. At the time, I thought he was not the right person. Later, as years went by and no one roused so much as a faint tremor, I concluded that I had no interest in sex.

"Why do you always wear such gloomy colors?" Mrs. Chase asked me, at another conference.

"I like them."

"With your dark hair, you would look very nice in red, or in a bright blue-green. Brown makes you look so sad."

I shrugged.

"It's important to look nice. It shows self-respect."

I shrugged again.

"You put people off, dressing like a hobo and acting so

serious all the time. Don't you care if people like you?"

I shrugged yet again. Mrs. Chase was almost sputtering in her frustration. She could see so clearly what I needed to make me happy, and there I was, stubbornly, stupidly, resisting her help. It was so simple. If I was nice to people, if I smiled and talked and dressed nicely, then people would like me. If people liked me, then I would be happy. The equations were straightforward.

What Mrs. Chase did not understand, and what I did not know how to explain, was that I did not feel unhappy. She assumed that anyone who walked around in baggy brown flannel shirts, and who spent most of her time by herself reading and drawing, and whose only apparent friend was a roughneck boy two classes ahead of her, must by definition be unhappy. The term "low self-esteem" had not become the catch-all popular diagnosis, the way it has since, so Mrs. Chase did not have a label to put on what she saw. Still, she was sure I had a problem. Since I did not think I had a problem, it was not surprising that I was not eager to be fixed.

When I told her I was not going to college, she finally gave up and decided there was no hope for me. I was not only odd, I was ungrateful. For three years I had been her great hope, a student smart enough perhaps to go to Stanford or Berkeley or Cal Tech. She had sweated through the application process with me. She personally saw to it that I got the recommendations I needed. She had had glimpses, at least, of my mother's frantic deathbed aspirations for me. The acceptances, when they came, were a triumph, not just for me, but for herself, for the school and for the town. And I had torn them up.

"You always were an odd child, Pat," she said. This time,

instead of voicing a sympathetic desire to help, the words were spat at me in furious disappointment.

I said nothing. I was not really looking at Mrs. Chase, or listening to her. Two images were in my head. I saw my mother's face, cold, still and emaciated. The skin was tight and papery over her fine bones. The face looked like the desiccated remains of a dead bird. Inside myself I felt a cold stillness corresponding to hers, a bone-deep conviction that effort and ambition were meaningless, a trick on the part of God to distract us while the final trap was prepared and sprung.

Then I saw my father weeping, clinging to me, pleading, "Don't leave me, honey."

The first image was my own, not to be shared with anyone. The second was not mine, but still I could not share it. I could not bring myself to make public the spectacle of Smoky Lloyd, feisty, likable Smoky, blubbering and clinging for support to his eighteen-year-old daughter. The sight was embarrassing and I didn't want anyone to know about it. So I didn't say anything, to Mrs. Chase, or to anyone.

After graduation, I went to work full time at the Mercantile. Except for one brief experiment, I had been there ever since.

I tried the experiment about twelve years ago, when I was twenty-two. By then, Pops was over his bereavement and happily occupied playing the elusive bachelor to all the widows, divorcees and spinsters in the vicinity of Kilgore. I decided I had to go away from Kilgore and live in a city. I thought I must be missing out on a vital part of human experience, living in the same place where I grew up. I thought, too, that all the odd children must congregate in cities, where they would be less conspicuous, and that perhaps I might meet some of them. I moved to Chicago.

I lasted six months. The first month I spent in a state of nervous confusion. The last five I spent in a downward spiral of loneliness and torpor. All my normal thought processes were rattled by the noise, the constant motion, the ever-presence of humanity. Surrounded by walls, cars, billboards and people, I could not daydream. Without my daydreams, I was lost. Without my daydreams, I was left with outside reality. Outside reality was a mindless job, solitary evenings in a tiny, anonymously modern apartment, and boredom, endless, un-relieved, mind-numbing boredom.

I had no idea how to survive in a city. I was as helpless as a boy from the Bronx dropped by helicopter five hundred miles deep in the Alaska wilderness. To me, the million strange people seemed as inanimate and inscrutable as a mil-lion trees indistinguishable from one another to the untrained eye. If there were odd children like myself among the million, I did not know how to recognize them. If I had recognized them, I was far too shy to make their acquaintance. I did not make the acquaintance of anyone, odd or otherwise, apart from people I saw at work.

At the end of six months, I gave up. I packed up my truck and headed back west. Later, almost the only things I re-membered distinctly were the two drives, first the eastward progression of shrinking landscapes as the land grew richer, the hills less rugged, the farms smaller, the colors more vivid and bright, and then the reverse, the land spreading itself wider and wider, and everything becoming more sparse, as if the same quantities of rainfall, plants, colors and people were being scattered over a larger and larger area.

When I came back to Kilgore, Pops wanted to throw a big party for me. I wouldn't let him. The only thing worse than being surrounded by a million strangers was to be the center of attention in a room full of people I did know. He had to content himself with greeting every person who came through the door of the Mercantile with the news, "Pat's back. Got back last night. Just couldn't stand the wild city life, right honey?"

Then he would put his arm around my shoulder and give it a squeeze. "Pat never has been much of a one for parties and night life. Her mom and I never had to worry where she was at eleven o'clock. And now she's right back where she belongs." A few details had changed. To find employment in Chicago, I had had to buy some new clothes. For once they were clothes that did not look like oversize surplus from the Chinese army. Since I had them, I continued to wear them. At least a dozen different people asked me if I had lost weight or redone my hair, neither of which was the case. It was their tactful way of complimenting my new wardrobe. They couldn't compliment my new clothes directly. It would have been a tacit admission that they had noticed how slovenly I looked before.

Soon after I came back, I took all my savings out of the bank and bought a piece of land, not much, just about forty acres five miles outside of Kilgore. There was nothing on the land except a falling-down shed and an old foundation where the house had stood before it burned down. With the cattle market in a deep slump, land was cheap. My piece was too small to be good for much, anyway. It might support a cow or two, or half a dozen sheep. It had seven trees, cottonwoods and box-elders, scattered around the old foundation, plus a handful of scrub pines on the ridge behind the house.

The best part of the land, the reason I bought it, was a huge rock outcrop along the top of the ridge. The back side of the ridge sloped away gently, but the near side, above the old homestead, dropped right straight down to the creek bottom and the level land where the house had been. At the top of the ridge, wind and rain had scoured away the soil, leaving a bare skeleton of red-brown rock that loomed over the narrow valley like the wall of an ancient castle.

If a blue mood took hold, if Pops was getting on my nerves or if I began to wonder if I would ever belong to the human race, I would climb up there. I would scramble up the steep side hill of bunchgrass, yucca and prickly pear, and perch myself on one of the ledges. Sometimes I took a book or a sketch pad. Sometimes I just sat, looking out across the miles and miles of living landscape.

From the outcrop, I saw none of the conglomeration of dead objects with which mankind surrounds itself, no lumber, concrete, plastic or metal. Everything to be seen was alive. Amid the dry, fragile soil, the carved buttes, the changeable creek beds, the harshness of summer heat and the dry, bitter winds of winter, I felt as I did nowhere else the fierce tenacious pulse of life itself. Nothing favored life here, and yet everywhere I looked, there were living things, the tiny pioneering lichens breaking the soil for other seeds, the sinewy, dry vegetation, cautious and pragmatic, laying its miles of water-gathering roots before venturing any large display of greenery. The will to survive became a palpable presence, infusing my spirit, and before long I did not care whether I ever joined the rest of the human race.

2

"EXCUSE ME, WHERE DO YOU KEEP the Tampax?"

The voice came from behind me. I was on my knees beside several open cartons of cold cereal. It was quarter past eight, almost closing. I was restocking shelves, to fill up what was usually a dead hour of the evening. At that moment I was working on the Sugar Pops on the bottom shelf.

I turned to see who had spoken. The first thing my eyes took in was a pair of elaborately tooled black cowboy boots, very narrow and pointed. My own toes winced at the shape. I looked up to see who belonged to the boots. She was slender and very blonde, with curly hair falling around her shoulders. She repeated her question and then, before I could answer, she went right on, "The store at the truck stop doesn't stock Tampax. I suppose they don't have much call for it. They had twenty-seven different brands of condoms and a

21

pretty good supply of deodorant and aftershave, but only one lousy brand of tampon. It was one I refuse to buy. It's plastic and it pinches on the way in. I'm a little particular about what things I put into that part of my body."

Several questions leapt into my mind, such as how many other things one would put into that part of the body, and which other parts of the body might she be less particular about. Since I couldn't ask them, and I had long since blanked out the question that had started the whole conversation, I just stayed there kneeling and staring at her. "Have I embarrassed you?" she asked. "I forget sometimes that people are modest. I thought since you're a woman you would sympathize. Or maybe you buy the plastic kind and I've made you mad."

"You haven't made me mad," I finally managed to say.

"I'm glad of that, anyhow. I often stick my foot in my mouth. It seems to happen, when you talk before you think. I've lost a couple of jobs that way. I didn't remember quick enough that I was talking to a guy who could fire me. I get caught up in what I'm saying—it sounds so persuasive, you know—and before I know it someone's mad at me, or blushing, or something."

At first I had been thinking, this woman is cuckoo. Now that I'd had a chance to take a longer look, I could see that she had not been wholly serious about a single thing she had said so far. She was grinning, in a way that was part friendly, part kidding, and it struck me then, how pretty she was.

"I'd say you don't have that problem, talking before you think," she said.

I started to shake my head no, in agreement, but her

thoughts had already galloped ahead and she was talking again. "I'll have to work on you. I like it when people talk without thinking. That's when they say the most honest things. The brain is a big filter. It filters out the truth and leaves all the things that are safe and polite, and those are what come out. My name is Alma Rose, by the way."

She stuck out her hand and looked expectant.

"I'm Pat," I said and shook her hand. Her expectancy was as absolute and yet disarmingly vulnerable as a baby bird with its mouth open. A person couldn't help responding to it.

"Is this your store?" she asked.

"It's my father's. I work for him."

"So you grew up here."

"Yes."

"I couldn't work for my father. I'd go nuts. We don't agree about anything. Or maybe we agree about one thing, that I'm never going to amount to much. He's in banking, so I wouldn't want to work for him anyway. Do you get along with your dad?"

I shrugged. "Well enough."

She looked at me intently, as if she were sure a story must lie behind my answer and she wanted to hear it. She was actually silent for a full ten seconds, waiting to see if I would elaborate. Her pause was not rewarded. I could be silent longer than anyone, and certainly longer than Alma Rose.

She grinned suddenly. "You're going to be a hard nut, I can tell. I'd better get that Tampax. Do you have a bathroom, by any chance?"

I pointed, first to the Tampax, then to the bathroom.

When she returned, she said, "That's the cleanest ladies' room I've seen in weeks."

"That's because I have to use it myself."

"Does that mean the men's room is a filthy mess?"

"Nah, it becomes a habit, keeping things clean."

"Not for everyone," she said. "Do you have some Diet Coke cold somewhere?"

"One can?"

"Yes."

"I'll get it for you."

I wished for a moment that I had to hack through jungles and beat back man-eating tigers to fetch that can of pop. Someone so pretty and so charming should have trophies laid at her feet. Unfortunately, there were no jungles or tigers between me and the cooler. There was only an aisle of potato chips and Hostess cupcakes, and a few yards of linoleum floor. In that span, I couldn't see any way to make my square, functional self into a person worthy of her continued attention.

It crossed my mind to try the endearing buffoon approach, to trip and look like an idiot, and then say something self-satirizing and devastatingly funny. The problem was, I couldn't think of anything devastatingly funny ahead of time, and I wasn't fully confident that something would leap into my head as I landed on the floor. So I walked to the cooler for the Coke and walked back again, in a perfectly ordinary way. Alma Rose thanked me and paid for the Coke and the Tampax. I expected her to leave then, but she didn't. She flipped back the tab on the can and tilted her head back to take a long, appreciative drink. I watched the small ripple of her throat as she swallowed.

She put the can down on the counter and leaned her elbows there, as if she meant to stay for a while. "So, tell me about Kilgore," she said.

"What about it? Are you looking for a place to move to?"

"Hell no. I'm just here for tonight, for my rest stop. My rig's out at the truck stop."

"You own your own rig?"

"I wish. The company owns it. Usually I stop a little further east, but tonight I decided to stop here. I like the name, Kilgore. I always wanted to stop and see what it looked like. So what is it like?"

"Small."

"That's all?"

"Pretty much."

"What's kept you here, then?"

The answer to that would be my whole life story.

I said, "I don't like people all that much, I guess. Not in quantity."

"What do you like?"

"Most other species."

"Even magpies?" she asked.

"I don't mind magpies."

"What about rattlesnakes?"

"I don't mind them either, so long as I don't step on one."

"What about box-elder bugs?"

"Now you're pushing it," I said.

She laughed. "I used to live in a place that had box-elder bugs. You couldn't put a glass of iced tea down for two minutes before there would be an elder bug in it. I wanted to invent a glass with some kind of flip-up lid to keep the elder bugs out when you weren't drinking. Do you suppose there would be any demand for it?"

"There would in Kilgore, but it's not a very big market."

"Oh, well, it was a nice idea." She took another drink of Coke.

"I guess they're not as bad as cockroaches," she said. "The place I live now has cockroaches. I lie awake at night and listen to them skittering around on the counter. Just as well I'm on the road so much."

She stayed another half hour, leaning on the counter and talking. She didn't need any priming. The talk just kept pouring out of her, and I was content to listen. She had a high, lilting voice that sounded young, much younger than she looked. It reminded me of some country western singers, not the deep-toned twanging belters, but the sweet-voiced, delicate girlish ones. They make you think about kittens and little pink flowers, but underneath they're probably as tough and durable as beef jerky.

I learned a lot about her in that half hour. She'd been driving a truck for a year and a half. She had an ex-husband somewhere, she didn't know where. He'd left her a few years ago and she hadn't heard from him since.

"I was too restless for him," she said. "I wanted to move every year or two. For a while, he put up with it. Then finally he said he was going to move back to Minnesota and find himself a woman who would stay in one place and have kids."

She had grown up in St. Paul, in a nice house in a prosperous neighborhood. That seemed incongruous to me. From the way she lived, I expected her to come from a tough background, a broken home or a poor family, something that might leave her rootless. Instead, her father was a banker. Her parents were still married and still lived in the house where she grew up. Her older brothers and sisters had been to college and worked as professionals. She had been to college herself, though she never graduated.

"I'm the black sheep, needless to say," she said. "But you must not be, since you've stayed and worked in your father's business."

"No, I'm hardly a black sheep," I said. Was it possible for an only child to be a black sheep? It was one of the compensations, to be spared comparisons with brothers and sisters.

"How many are there in your family?" she asked.

"Just me and Pops."

"Your mother died?"

I nodded, not inviting further inquiry.

For a moment she looked as if she was going to ask anyway. Then she shifted gears. "I wish I got along better with my family," she said. "Especially my dad. Nothing I do suits him. I tried to study business in college but I couldn't choke it down. So now I drive a truck, and that definitely doesn't suit him."

Her face fell into an expression of sadness, following lines already deeply traced. The mood must come on her often. I wanted to reach out a hand and smooth the lines away. She had a lovely face, with fine bones and curving lips. It didn't seem right that such a face should settle into a permanent look of sadness. It seemed like an aberration from the natural order.

I was not the sort of person who puts a comforting arm around the shoulder of a stranger. I stood still where I was, a few feet away on the other side of the counter.

After a moment, she gave herself a shake and said, "I must be boring you with all my woes. I'd better be going so I get some sleep." She looked at her watch. "Yikes, it's late. What time do you normally close?"

"Eight-thirty. But it doesn't matter. I wasn't going anywhere."

"I've enjoyed being here. Maybe I'll stop by again sometime."

"You'll be welcome," I said, with no expectation that "maybe sometime" was likely ever to come.

3

THAT SHORT VISIT FROM ALMA
Rose shattered the serenity of my existence. In one hour, she had wrecked sixteen years of work getting my life around to where it fit without pinching too much. Before she appeared, I had not wanted anything. Now I wanted her to come back and talk to me some more.

I had learned how to be content with what I had. My work I could do automatically. That left my mind free to think about the books I had been reading, or a sketch I wanted to make, or my collies. I wasn't lonely. Though I didn't have close friends, I knew everyone in town. People generally paused to visit for a minute or two whenever they came into the store.

My only real friend, Chuck Eiseley, had drifted away once he got married. His wife couldn't understand him having a girl for a friend. After a while she made it too uncomfortable for him to spend any time alone with me, and I couldn't stay friends with someone I never saw alone. Then his dad died, and Chuck sold their ranch and moved away to work in the oil fields, where he had better hours and better money.

Right before he left for good, he came by the house to see me. It was January and colder than hell.

"Brought you something," he said. "I won't have any use for them anymore."

He opened his jacket and pulled out two black and white border collie puppies. "They're both bitches. They were the best two in the litter. Maybe now you can use all that stuff I taught you."

Even when he was a kid, Chuck had had a gift for training dogs. Unlike most of the ranches around Kilgore, the Eiseleys ran sheep, and the collies were working dogs. I didn't have Chuck's gift for training them, but he had taught me all the technical information I needed.

"You'll have to get yourself a few sheep and put them on that land of yours," he said. "So the pups will have a way to learn."

"I guess I will," I said. I felt like crying, but I didn't. Chuck was already looking awkward enough. To have me cry would have put him into an agony of embarrassment.

"I guess that's it then," he said. "Beth's in the car. I'd better not keep her waiting."

"Good luck," I said.

We didn't hug each other. Except for that abortive kiss, we probably hadn't touched each other since we outgrew our childhood wrestling matches. At fourteen, Chuck began his growth spurt and didn't stop until he was six-four, which took any sport out of wrestling with me.

He had always had a strong melancholic streak. In high school, it took the form of getting drunk a lot, driving too fast, brawling with anyone he could find who was as big as he was, and, occasionally, engaging in a long and serious conversation with me. The conversations were not intellectual. Chuck was not an intellectual. He was a big, strong, straightforward boy who liked work and liked animals and had somehow grown up with an unshakeable belief that he was no good for anything. The rage that resulted from that belief could take hold of him at any moment, and then he would drink or go in search of someone with whom he could pick a fight. He never unleashed his anger on me, though. I think I fell into the same category as his dogs, mute, helpless creatures that were his to cherish and protect and teach.

We had become friends when I was in third grade and he was in fifth. Since I was a year ahead in math and he was a year behind, we were in the same group. The school was so small that the boundaries between grades were fluid anyway. I often helped him with his math homework. Even though I was a girl and younger, he did not resent it. I think it was because I had already acquired the reputation of being a great brain and hence outside the ordinary standards of comparison and competition. I was an anomaly, almost a different species. It was no more shameful to be coached by me in math than it would be to lose in a game of one-on-one with Wilt Chamberlain.

Neither of us had many friends. The other kids were put off by my overwhelming shyness, and they were afraid of Chuck's temper. However, I wasn't shy when I was explaining long division, and Chuck didn't lose his temper with girls younger and smaller than himself, so we became friends.

Sometimes I went out to his family's ranch for a Sunday afternoon, if it was a season of the year when his time wasn't all taken up with work, lambing or shearing or haying. It was on those Sunday afternoons that he showed me about the dogs. "The main thing is never to lose your temper," he said. I tried to imagine the look on the face of the school principal, or Mrs. Chase, or the sheriff, if they had heard him say that. "If you get mad, all you do is scare them. They don't learn anything from it."

His whole manner changed when he took a puppy out to a field for a lesson. He became slow, careful, soft-spoken. The dogs watched him intently. He never spoke in a loud voice or gestured broadly. He used understatement to hold their attention, the way a skilled orator can use soft, slow speech to pull the audience further and further into his spell.

In my junior year, he had to shoot one of his dogs.

"He went bad. I don't know why. He killed a sheep last night, so I put him down."

He spoke matter-of-factly. It was one law he did not question.

The next night he was arrested in Seco Springs. First, he had slugged a guy in the Antler Bar, for no reason except that the guy was bigger than Chuck and talked too loudly about his Harley-Davidson. Then he had ripped a stuffed ram's head down off the wall and used the horns as a battering ram to smash the glass on a whole row of photographs of the leading businessmen of Seco Springs. The pictures hung on one wall, between the rack of pool cues and the doors to the bathrooms. Chuck had just walked down the line, bam, bam, bam, with the sheep's head, until a couple of policemen grabbed him. He had agreed to pay for the damage, and got a suspended sentence.

I didn't cry, even after the door closed behind him and I was left with just the two puppies wriggling in my arms. I was due at the store in an hour. Before then I had to make a place for the puppies in the utility room, and find dishes for water and food, and a blanket, and some expendable objects for them to chew on. By the time I was done, the moment for crying was past.

I still had Lulu and Tess. I had three younger dogs, too, Lulu's daughter Lucy, and two of Lucy's puppies that I was training to sell as working dogs. The two old ones were growing stiff-jointed and crabby, but they still liked to work sheep.

Much as I loved my dogs, I had no illusion that their company filled the place where Chuck had been. They were better than no company at all, but they didn't talk to me, they didn't know when I was making a joke, and I didn't pretend to myself that they understood if I came home and complained that Peggy Treadwell had been hounding me to join the October rummage sale committee. Over the years, I had got used to the idea that most of my conversations were inward, and that I should laugh inside myself if I had a thought that seemed funny.

When the door closed behind Alma Rose, I thought, there goes someone who might have been as good a friend as Chuck. I couldn't tell if I was regretful or relieved. The silly jingle of the cowbell as the door closed sounded like an alarm bell in my ear. If I made friends with Alma Rose, she would inevitably leave, as Chuck had done. I did not want to spend another ten or fifteen years getting used to my life. It was far better that she left now, so that I could hold on to my hard-won peace of mind.

4

THE FLAW IN MY REASONING WAS that my peace of mind was already long gone. My thoughts were not my own. Alma Rose paraded through them any time she pleased, with the arrogance of ownership. Sometimes she grinned at me, said teasing things, made jokes. Other times she looked so sad, I wanted to put an arm around her to console, or do something silly so that she would smile again. I replayed every word we had said in that hour.

Her face was right in front of me, in full detail. Her blue eyes were lightly made up with mascara. Her nose was narrow and a bit pointed. Her lips were full and curving, her teeth not quite perfect, but close. I could still see the way she drank the Coke, the way models do on TV commercials, eyes closed, head tilted back so that the jaw and throat make a beautiful line for the camera.

"I said, do you have any more strawberry ice cream hidden

34

away out back? There isn't any in the freezer case."

Gladys Gardner was standing across the counter from me, waiting for my mind to surface and start ringing up her groceries.

"I'm sorry," I said. "I was thinking about something else. I'll go look. Strawberry, you said?"

When I came back with the ice cream, Gladys said, "I thought for a minute there that you must have taken up one of those Chinese religions and put yourself in a trance."

"Daydreaming, I guess."

"You sure were gone somewhere. I asked about the ice cream three times. Spooked me a little, because you were staring straight at me the whole time."

"I'm awfully sorry," I said.

Gladys laughed. "I don't mind. But I was starting to wonder if I needed a magic password to bring you out of it."

If she had a magic password, I wished she would use it. Unfortunately, Gladys Gardner was no one's idea of a conjurer. She was a plump middle-aged woman with a round, sun-reddened face, wife of the foreman on the Coon Creek Ranch. The only incantation I could imagine her chanting over me would be something like, "You get yourself a good night's sleep, and I'll make you a big batch of cinnamon rolls for breakfast, and you'll feel a lot better."

On the other hand, her method would probably be as effective as anything got up in bat's blood and Latin spoken backwards.

I tried to distract myself. I drilled the puppies for hours. I ordered a dozen new books from my book club. I carved and painted some of the silly rock sculptures I kept in the front window of the Mercantile and occasionally sold to a stray tourist. I climbed up on my outcrop and drew sketches. Nothing worked. I grew irritable with the puppies and abandoned training for a while, lest my bad mood lead to an outburst that would undo months of training. The books, when they arrived, proved to be either dull, or trivial, or irrelevant. My sculptures, which usually took the form of frogs, rabbits and cows, now came out looking like painted lumps of rock. Instead of landscapes, my pencil traced aimless lines across the page, some of them suggestive of human features, but rearranged into disjointed bits.

I stayed away from Pops as much as I could. I was not worried that he would notice my mood and inquire. I was sure he would not notice, and that was worse.

"What's cooking out in the real world, Sweetie?" he would ask when I came in for work.

He asked the same question every day, and every day I answered some sort of familiar nonsense, "Mulligatawny soup," or "Pig's knuckles," or "Toast and black coffee, the world's on a diet." These days the menu in my head was blank, and I just said, "The usual, I suppose."

That was about the extent of our talk with each other. Pops did not really converse, with me or anyone. He told stories and then waited for his audience to laugh. Even if he had been the sort to converse, we would have been hard put to find a topic that interested both of us. The only activity we both liked was hunting, and we didn't even go anymore. When I was younger, we had gone elk hunting every fall, on a National Forest four hours drive from Kilgore. Then the rancher who used to lend us horses and gear retired and sold his place, and Pops decided to retire, too, to a bar stool where he could swap stories about hunting.

As always, when I came in for work, I found Pops in the middle of a story. This time he was telling Father Paul, the new Catholic priest, about Peggy Treadwell's latest rampage. Pops greeted me and then took up where he had left off, with Peggy heading out to the trailer park at the end of town to find out who had stolen two young spruce trees from the school grounds.

"You know Peggy, she sure does have a thing about those trailers," Pops said. "She was positive she'd find the trees planted beside somebody's back door. She went through the whole place, snooping into every back yard, but she didn't find them."

I could picture Peggy, with her pocketbook clamped under one arm for safekeeping, marching up and down the row of house trailers, peering into tiny back yards that barely had room for a clothes line and a few toys, much less two spruce trees that would spread to twenty feet across once they were grown.

"Peggy didn't know what to do then. She couldn't search the whole county. So she went to work on Marv, telling him it was his responsibility as school principal to find those trees. She talked him into calling an assembly at the school to make an announcement about it. Poor Marv. He didn't have a chance to stop and think, or he wouldn't have done it. Peggy doesn't give a person much chance to stop and think, especially not her husband.

"Anyhow, this morning, Marv called the whole school together in the gym and made a big speech. He went on and on about how mean and thoughtless it was, and how the kids had planted those trees themselves for Arbor Day six years ago, and all the symbolic meaning of planting a tree, and the scarcity of trees in Kilgore. He was trying to appeal to the kids' conscience, I guess, and once he got started, he kind of got carried away with the idea. He had all these things in his head that Peggy had been pounding into him since yesterday, and out they came. Finally he wound up to a big conclusion and said that if the culprits did not put the trees back, it would be a 'tragic breach in the fiber of trust that holds our community together.' That's exactly what he said.

"When he was done, the whole gym was as silent as a church. Nobody dared move, for fear they would look like the culprit. Except that way back in the back, there was one boy waving his arm to get Marv's attention. Everybody turned around to stare, all expectant, as if maybe there was going to be a public confession of sin, the way there is at a prayer meeting. The boy stood up and it was Chip Wilkins, and I think right there Marv knew what was coming and wished he didn't. He said, 'Do you know something about it, Chip?' And Chip said, 'Well, it was my dad. I mean, he does the school grounds, so he does those trees, too, and he said they had some kind of a blight. He said we had to burn them quick, or the blight might spread to the other spruce trees in town, like the big ones by the Catholic church. So I helped him dig them up, and we burned them. I didn't know we weren't supposed to. I didn't know they were holding the town together.' Chip looked like he was going to cry. He's only about nine.

"Poor Marv. If he had only had time to think, he would have asked Gus Wilkins first thing, but Peggy had gotten him all rattled. So there he was up in front of the whole school, looking like a donkey and trying to tell Chip it was OK, the town wasn't going to fall apart, and trying to say how glad he was that it was all just a big misunderstanding."

Pops laughed and laughed, and I laughed too, and so did Father Paul, who was a big, blond, vigorous man, not at all like his bald and sour predecessor, Father Sullivan.

If it had been me telling the story, I'd have finished in two sentences. Peggy thought somebody stole the spruce trees at the school. It turned out Gus Wilkins dug them up because they had a blight that might spread to the other spruce trees in town. It wouldn't have sounded funny and instead of standing there laughing about Marv's plight, Father Paul would probably have rushed off in a panic to check on the health of the magnificent stand of spruce trees that lined the north boundary of the church parking lot. That was why Pops told the stories, and why I did the accounts for the Mercantile.

Like most of Pops' stories, this one was true up to a point. I had heard the sober version an hour earlier, from Marge Gorzalka. It had not been a special assembly, it had been the regular Wednesday assembly. And Pops had embellished Marv's speech by about triple, to make a better story. In a week or a year, I knew, Pops' version would be the one people remembered as the true one.

Father Paul left, and Pops went on telling me the lesser news. His recitation kept me company while I tidied up the produce bins and began checking shelves to see which items needed to be restocked. While I worked, Pops hovered just behind, talking.

If nothing else, his talk now served as a diversion, and I was glad of it. It didn't work indefinitely, however. Before long, Alma Rose would be back, and her voice inside my head would gradually drown out whatever Pops was telling me.

Even my logical brain was beginning to fail me. I made three major errors doing the month's books, and it took me several hours to sort them out.

"This is nuts," I thought. "You talk to a stranger for an hour, and all of a sudden you can't add a column of figures right."

I was almost considering going on a fast, or talking to the minister, to try and purge whatever bizarre devil had taken possession of me. The trouble was, I didn't honestly want to purge that devil. I wanted her to come back in the flesh and talk to me again. After a hundred replays, the conversation still felt like a rare and heady drug, far too powerful to be legal.

5

"HEY, PATAGONIA, WANT TO COME have a burger when your shift is done?"

This time I played the endearing buffoon whether I meant to or not. The cardboard tray of yogurts I was unloading into the dairy case simply took flight out of my hands, performed a midair somersault and landed head down on the floor. A gloopy spray of yogurt flew in all directions, including onto those beautifully tooled black cowboy boots.

We both stood for an instant staring at her boots, me in horror, her laughing.

"Next time I'll stand a little further away when I talk to you," she said. I scrambled to find a roll of paper towels to clean up the mess.

"I'll do the boots, you worry about the floor," she said. She knelt down and delicately wiped her boots and pantleg, while I, not at all delicately, tried to scoop the pool of pink goo back onto the cardboard tray. Midway through the process, the cowbell jingled. I heard Pops' voice from the end of the aisle, loud and jovial, the way it was after a couple of beers.

"Why didn't you just tell me you didn't like yogurt, honey, instead of dumping it on the floor?"

I looked up and Alma Rose stopped wiping her clothes and turned around. Pops was not looking at me or at the mess on the floor anymore. He was looking at Alma Rose with the kind of gaze that men describe as appreciative, but that to me, at that moment, looked like a leer.

"Heck of a way to treat a visitor, throwing yogurt all over her," he said. "Especially such a pretty visitor."

If he had been wearing a ten-gallon hat, he'd have swept it off his head and bowed. As it was he grinned and winked. "Pat's quite a brain, but she's never been what you would call graceful."

I clenched my teeth and went back to wiping the floor while Pops chatted on amicably with Alma Rose.

"You're not from around here, because I know everyone who is," he said. "But you sure do brighten up the neighborhood. Makes me wish I was twenty years younger. I'd show you some real hospitality. You just passing through on your way to the National Parks?"

"Actually, I'm on my way to Cleveland with a load of paper products."

I almost covered my ears, because I could already hear the line that was coming next.

"What's a pretty girl like you doing driving a truck?" Pops asked.

I glanced up to see Alma Rose's reaction, just in time to

see her lick her index finger and make a tally mark in the air. "Seven hundred and forty-eight," she said with a slight smile in my direction. Then, to Pops, she added, "Somebody has to do it."

The irony in her tone passed him by. "Seems to me there are plenty of big, strong, ugly guys to do the truck driving. You pretty ones should do something where folks get to look at you."

"Maybe some of us pretty ones don't want to be looked at."

"I don't believe it for a minute. There isn't a woman on earth doesn't want to be looked at. Some just don't admit it. Even Pat here wants a man to notice her now and then. Did you meet Pat by the way? This is my daughter Pat. And I'm Walter Lloyd, but everyone calls me Smoky." He stuck out his hand. Alma Rose shook his hand and said, "Glad to meet you, Smoky. Pat has mentioned you."

"So you two know each other already?"

"We do, a little."

"I don't know what I would have done without Pat all these years. She's the best help anyone could ask for. I'm lucky some young fellow didn't snatch her away and marry her."

"You're lucky she didn't snatch herself away and hit the road," said Alma Rose.

"No, Pat wouldn't ever do that. She's not that type. She went to the city once and didn't last six months. Got homesick."

I had done all I could with the paper towel. "I'm going to get the mop," I said. I picked up the cardboard tray full of spilled yogurt, carefully, since it was now sodden. I carried it out to the trash barrel in the back room. I could hear Pops, still talking, and now and then a brief answer from Alma Rose.

When I returned with the mop and bucket, Alma Rose said, "I'd better be going. It's been nice chatting, Smoky. I'll see you around, Pat."

"Let me give you a lift," said Pops. "You going back out to the truck stop?"

"Thanks, but I can walk. It's not far. I walked when I came in."

"I'll keep you company walking, then. There's some tough characters who come off the Interstate after dark."

"I know," said Alma Rose. "A lot of them are my friends. You can walk with me if you want, but I don't need protection."

"I'm always glad to spend time with a pretty woman," he said, as he followed Alma Rose out the door.

Behind them, the cowbell gave out its familiar jingle, mocking. I dumped the mop, walked back to the sporting goods section, grabbed a baseball bat, and headed for the door, ready to demolish that silly, quaint bell. It was one of Pops' flashes of marketing genius. The tourists, the few who came in, loved it. First, they would say, "What a darling little rabbit," and buy one of my ridiculous rock carvings. Then they would add, "I just adore that cowbell over the door. It's so genuinely RURAL, somehow. I think this town is a real find, don't you, dear?"

"You're goddamn right, it's RURAL," I muttered, and swung the bat, viciously. My aim wasn't good. The bat glanced off the bell, setting off a wild clanging, and then left a deep dent in the wood trim above the door.

"The hell with it." I returned the bat to the rack and picked up the mop again. What was wrong with me, that I had stayed here all these years?

I mopped up the yogurt and then, since I had the mop out anyway, I did the whole store. By the time I finished, it was almost nine and I still had to close out the cash register. I didn't care that it was late. I wasn't in any hurry to go home. If Pops was there, I didn't want to see him, and if he wasn't there, if he was still up at the truck stop having a whee of a time, I didn't want to know.

As I was counting up the cash for the night, the cowbell clanged and I grimaced. "Hi Pops," I said. I didn't look up, or I'd have lost count of the stack of ones in my hand. I wrote twenty-nine on the scrap of paper I was using for a worksheet, then looked up to see why Pops hadn't answered.

"So, you hungry?" Alma Rose was leaning with one elbow on the counter and grinning at me. "Your dad sticks tighter than a cockleburr. He'd have stayed around all night if I hadn't said I was going to take a shower and go to bed. I even had to get my towel and go into the shower rooms."

"He likes pretty women," I said.

"So I gathered. You never did answer me about the burger, unless splattering me with yogurt means no."

"Splattering you with yogurt means nothing, except that I'm clumsy."

"Are you sure of that?"

"Yes, why? What do you mean?"

She laughed. "Never mind. I just thought it might mean something else, too. What about the burger?"

"I'd like one, if you don't mind waiting until I finish."

When I walked into the truck stop with Alma Rose, the waitresses all greeted me. I knew them and they knew me, not because I ever ate there, but because they all came into the Mercantile.

"Hi Pat, what's the occasion?"

"It's about time you found your way out here. Maybe we'll wean you away from Marge's turkey sandwiches."

"Who's your friend? She in town visiting?"

"I know her. She was here a couple of weeks ago. She drives a rig for Con-Way. She a friend of yours, Pat?"

I glanced at Alma Rose and shrugged. "I guess so."

"Good thing she's a lady. The men are nothing but trouble."

"Talk as sweet as candy, but they're always on their way to someplace else and don't you forget it."

The waitresses strolled away, laughing among themselves.

"Do you know every person in Kilgore?" Alma Rose asked.

"Probably. For sure they all know me."

"And they know everything about you?"

"Depends what you mean by everything."

"They know that you eat turkey sandwiches for lunch. They know your dad and where you work. Now they know you've made friends with a lady trucker."

"And by tomorrow, they'll know I spilled a case of yogurt on you," I said. "It's true. People know a lot about me. I'm Smoky's girl, the one who was so smart in school, the one who turned down three scholarships to good colleges, the one who never talks and who's never had a boyfriend, unless you count Chuck Eiseley, and he always was a bad kid."

"You got a bad conscience?" Alma Rose asked.

"Why do you say that?"

"You sound as though you expect everyone must despise you, because you turned down three scholarships and never had a boyfriend."

"Don't you think they probably do?"

"I got the feeling from those waitresses that they liked you, and that they hadn't thought much about how many boyfriends you'd had, because they were too busy counting up their own. What I think is that you're pissed at yourself. You assume that everyone else must be pissed at you, too."

I remembered the dent I had left in the door trim at the Mercantile and smiled.

"I'm mad at something, anyhow," I said, and told her about my assault on the cowbell.

"Now there's something I'll bet no one in town knows about you. That quiet, brainy Pat Lloyd would pick up a baseball bat and launch an assault on a harmless, tourist-pleasing gadget. So what else don't they know? I intend to find out all your secrets."

"You do, huh?"

"You bet. I can't resist a secretive type. I can become as single-minded as a cat outside a birdcage. Some people, like your dad, tell me all I want to know in the first five minutes. Other people, like you, take a lot of unraveling."

The waitress returned and we ordered cheeseburgers and coffee. The conversation ambled forward in comfortable cowpath fashion. Alma Rose never ran out of things to say. She talked for a while about her ex-husband. He was straight and true as a carpenter's level, she said. His name was Jim. She talked about jobs she'd had and places she'd lived. "I've finally got a carpet with no stains, but the walls are so thin, I can hear my next door neighbor read the newspaper."

She told me, too, about quarrels, love affairs, about depressions and self-doubts. She seemed not to draw the boundaries that other people did in making an acquaintance. I felt a bit startled, but honored, to be told so much. I found myself growing more talkative in return.

It puzzled me that the connection with Alma Rose seemed so easy. We were not at all alike. Chuck and I had at least had our isolation and awkwardness in common, but Alma Rose and I did not even have that. She was lively, talkative, friendly, pretty, and very likely a bit unreliable. I was quiet, plain, and as steady and reliable as they come.

By the end of the evening, I had a theory. It wasn't that there was any special kinship of spirit between Alma Rose and me. It was simply that Alma Rose had such a brilliantly alive, open and outflowing spirit herself, she could have struck sparks off a stone. The only puzzle now was why she had chosen this particular stone to strike sparks off.

6

ALMA ROSE TURNED OUT TO BE
saying truth when she said she meant to find out all my secrets. There was no question she wouldn't ask, no topic too
personal to be discussed.

"So why did you turn down all those scholarships?" she
wanted to know.

She had appeared late one night, long after I had come
home from work. To my relief, Pops was gone, probably out
for the evening with his buddies at the Trail Bar. The night
was warm for May, and we were sitting out on the porch, in
the greenish half-light cast by the street lamp at the corner
of the yard. A soft breeze carried the scent of pine and sage,
sharpened by spring rain, and the low throb of idling diesel
engines from the truck stop.

Alma Rose lounged back in her chair, hooking one leg
over the arm. She was waiting for my answer, and when she

made up her mind to it, she could be patient. The answer was simple enough, but even now I had difficulty saying it.

"My mother had just died. Pops needed me here. He fell apart completely. And anyhow, I didn't have the heart for college. Striving seemed pointless when you just die in the end."

"Do you still feel that way?"

"No." I smiled a little. "I've discovered that there may be a lot of years to get through before you do die. You have to find some way to make them tolerable."

"What a depressing view of life!"

"That isn't how I normally think. Only when I'm thinking about Mom."

"I've never lost anyone so close. Except maybe my Aunt Rose. She was a sweet, wonderful person. She killed herself when I was sixteen, and I've never understood why. She had two kids about my age."

"What happened to the kids?" I asked.

"Frank Jr. has done the proper things. He went to law school and got married. Liz cracked up. She's been in and out of drug treatment programs ever since. My dad has done all he could for Liz, helping pay for her treatment, finding jobs for her. He has a highly developed sense of duty. If there is a right thing to be done, he does it, without fail, especially if it is something unpleasant. He doesn't like Liz at all. She's a loud, obnoxious person, and she was that way as a kid, too, long before Aunt Rose died. My dad never took any interest in her when she was little, but the moment she became seriously messed up, and not just generally unlikable, he was right in there, standing by her. That's the way he is.

"He's always been such an exemplary person. My whole

life growing up, I felt that there was some standard out there that I was supposed to meet. Only I never knew what it was and I never seemed to meet it. Instead I have some irresistible force in me that propels me right off the rails and into a ditch."

As she talked, she had been looking out into the darkness beyond the circle of the street light. Now she turned to look at me.

"You don't seem to have gone off the rails ever in your life," she said.

"My mother would say I had," I said.

"She wanted you to go to college?"

"You could say so. She put herself through nine months of hell trying to make sure I did go." I paused, because my throat was getting tight. After a moment I went on. "Her date with death was sometime in the summer after my junior year, but she said to God, sorry, I can't make it, I've got something I have to do first. And God said, OK, but you'll have to pay. And she paid, all right."

"What do you mean, she paid?"

"She had surgery six different times, taking out little bits of this organ, then that organ. Even the doctors thought it was pointless, but she was frantic. I remember, she used to read over my application essays, and maybe make a comment here or there. While she was reading, I could see the sweat making drops on her forehead and her upper lip, from the effort of holding up a piece of paper and focusing her eyes, and from the pain. She wouldn't take much morphine, for fear she wouldn't be able to think clearly. When she was done reading, she would lie back and close her eyes for a minute, and then she would say, 'That's a beautiful essay, Pat.'

And then she would rest for another minute, and then she would say something like, 'In the bit about Leonardo DaVinci, there is one sentence you might shorten a bit.' And then she would rest again and then she would say, 'It's a minor point, though. They'll accept you whether you change the sentence or not.' And then she would smile a little, to make sure I knew she was joking with me."

I was silent, thinking about that smile of my mother's, with the sweat still on her lip. Alma Rose was silent for a while, too. Then she asked, "Did she live to see the acceptances?"

"No, she missed them by three days," I said. "At her funeral, Leonard Kinley kept talking about how she was in God's care now, and how God was a loving being who gave his only son to ensure our salvation. But all I could think about was that if God was a being with one single shred of kindness, he would have let her live three more days so that she could see that first letter. Maybe it was supposed to be a lesson that humans are mere worms in the eyes of God, and that we should be grateful for any crumb of kindness God does toss our way. If so, the lesson was lost on me. I just thought, God is either cruel and capricious, or else nonexistent. When you're eighteen, your own woes seem big enough to engulf the whole world. Maybe if it happened now, I could tell myself that it wasn't deliberate cruelty, that it had happened because God was momentarily distracted by someone else's troubles."

"But how could you not go, if your mother wanted it so much? Didn't you feel a huge obligation to carry out her wishes after she was dead?"

"I was worried about Pops. He would get so desperate at

any hint that I might go away and leave him. He seemed so helpless and lost without my mom. I guess the living won out over the dead. My mother wouldn't get any joy out of my going, but Pops would most certainly suffer. I couldn't do it."

"How old was he?"

"Who, Pops?"

"Yes. How old was he when your mom died?"

I thought for a minute. "Forty-one."

"Forty-one. Seven years older than you are now."

"Yes, why?"

"When you describe him after your mother's death, he sounds like someone either very young or very old. Not like someone right in the so-called prime of life."

"I doubt he felt as though he were in the prime of life right then."

"But neither were you," said Alma Rose.

"What do you mean?"

"You were eighteen years old, for Christ's sake. And you're supposed to be making sure that he doesn't suffer." It was true that I had always thought of Pops as old. I had never done the arithmetic to realize that he had been almost as young as I was now.

"I was stronger than he was," I said. "I felt very strong, then, like I knew I could endure. And he didn't seem strong at all. I knew I wouldn't crack, no matter what happened. I wasn't so sure about him."

Alma Rose was staring at me with a look of amazement.

"Did you feel anything at all?" she asked.

"About my mother? Of course. I was miserable."

"But you knew you wouldn't crack. Here is this teen-aged girl, who has just lost her mother, her faith in God, her hopes for the future, whose father is a hopeless wreck, and she's saying to herself, ever so calmly, 'I know I won't crack.' Didn't you ever just want to start bawling and have someone big and strong and kind come put their arms around you?"

"I never thought about it. I mean, it wasn't something that could ever have happened, so the idea never occurred to me."

"The idea! Listen to you. The Idea. Wanting to break down and bawl is not an Idea."

I felt my jaw muscles grow tight. Why was it so hard to explain, even to Alma Rose? For that moment she had joined forces with Mrs. Chase and all the other people who seemed to think there were things inside that I was not admitting, when the truth was, those things simply weren't there.

I was searching for words to explain when I heard the sound of a pickup truck approaching. A set of headlights turned down our street. Pops had returned from his night out.

"Back again, are you?" he greeted Alma Rose. "Couldn't keep you away from the prettiest spot in five states, not once you'd seen it."

"Which five states were you thinking of?" I muttered, while Alma Rose answered something pleasant.

She didn't stay long after that, just long enough to receive a few gallantly exaggerated compliments from Pops. Then she made her excuses about needing to rest, and left.

When she came again two weeks later, she found me in the back yard, replacing a rotten post at the corner of the dog run. It was a Sunday afternoon, and Pops was in the house watching a stock car race on television. I could hear the whine of engines and the chatter of the announcer through the open windows.

Alma Rose cocked her head toward the sound for a moment, then said, "Why don't you take me to see your forty acres?"

"Gladly," I said. I left the post hole digger propped upright in the half-dug hole and called the dogs to come with us.

We parked outside the gate to my land, and Alma Rose got out and stood leaning on the gatepost, looking. She barely glanced at the objects of practical importance, the fence, the trees, the creek that provided water for my six sheep, the level ground where the house had been, the small wooden pens I used to drill the dogs with the sheep. She was gazing at the outcrop.

"Let's go up," she said.

She climbed through the fence and set off at a lope. By the time we reached the top, we were puffing hard. She sat down on a ledge and pulled her knees up to rest her chin on them while she looked at the view.

"It reminds me of the cliffs along the coast," she said. "Except that the swells here are a little bigger than they are on the ocean."

I followed her gaze out across the expanse of semi-desert, the rough hills and buttes, rising above the deep, wandering troughs of the creek bottoms and scored by the narrow gullies of seasonal runoff. At the horizon, the rise and fall of land blurred into light and dark shades of brown until it met the single blue of the sky.

As we watched, the wind raised a swirling cloud of dust from the brow of the nearest hill. If I ignored the hot dry air, the baking rock, the scent of drying vegetation, I could almost see the swirling wisp as a veil of spray, lifted from the crest of a wave.

In fact the hills were still faintly green, from the spring rains, but I wondered if that green was visible to someone whose ideas of color had been shaped in the rich Midwest. The only obvious greens were the cottonwoods along the creek below us, and the occasional clusters of pine trees, so dark they almost looked black.

The dogs had taken shelter from the sun in hollows among the rocks. Alma Rose and I sat for a few minutes, not saying anything, just looking. I didn't mind the heat. I could sit up here for hours, and with Alma Rose for company I could have sat indefinitely. It was a change, for her to be so silent. The change was brief. Rather suddenly, she shook herself, the way a horse does sometimes when it's bored or decides the saddle isn't sitting right.

"You'd have to like your own thoughts to live out here," she said.

She stood up and stretched, then spread her arms and leaned back against the wind. The sleeves of her blouse fluttered. The wind flattened the thin material against her back, so that the line of her backbone was visible.

"You're so thin," I said.

She glanced over her shoulder at me and grinned. "That's what happens if you live on coffee and Diet Coke."

I stood up, too, and immediately the dogs leapt to their feet and danced around my legs, growling and nipping at one another in eager expectation.

"Want to show me their tricks with the sheep?" Alma Rose asked.

"I'd love to."

We picked our way back down the rocky slope toward the small gully where I had noticed the sheep grazing. When we were close, I snapped leads onto the collars of the two puppies and handed them to Alma Rose, to keep them out of the way. All the dogs were alert and excited, now that they knew we were headed for the sheep and not back to the pickup.

"Tess, stay! Lulu, Lucy!" I called them to attention, then gestured with my hand and whistled.

The two collies set off at a trot toward the sheep, low to the ground, eyes and ears intent. Seeing the dogs, the sheep started up and clustered together, nervously. I whistled and gestured again, toward one of the pens. The dogs moved closer, and the sheep scooted away. Though they did not realize it, they were moving in precisely the direction that I and the dogs wanted. First Lucy, then Lulu crept forward a few steps, pushing the flock a little this way, a little that, but always in the direction of the pen.

When they were close enough, I whistled and gestured downward with my hand. Both dogs stopped and crouched, bellies down on the ground, eyes and ears fixed on the sheep. The sheep milled in a tight circle.

I opened the gate to the pen, then signaled to the dogs, who maneuvered the sheep inside. Even after I had closed the gate, the dogs continued to watch the sheep, circling the fence with their ground-hugging creep. Their attention was fixed, with fanatical intensity, on the silly, defenseless creatures in their charge.

"They look obsessed," Alma Rose said.

"They are obsessed," I said. "It's like an electric current, setting all their nerves on edge. If they are not trained and disciplined, they often become neurotic, and sometimes vicious. All that nervous energy has to go somewhere."

"How do they know where to move, to make the sheep go the right way?"

"It's like moving something magnetic with a same-pole magnet. Move the magnet closer, and the object is pushed away by the force of repulsion. The sheep move away from the dogs in exactly the same way."

I opened the gate and signaled to the dogs to push the sheep back out of the pen.

"What would happen if each sheep decided to go off in a different direction?" Alma Rose asked.

"They wouldn't ever do that, unless a dog was too hasty and frightened them too much. Their instinct is to clump together for safety, like a big drop of water."

"Where did you learn all this?"

"From a guy named Chuck Eiseley. My best friend from school. His folks had a sheep ranch near the edge of town."

"Your best friend was a guy named Chuck. Did he look like a Chuck?"

"What does a Chuck look like?"

"I don't know. Big, husky, square. Like a football player, with a clean honest face. Maybe a crewcut. Maybe freckles. I'm trying to imagine you being pals with a guy named Chuck."

"He fits your description," I said.

"Does he?" She laughed.

We strolled back to the pickup. I opened the tailgate and the dogs, except for Tess, leapt in. Tess I had to lift now, because her hindquarters were weak.

I invited Alma Rose to have something to eat, but she said that, as usual, she was supposed to be sleeping.

"You keep strange hours," I said as I dropped her at the truck stop.

"I know. I'll see if I can make them even more strange the next time I come."

7

NEXT TIME, I THOUGHT.
It was the first time Alma Rose had mentioned anything resembling a future plan. She had said, "Next time," and that meant she intended to come back. I soaked in the thought, like a newly crowned queen in her bath, enjoying the luxuriant sensation that the world had organized itself for my pleasure.

My mind made endless calculations of the number of days it was likely to be before the bright yellow Con-Way rig rolled into town again. At first, when my hopes were highest, I thought she might stop on her return trip, in three or four days. Four days went by, with no sign of her. The disappointment made a path for reason to re-enter the calculations. Her other visits had come about two weeks apart. Therefore, it was likely to be two weeks again. I settled myself into an attitude of patience. Patience was the state of mind more familiar to me than any other. I ought to be good at it by now.

Until now, I had seldom had reason not to be patient. It had been easy to be patient when I had nothing to anticipate. Now the only things I could think about for more than ten seconds at a time were my conversations with Alma Rose, the ones already past, and the ones I could imagine in the future. I could envision, in detail down to milliseconds, the moment when the cowbell would jingle and I would hear her lazy, lilting voice say, "Hi, Patrouchka, got any Diet Coke today?" Then I would look up and see her smiling, with the teasing-friendly look she had, a little bit cocky maybe.

By the time I got this far in the scene, I could feel my pulse racing, and I thought, "Patrouchka, if that's who you are, you are getting downright crazy. You'd better go check the inventory lists and see if you need to reorder anything." I would be lucky if I got halfway down the first page before my mind was back at the sound of the cowbell jingling. Sometimes I ignored a live customer because I mistook the real cowbell for the one that played so regularly in my head.

With my mind busy breaking time down into milliseconds, the days went slower and slower and slower, until they seemed to me to be moving at the pace of geologic change. Barely a week had passed since her visit, and I thought, even I could have created the world in seven days, if seven days always moved this slow.

Then the weather decided to have a contest with time, to see which of them could win the prize for torpor. The sun seemed to just sit in the sky, dead still. Here and there a puffy white cloud would hang in the air, dead still. If a person kicked up a little puff of dust from the ground, that dust would hang there, too, dead still.

Nearly everyone who came into the Mercantile would pause just inside the door, in the relative coolness, and pant for a moment, and then say, "God-dang it's hot out there. I don't think I've ever seen it so hot. Do you ever remember it being this hot?"

I'd shake my head, and the person would add, "Marge ought to move her grill out onto the sidewalk and save herself some propane," or else they would bemoan the lack of air conditioning in their pickup.

As yet the weather was only a source of discomfort, not of worry. It would have to last a few more weeks to be called a dry spell, and a few months after that to make it to a drought. Still, the heat did wear on the nerves, and my nerves were in a state where it didn't take much to wear on them. I became, if that was possible, even more taciturn with the customers.

"My garden is shriveling away to nothing," Peggy Treadwell complained to me one day. "Pat, do you know any way to keep moisture in the ground in heat like this?"

I shook my head. "I've never grown a garden," I said.

My mother had grown a garden, large and flourishing green in the midst of Kilgore's red-brown dust. Our water bills had been exorbitant in the summer months.

"I sprinkle the garden every day, but the water dries up as fast as I put it on," Peggy said. "What did your mother do during these hot spells? She must have had some trick."

"I don't know of any trick," I said.

This was not entirely a lie. I knew what my mother had done, but it was not a trick. She had let the water run for hours and hours on end, until it finally did soak deep into the ground. I thought, if Peggy Treadwell can't figure that much out for herself, she doesn't deserve to have a garden that makes the whole town envious.

I was being ungenerous, but I did not particularly like Peggy Treadwell. She was a conspicuously virtuous person, very busy in church affairs and charities. She had always struck me as the sort of do-gooder who collects mountains of free canned goods to give to the town's poor families at Christmas, at the same time that she's telling everyone what delinquents their kids are, how they'll never be good for anything, and how it's a good idea to keep a close eye on your purse if you venture into "that part of town," meaning the trailer park out beyond the water tower, where most of the poorer families lived.

All too often, I was the ear into which she clucked her outrage at the number of beer cans she had noticed in the trash can at this trailer, or deplored the grubby faces of the children at that one. "I wouldn't be surprised if a lot of them are on drugs," she would say in dark tones that hinted that she knew more than she was saying. Then she would add, "Of course, a good many of them are Catholics." Her tone implied that it was all to be expected, that to be poor, to be a drug addict or a slob, or to be a Catholic were all one and the same.

It made her doubly irksome that she liked me. To her, I was the model of the good student and dutiful daughter, and yet slightly pitiable because I had never married. She could point me out as an example to others while simultaneously offering me consolation and advice, a delicious combination. I sometimes wished I had the boldness to tell her what I really thought, and blow her approval of me sky high.

"It's a shame you didn't keep up your mother's garden after she died," Peggy was saying. "You must have inherited some of her green thumb, if you had ever put it to use."

"Perhaps," I said.

"I always wondered what her secret was. She never would tell me, no matter how much I asked. She would always say she did it with good soil and plenty of water and a hoe."

I could see my mother with the impish look she often had, before she got sick. I could hear her speaking the plain simple truth about her garden, and see her watching in amusement as Peggy Treadwell tried to burrow beneath her words to find the 'real truth.' I thought, to someone like Peggy, the 'real truth' was always something buried underneath, in the dark, or acquired at blackest midnight through a pact with the Devil.

The weather now had a heavy, portentous feel to it. If I'd been inclined to see the weather as a carrier of omens, I would have felt a dread of the immediate future. This was not one of my superstitions, however. I had never been able to discover any predictable connection between the weather and human affairs, apart from the predictability with which the humans complained about the arbitrariness of the weather.

Still, I couldn't help feeling a primeval prickle on the back of my neck every afternoon as the dark roiling clouds moved in, and the thunder rumbled, and a few sharp gusts of wind whipped the dust into a frenzy and brought a brief, startling chill to the air. Each day, half a dozen gigantic raindrops landed with a splat against the front plate-glass windows and traced a snake path downward through the coating of dust. No real rain came, though. In half an hour, the clouds moved on, the sun blazed down again, and the air settled back into smothering stillness.

The drama repeated itself every afternoon for days. We all wished the sky would let loose a howling, drenching storm and get this ugliness out of its system. Nothing came of our wishes, neither rain, nor a break in the heat.

"Don't know as I'll want to go to the rodeo, if it stays this hot," someone said. "There's no shade at all in that grandstand after two o'clock."

As other people echoed the same sentiment, I knew that the town had reached its extremity of discontent. The rodeo in Seco Springs was the biggest event on the calendar in Kilgore.

We did have some other events on our calendar. Over in Seco Springs there were the county fair and the Shrine Circus every year, and in some years there might be a visit from the Harlem Globetrotters, or a campaign stop by a presidential candidate, or a concert by a country western singer. Here in Kilgore, we had the home basketball games at Kilgore High, the Sunday afternoon calf-roping out at Bud Donelly's, hunting season, and the Christmas pageant and spring concert at the school. There were church events, too, but they were smaller, partisan affairs, divided between the Catholics at St. Thomas and the more or less generic Protestants at the Church of Christ, and skipped altogether by a large group who didn't bother with either church.

Except for the basketball games, the rodeo was the only occasion that was of interest to almost everybody. It lasted four days, from Thursday to Sunday, and everyone who could get an afternoon free went to see it. For people to suggest that it was too hot to go to the rodeo meant the heat had passed imagination. If it was too hot to watch the rodeo, then it was too hot to eat, sleep or make love, and far too hot for a thermometer to give an idea of the temperature.

8

"I GUESS **I'LL** SKIP THE ICE CREAM today. There'd be nothing left but a puddle by the time I got home," said Alice McNeil. "As far as that goes, I may be nothing but a puddle by the time I get home."

The McNeils' ranch was twenty-five miles out of town. All but the first two miles were on gravel, the same gravel road that ran past my land.

"Creek's getting real low," she added. "It's a good thing we had a wet spring, or we could be in a bad way."

"How are the cattle holding up?" I asked.

"Not too bad, considering. The flies are awful but there's still good feed. You and your dad going to the rodeo?"

"Pops is. I don't know about me."

"I don't know about me, either."

"Hey, Mom, come look! We just made a bear track in the tar. The road's so soft you can stick your thumb down into

67

it." Her children clustered around her, pulling at her sleeves with hands that were smeared black.

Alice sighed. "I sure wish this weather would break."

"So do I," I said.

By now it had been over three weeks since Alma Rose was here. I had had no word from her and I was getting a little desperate, though I knew she would not call or write. She considered the phone and the mail to be instruments of enslavement.

"As soon as someone thinks you might call, they start expecting it as a right. Before you know it, you're tangled up in obligations to call this person Tuesday and that person Saturday. Your life turns into one big appointment book."

So I had not been hovering by the phone, awaiting word. I expected none. I did not even know what city she lived in. Not expecting word did not stop me from stewing when I didn't hear any, however. She had said she was coming back, and even two weeks had seemed like an inhumanly long time to wait. Now the weeks might be stretching out indefinitely into the future. I had no way to know.

That Tuesday, I got a postcard in the mail, a picture of an alligator in a dank-looking swamp. I turned it over to read it. The writing looked rapid and casually untidy.

"The darned company sent me on a different route this week, and then the tractor broke down. Three days in the shop. Be glad you don't spend July in Louisiana. See you soon. A.R." It was postmarked Baton Rouge, a few days ago.

Soon might mean another week, at the least.

I decided to go to the rodeo with Pops on Sunday when the store was closed. I hoped it would be a distraction from my repetitious and anxious thoughts.

The weather still had not changed. The truck was a sauna when we set out for the rodeo late in the morning. Most years, every seat in the grandstand was filled for the Sunday show. This year, the stands were almost half empty. The people who were there took on a mood of fellowship in the face of adversity, everyone very friendly to strangers, everyone joking about what fools we all were to be there. Anyone who went to the concession stand for cold drinks would offer to bring them back for his neighbors as well, and he would be sent off on his mission with cheers. Pops made half a dozen trips, happily in his element at the center of joking and sociability.

The rodeo itself was no different from any other year. It was always a hot, dusty business for the participants. The horses were dark with sweat before they began, but they did not appear to have lost enthusiasm. The best bulldogger of the day brought his steer down in six seconds, and a bareback bronc rider scored a seventy-eight on an ugly red roan named Porkbelly who bucked with single-minded vicious intensity.

Midway through the show, the thunderheads rolled in, as they had every day for three weeks. During the team roping, the rumbles of thunder became noticeably louder and closer. A few people in the crowd glanced nervously at the lightning arcing across the sky to the west, directly in our view. Here and there a rain squall could be seen, a gray veil hanging from the clouds.

The saddle bronc riding had just begun when there was a simultaneous flash and buzzing crackle, and then a booming explosion of thunder. For about five seconds, the whole place went still. The clowns, the pickup riders, the cowboys manning the chutes, the crowd of spectators in the stands, the crowd of contestants perched on the fences around the arena, none of them moved.

Rain began to fall, first the usual half dozen giant drops, but within seconds a pelting downpour, accompanied by roll after roll of thunder. The fence sitters reacted first, fleeing for cover like a flock of sparrows startled from a power line. The pickup riders hesitated a moment, then galloped out of the arena toward the sheds behind the judges' stand. The clowns followed. The spectators crowded toward the back of the stands, where the roof gave a little more shelter.

The next contestant in the bronc riding stayed where he was the longest. When the storm broke, he had been climbing up the side of the chute in preparation for mounting his bronc. Probably he feared he might be disqualified if he didn't go ahead with his ride.

In a shout barely audible over the roar of rain and thunder, the P.A. announcer said, "The saddle bronc riding will be suspended for a few minutes. Andy, you'd better get yourself out of that chute and under a roof before you drown."

The cowboy named Andy scrambled down from the chute and ran to join the others who had taken refuge in the sheds and pickup cabs and trailers out behind the arena. His mount stood where he had left it, still in the chute, looking morose with its head drooped toward the ground.

The storm lasted nearly twenty minutes, a long time for this sort of thunderstorm. When the rain had passed and the thunder subsided to distant rumbles off in the east behind the grandstand, a warm south wind began to blow.

"Out of the washer and into the dryer," a half dozen people commented. That's exactly what it felt like, as the warm rush of air sucked the dampness out of our clothes.

The wind worked quickly on clothes, but the arena was going to need more than a few minutes of drying. Every low spot was now a puddle, and some of them looked big enough to go fishing in.

The P.A. announcer came to life. "Let's get this show going again. Andy, are you ready back there? Put your waders on and come on out."

The pickup riders trotted back into the arena. The fence sitters came back one by one and resumed their perches. Then the clowns reappeared, and one of them had put on a pair of bright yellow hip waders. He cavorted around the ring, splashing through all the biggest puddles. The crowd cheered.

"Hey Barney, you going to lend those things to the cowboys before they ride?" the P.A. announcer shouted down to the clown.

The clown shouted something back.

"You say you'll swap them even up for a pair of leather chaps? I don't know as you're going to find any takers."

The clown shouted again and pointed to his backside.

"You say it's a good deal for the cowboy, 'cause the waders don't have that big hole in the backside if he lands in a puddle. What do you think, Andy, want to swap?"

Andy's demeanor did not suggest that he was in a joking mood as he climbed up the side of the chute and eased himself down onto the soaking wet saddle. The bronc, a sorrel not aptly named Sunspot, appeared to share his rider's lack of enthusiasm. When the gate opened, he didn't move. After much urging with shouts and swats from cowboy hats, he gave a few half-hearted crowhops out into the ring. Spur as he would, Andy could not make him do more.

It appeared that Sunspot, as he stood head down in the rain, had had one of those flashes of philosophical insight that dark moments often bring. He now understood that in the contest between man and animal, the animal never wins in the end. No matter how hard he bucked today, no matter how far and hard he tossed the hateful Andy from his back, the whole process would happen again tomorrow. The aggravating strap would be cinched around his flanks and he would have to buck again, with equal futility. Then, when the rain came, it would be the man who stood under shelter and he, Sunspot, who got drenched. Old Sunspot decided to concede, then and there, rather than waste his energy.

Unfortunately for him, his moment of insight did not go quite deep enough. He did not understand that a willingness to go on losing these daily battles saved him for another day from losing the whole war. For a bucking horse, surrender meant death. A bucking horse who wouldn't buck had no possible use. He wouldn't be earning his keep and his fate would be a swift trip to the pet food cannery.

The buzzer sounded, the rider clambered off his back and up behind one of the pickup riders, and Sunspot was chased out of the arena. The score was as mediocre as the ride had been. Andy hadn't even lost his hat.

The rest of the bronc riding churned the arena into a sea of slop. Most of the riders kept their seats for the full ten seconds, and then made a frantic leap onto the back of the pickup horse. Perhaps they were given double determination by the thought of landing their handsome leather chaps and bright colored shirts in a bath of muck.

The calf ropers weren't so lucky. Like it or not, they had to get down in a mud-wrestling match with a slippery kicking calf. The barrel racers suffered too, their times slowed by the heavy going and the horses' scrabble to keep their footing on the turns. None of them came close to the best times from the previous days.

Finally came the Brahma bull riding. The crowd anticipated it with the same sort of eagerness as a crowd at a car race anticipating a crash. No amount of pride in hand-tooled leather chaps could keep all the bull riders on the back of their mounts for the full ride. Even if they did stay on until the horn, they still had to dismount as best they could into the slop. There weren't any riders to pick them off the back of the bull.

The clowns reappeared. They had shed the cumbersome waders in preparation for their one serious task, the protection of the bull riders. One of them rolled a large red and white barrel into the ring and set it on end, as a safety hatch.

The show was as good as everyone hoped. The bulls bucked and spun furiously, sending showers of mud in all directions. The mud did not slow them in the least. A bull with a man on his back became a creature possessed, blind to anything except his own fury. The mud was of no more consequence to him than the moon.

One after another, the peach and crimson and green plaid shirts landed splat in the mud. Then the clowns, spattered with dirt, pranced in to lure the bull away while the cowboy slipped and slid across the arena to the fence and safety.

The moment of ultimate satisfaction came with the second to last bull. He shed his rider with ease and then set off full tilt on the heels of one of the clowns. The clown leapt into the shelter of his barrel. The bull charged the barrel, tipped it over and rolled it thirty yards across the ring through the slop, with the clown still inside. When the bull was finally teased away by the second clown and chased out of the arena, the first clown emerged from the barrel. His face and clothes were now completely brown with mud. He turned and shouted something up to the announcer's stand.

"What's that you say, Clyde?" said the P.A. "You say you just saved yourself thirty dollars? How do you figure that?"

The clown shouted again.

"I got it. You say that's how much the beauty parlor charges your wife for a mudpack facial treatment."

The crowd cheered lustily, for the bull, the clowns, the barrel and the mud. The poor cowboy, who had gone headfirst into the slop just three seconds into his ride, was already long forgotten.

Filing out of the stands, the crowd emitted the cheerful buzzing murmur of an audience that feels it has gotten its money's worth. The first half had been good rodeo. The second half had been a good spectacle. All in all, it had been a good show. Best of all, the temperature had dropped twenty degrees. Once we had left behind the popcorn and hotdog smell of the rodeo grounds, the air was filled with the fragrant scent of sagebrush and dry earth just soaked by a summer rain.

"Hell of a ride Myers had in the bareback," Pops said as we pulled out onto the Interstate. "About as good as I've ever seen."

"He drew a good horse," I said. "That roan bucked like he meant it."

"Still, Myers had to stay on him. And he showed a lot of style doing it. He ain't at the top for nothing. The saddle broncs weren't much today. Hard to buck with all that mud sucking around their feet. They looked kinda discouraged. The bulls didn't seem to notice, though."

Pops chatted on about the rodeo for most of the drive home, and I listened. I realized, with a start, that for nearly four hours I had not thought about Alma Rose. Now that I had remembered, she returned to her accustomed place, hovering on the fringe of my thoughts. Still, I felt reasonably contented, leaning back in my seat with the breeze blowing in the open window across my face. There were huge cumulous clouds rolling across the sky, left over from the storm. Where the evening sun hit them, they looked as solid as carved marble, blazing white with contours shaded in gray. Among them, patches of clear sky turned a deepening blue, and below them the hills glowed more brightly gold as the sun dropped toward the horizon.

It's almost enough, I thought. The mild air, the rich fragrance, the warm, vivid light, the rugged outlines of the hills, all had come together into a moment of natural perfection. It was almost enough, but not quite.

Arriving home, I found a note wedged in the crack between the screen door and the casing. It was scribbled on a sheet torn from a notepad.

"Where are you? At the rodeo, I suppose. Everyone at the truck stop was grouchy because they had to work and couldn't go. I thought sure you'd be here on a lazy Sunday afternoon. Them's the breaks. My schedule is every which way these days. I can't stick around to see how soon you get back from carousing with the cowboys. Next time . . . A.R."

Next time. Damn the rotten luck. It was the first time in four months I'd been away from Kilgore for a whole afternoon. She had to pick that one afternoon to come through town. Next time. That might be another two weeks, or another month.

What an absurd way to live this was, with my moods at the mercy of someone who might or might not appear on some day or another in the future. Who was this person anyway? What was she to me? Was she a real friend, or just an obsession born of too much empty time for thought?

Inwardly I was hearing sermons. "Stop thinking about her," the preacher shouted at me. "Live your own life. She is certainly living her own. You're just a random stop for coffee in her schedule. She has to stop somewhere on this thousand mile wasteland of interstate. So don't waste your time. Go back to the things that have always made you happy. Stop thinking about her."

The preacher spoke with the fervor of a Calvinist who thinks it will do his congregation good to be convinced that they are worthless sinners. I was easily convinced of my folly, but I was not stopped from pursuing it any more than humankind has ever been stopped from sinning. "Don't think about it," and "Don't sin," must be two of the more futile instructions human beings have ever given themselves.

9

"HALLOO, ANYBODY HOME?" THE shout came from the front room. I was sitting at the kitchen table finishing breakfast. Pops had left for work a few minutes earlier.

I knocked over my chair getting up, so Alma Rose found me still in the kitchen, stooped over to put the chair back on its legs.

"Still clumsy, are you?" she said with a grin, then added, "I was starting to worry I might not ever see you again."

"I don't move very far," I said. I was standing backed up against the kitchen table. I could feel the edge of it pressing against my legs and it felt like a fence that was keeping me there, right where I had always been.

"You're here today anyway," she said. "And I've got the whole morning."

"Did you drive all night?"

"Most of it. I had dinner and a rest at about two. I had it all figured out, so that I could get here at breakfast time."

At the mention of breakfast, I started up and rushed to be hospitable. "Can I fix you something? I'm sorry. I should have offered right away. There's cold cereal, or eggs. Or I could make pancakes, if you don't mind waiting. The coffee's all ready."

I went over to the cupboard to get a cup.

"There's milk in the fridge. I know you don't like it black."

I hurried to the refrigerator to get out the milk.

"Go ahead and pour the coffee yourself," I said.

As I was closing the refrigerator door, I remembered the eggs and opened it again.

"Would you like eggs? There are plenty."

Alma Rose had not moved from where she had been standing, just inside the door to the front room.

"I don't want any breakfast. I'm fine," she said.

I was back at the stove now, with the cup in my hand.

"Not even coffee?" I asked.

"Not even coffee," she said. "And calm down a little. I was nervous enough before you started jumping around the kitchen like a drop of water in a hot skillet."

"Sorry." I put the cup down beside the stove and backed up against the counter, as if leaning against something again might make me calm down.

"So what do you want to do, if you don't want breakfast?" I asked. "There's not much entertainment in Kilgore. The bars aren't even open. There's no Tuesday matinee." I was babbling, because I didn't know what else to do when Alma Rose was silent. "Do you want to go out to my land again? Or we could sit in the front room where the chairs are more comfortable."

"I don't want to go for a walk, and I don't want to sit in a comfortable chair," she said, abruptly.

"Is something wrong?" I asked. She had sounded almost angry.

"Nothing's wrong, except that what I want suddenly looks a lot more difficult than it did when I was thinking about it for all those hours in the cab of my truck."

I was mystified now. I waited for her to explain, but she didn't. She was tracing one of the floor tiles with the toe of her boot.

I asked, very hesitantly, "Are you short of money? Do you need a loan?"

"Oh, for Christ's sake. No, I don't need money." She jammed her fists in her pockets and paced around the room. After a minute she stopped and looked at me. "Are you really that . . . I don't know what . . . detached? You really don't have the faintest idea what it is that's difficult?"

"Maybe I'm obtuse. I know I can't read minds."

She set off pacing again. "Maybe it's me who is obtuse. Maybe I don't understand you at all."

"What are you trying to understand? I'll tell you anything, if you ask."

"Just ask. It sounds so simple. Do you think about me at all, when I'm not here?"

I looked away. "I think about you quite a lot." I had said I would tell her anything, but now I couldn't bring myself to say the whole truth, that I thought about her constantly. I would sound obsessive.

"And what do you think about me?" she asked.

"About our conversations. About what we might talk about the next time you come."

"And that's all?"

"Pretty much. I always look forward to your coming again." It sounded like lukewarm tea, even to me. I remembered the way her jawline and throat looked when she tilted her head back to drink a can of pop. I pushed the image aside. How could I tell her I thought about the way her throat rippled when she swallowed a Coke?

"Well, I think about you now and then, too. Do you want to know what I think?"

"Yes."

"I think about . . . " She stopped again. "Hell!"

"You think about hell?"

She laughed then. "No, I don't think about hell. Though I'm probably a good way down the road to it. What I think is . . . I don't know how to explain. Sometimes I get a feeling . . . but probably I'm just crazy."

"You feel like you're crazy?"

"Are you intentionally misunderstanding me?" she asked, laughing again.

"No, I'm totally at sea."

"How can you be at sea when it's so clear?" she said grumpily. Then, quite suddenly, she asked, "Are you still a virgin?"

I had given up on trying to follow the zigs and zags of her thoughts. Whatever logic connected them was not yet divinable. She was angling her way toward something. If I kept answering her questions, maybe she would zig and zag until she reached whatever end was in her mind.

"Technically, no, I'm not a virgin," I said.

"What do you mean, technically?"

"I mean that I've slept with men a few times. Seven times. I'd just as well name a number, since I know it."

"And?"

"What do you mean by 'And'?"

"How was it? Did you like it?"

I shrugged. "Sometimes."

"So why do you say you're only technically not a virgin?"

"Because I have yet to discover what all the fuss is about. I mean, orgasms are very pleasant. I should say, they're exceedingly pleasant. Also, they can be useful when I'm having trouble getting to sleep. But for people to write mountains of poetry, and throbbing romantic symphonies, there must be more to it. Evidently I've missed something. I have yet to feel anything that would drive me to write a four hour opera full of swelling passion and tortured dissonances. Most of the time when I think about sex, it seems comical. If I think back on Gary Siebenaler and me fumbling around on the way home from a basketball game, bonking our heads on the door handles, it hardly seems like material for poetry."

Alma Rose laughed. "I suppose not, if that's how you think about it."

"Do you stop thinking that way, if you feel strongly enough? You went as far as getting married. You must have felt strongly then."

"For a while I did. I never stopped noticing if I bonked my head on a door handle, though. As long as we were in love, we could laugh about it."

"Have you been in love with anyone else besides your husband?"

"Yes."

"Very many times?"

"A few, here and there."

"How did you know?"

"How did I know?" She looked astonished. "You just do. How do you know when you're hungry? How do you know when you like a song on the radio? You don't have to think about it. You just find yourself trying to tune in the station better. Was that a serious question?"

"Yes." I looked down at the floor, embarrassed for myself.

"Maybe I'm not crazy, then," she said.

When I looked up I found that she was staring at me intently. She looked the way Chuck used to when he was about to challenge me to a game of checkers or a wrestling match. Her gaze was measuring, as if she were preparing for a contest and were trying to gauge the skill of her opponent.

My own muscles grew tense, as if I were preparing for a contest also. I held my breath, waiting for her to speak. I wasn't sure what I expected her to say.

She stayed silent. She just held my gaze, smiling, as if the first stage of the battle were to be fought with looks only, like those childhood contests to see who could go longest without blinking. For sure, I was not going to be the one who blinked, or in this case, spoke. The silence lasted quite a while. Then I saw her pull in her breath, ready to say something.

"I think I . . . " Before she got three words out, we heard a clumping tread on the front porch and a loud knock, which set off wild barking in the kennels out back.

"Pat, you home?" came the shout. "I've got a package."

"The mailman. Or rather the mail woman," I said, and shouted back, "Come on in."

I walked into the front room and Alma Rose followed.

"Nice morning, now that the weather's cooled off," said Cora Eastman. She handed me the package and glanced at Alma Rose. "You must be the lady trucker I've heard about."

"I'm the one," said Alma Rose.

When we were alone again, she asked, "Are you expecting any other visitors?"

"I wasn't expecting that one. She leaves the mail in the box, unless there's a package. She's a little early today, too."

I carried the box into the kitchen and set it on the table.

"Aren't you going to open it?" Alma Rose asked.

"It's just some books I ordered," I said.

"I can't believe you don't open it. I can't leave a package five minutes unopened."

"OK, I'll open it." I found a knife and cut the tape that held the box closed. Alma Rose came and stood just behind me, watching over my shoulder as I unwrapped the books.

"They're mostly biology and natural history," I said. "Plus a couple of novels."

I picked up one of the books and held it so that she could read the cover. She moved closer and some part of her body brushed the cloth of my shirt. The touch was barely there, a cat's tail or a breeze catching a wisp of hair, but the sensation spread in ripples across my skin.

"Science and novels," I said. "Sort of like dinner and dessert. I like the novels best, but too many of them would be like too much dessert. I might disconnect from reality completely."

I kept on talking, holding one of the books in my hand. My rational faculties had gone on autopilot, carrying on a discourse to create the illusion that my mind was present, while in fact the whole of my attention was fixed on the nerve endings in my back. My skin was prickling with the sensation of something almost but not quite touching it. Alma Rose had not moved. I was conscious of only one desire, that she would continue to stand there and that my skin would continue to prickle. I kept talking because I thought that as long as I was talking she would stay where she was.

I could feel the warmth of her breath near my cheek. My own indrawn breath caught a hint of perfume, overlaid with other smells, the cigarette smoke of the truck stop, the metallic and petroleum smell of machinery. I stared at the book. If I turned my head, my nose would probably bump her chin, which would be awkward. So I stood there, rigid, telling her far more than I realized I knew about the author of the book in my hand.

I heard her chuckle, and abruptly stopped my monologue. "Sorry. I don't know why I'm telling you all this," I said.

Her chuckle became a laugh, then. "I think I know why," she said.

I never knew quite how she did it, since I can never manage such maneuvers, but I found that she had turned me half around to face her, and her hand had slid behind my head and she was kissing me. For a second or two, I was paralyzed. Then I kissed her back. Then I thought, this must be what it's like when all the angels God kicked out of heaven get together to have a really good party, because I felt as though every imp of mischief in the universe were running wild and drunk with glee through my body.

Part Two

10

"YOU'RE CERTAINLY CHIPPER THIS afternoon," said Mrs. Kinley, the minister's wife. She was smiling in what seemed to me a very pointed way.

I nearly dropped the bottle of catsup that I was packing into her grocery bag. Could she tell? Was I wearing some badge that announced that I had spent the morning in bed with Alma Rose?

As surreptitiously as I could, I took a sniff of my skin. Maybe the smell of sex was all over me, despite the twenty minute shower I had taken before lunch. My skin smelled like soap.

"And when will the litter be due?" Mrs. Kinley asked.

I remembered then that I had been telling her about my plans to breed Lucy and raise another litter, now that I had sold the two puppies I had been training.

I collected my wits and said, "Probably in the spring. She's due in heat in January."

It was November now.

"My brother-in-law might want a puppy, if you sell them at eight weeks," Mrs. Kinley said. "They live in Nebraska, but it would give me a nice reason to visit. Keep it in mind."

"I will," I said.

"I hear you had to put one of your old ones down. I was sorry to hear it."

"Yes, old Tess. She couldn't walk anymore."

"That's why Ed wants a puppy. He just put one of his down and he thinks the other might not last another year. He's always had border collies, just like yours."

"You came from Nebraska, too, didn't you? Before you married?"

"North Platte. All the rest of my family have stayed right around there."

"How come you didn't?"

"I married Leonard, and he came from Idaho. Before we married, he took out a map and drew a line from north to south, right down the eastern boundary of Montana, Wyoming, Colorado and New Mexico. He said, 'I'm not living east of that line. You pick any town you want that's west of there.' So we ended up in Kilgore, because the church needed a minister."

"How did you ever meet him in the first place, being from Nebraska?"

She smiled then, the way happily married people always seem to smile when they are asked how they met their spouses.

"My sisters and I went to see the Passion Play, over in the Black Hills, and Leonard and his parents had the seats next to ours. During the intermission, Leonard started talking to us. By the end of the evening, he had offered to escort us to Mount Rushmore the next day. For some reason, Leonard picked me out of the batch of us. He used to drive four hundred fifty miles to North Platte to visit when he had a couple of days free from the seminary. He could do it in six and a quarter hours, if the roads were dry. It wasn't all Interstate then, either."

I thought about the Leonard Kinley I knew, a stout, friendly, easygoing man, bald, blue-eyed, the father of four daughters and a son, all now in their teens or beyond. I tried to imagine him as a young man, cruising through the night at seventy or eighty miles an hour along the ruler-straight Nebraska highways.

"I hope your courtship wasn't too long a one," I said.

"Two and a half years. We had to save up money, and he had to get a parish of his own. And of course we had to agree on a town, which wasn't easy." Her eye took on a combative sparkle, and she added, "If he was going to draw that line of his, then I was going to be good and sure I liked the town."

I suspected that the debate about the town had been the first of many marital debates, and that Mrs. Kinley had entered into all of them with relish.

"How could you stand to wait two and a half years, only seeing him for a day or two every now and then?" The question had a home interest for me.

"We didn't have any choice," she said. "Not like kids nowadays, who get married first and wait until afterwards to worry about money. That is, if they bother to get married at all." She shook her head at the sad state of self-discipline in the modern world. "Speaking of marriage, Pat, when are you going to find yourself a nice young man?"

I thought, I must look chipper indeed. It had been several years since the marriage brokerage network that operated among the matrons of Kilgore had concerned itself with my case. I had been written off as hopeless, someone old enough that the usual teasing hints would be painful rather than gratifying. I must have shed a few years, if she now thought I was a suitable target for such banter.

"I'm content enough as I am," I said.

"You should be thinking about the future. How will you manage this place all by yourself, once your father retires?"

I'm managing it all by myself right now, I thought. I could hire someone to do what Pops still did, which was to tend the cash register seven hours a day.

"It isn't the same, having hired help," said Mrs. Kinley, as if I had spoken my thoughts out loud. "You need someone you can talk over your troubles with at the end of the day. Otherwise the troubles wear you down and make you bad-tempered."

She picked up her bag of groceries. "You find yourself a nice, steady young man. I haven't lived all these years without learning what a person needs to be happy."

"Someone steady," I said with a smile, and she nodded.

After she left, I thought about Alma Rose lying sprawled, luxuriantly naked, on my bed. Whenever she came, I turned the thermostat up to seventy-two, because she didn't like to huddle under blankets.

"I want to be able to look at you," she said.

"No, you want me to look at you," I answered.

"Maybe that, too." She grinned and stretched her arms

over her head, so that her ribcage and hipbones stood out clearly around the taut hollow of her belly. She liked her body.

Someone steady, I thought. Alma Rose was beautiful, vibrant and captivating, but she was definitely not steady.

If she had been steadier, would I have been quicker to tell Pops that she was my lover? I wondered. I still had not told him and we still sneaked our time in bed, like high school kids avoiding the wrath of their parents.

Alma Rose teased me about my refusal to tell Pops baldly that we were lovers, so that we could go upstairs together at bedtime like any other couple.

"Are you worried he'll disown you?" she asked.

I shook my head. "It's not that." My fear was nothing so concrete and I could not explain it. My instinct had always been to guard my affections from the sight of other people. The risk of public scorn perhaps increased my caution, but did not create it in the first place. The idea of being castigated as a sinner was rather distant and abstract. What haunted me more immediately was the conviction that the affair could not last. When it ended, I did not want an audience.

I loved Alma Rose with my whole heart. I wanted to love her for my whole life and I wanted her to love me equally in return. Yet some small voice of objectivity and honesty persisted in speaking its view of the truth, that Alma Rose would not tolerate anything that felt like permanence. She came and went freely and that was as much the pattern of her nature as an annual migration is the pattern of songbirds.

My own nature was about as migratory as a sandstone butte. A thousand years of wind might move it, one grain at a time, into the next county. I would have liked to persuade Alma Rose to move a little more slowly herself, but I didn't dare. I sensed that if she felt the slightest constraint on her freedom, she might take flight completely.

11

ALMA ROSE CAME TO TOWN AS
often as her schedule allowed, usually a couple of times a
month. By now many people in town knew her and recognized her yellow rig.

She was not the sort to keep a low profile. If she came in
the afternoon, she hung around the store, talking with everyone, laughing and joking and sharing her troubles as if she
had known people for years.

"Compared to some of the truck stops I see, Kilgore's is a
high-class place," she said one day. She was perched on the
stepstool I used to reach high shelves. Gladys Gardner's son
Roy was there listening, in no apparent hurry to leave.
The afternoon stock boy, Blaine Eastman, was hovering
nearby, too.

"At least here the coffee's drinkable," Alma Rose went
on. "And there aren't any striptease pinball machines."

"What are those?" Roy asked, curious.

"They aren't actually pinball machines. They're video games. They show a lady on the screen, and each time you score a point, she wriggles around and strips off another piece of clothing."

"How far does she go?"

"Depends how good you are at the game," Alma Rose said with a laugh, and Roy laughed too.

"Where did you see those video games?" he asked.

"I've seen them several places. Pennsylvania. Texas. Wisconsin."

"You go all over, don't you."

"Yeah, I move around. I get bored with too much of the same thing. I like variety. It must be a rebellion against my overly stable childhood. You know, two parents, two station wagons, the same house in the same neighborhood with the same school for eighteen years."

"What places do you like the best?" Roy asked.

"Right now, I'm kind of fond of Kilgore," she said, with a glance and a smile toward me.

"It's not most people's choice," Roy said.

"I'm not most people."

She and Roy went on talking and laughing together for quite a while. On that day it was Roy. On another day it would be someone else, perhaps Marge, perhaps Peggy Treadwell, perhaps Hank Eastman or Joe Danziger.

I watched her and listened and tried to figure out how she did it. What went on in her brain, that she always had something to say? My brain only bubbled that way when I was alone. If there was a person to talk to, my thoughts froze up. I couldn't think of anything to say that sounded like the start of a conversation.

I thought it must be an inborn gift, like musical ability. Pops had it, but I had not inherited it. I took after my mother, whose extreme reserve had sometimes been mistaken for snobbishness while she was alive.

Because my mother had died tragically young, her image had been softened and warmed by people's memories. She came to be spoken of as a quiet, frail, lovely girl who loved music and flowers. I remembered quite distinctly, though, that when I was in high school, a lot of people thought she was standoffish and highbrow. She talked very little, she liked books better than dinner parties, and worst of all, she failed to devote herself to the charitable activities that were expected of all females, even if they worked as many hours as their husbands and then came home to look after the house and family.

At the time I was a little ashamed of her. I could not understand why she did not act the way other people's mothers did. As an odd child, my path through school was difficult enough, without having an odd mother on top of it. She was an adult. She should be able to cope with conversation and church committees.

But now I was an adult, and I was no more able than she had been to cope with these social necessities. I tried to be unobtrusive, so that people would not notice. I used silence as a camouflage, blending myself into the background.

The strategy had worked fine, until Alma Rose came along. She refused to go along with it. The quieter I was, the more she wanted to know what was in my head that I was not telling her.

"Are you thinking in there, or is your mind a blank?" she

would ask, pointedly.

At that particular moment I was tidying the store after closing. Since I was busy sweeping the floor, I probably had not said anything for several minutes.

"My mind isn't blank," I said. "My thoughts don't seem important enough to say out loud. People have enough on their minds without my adding every passing thought to the public clutter."

"How do you know which thoughts other people will consider important? People like knowing about you. If you're silent all the time, they have to guess what you're really like and what you're thinking. They might start to imagine you're planning a murder, or that you have communist sympathies, or who knows what. So what do you think about while you're sweeping the floor?"

I dragged my mind back to what I had been thinking about before Alma Rose demanded to know what it was.

"I was debating whether I ought to cut back on the amount of shelf space for canned vegetables and fruits, in order to make more space for snack foods. World-stirring, right?"

"I think it's interesting. It sounds like a debate between principle and profit. Also, it tells me you were not planning a communist takeover of the state capital, which is what I might have thought if you hadn't told me otherwise."

"You wouldn't seriously have thought that."

"Who knows what I might have dreamed up?"

"Then what happens if the truth would shock people more than anything they are likely to imagine?" I said. "For instance, if I told people every time I think about you lying naked in my bed."

"I don't think the truth can ever be more shocking than

what people are capable of imagining."

I thought about the Holocaust and about prison torture. I thought about people trying to take a hot air balloon over the Himalayas, or collecting thousands of key rings. People did startling or horrifying things. On the other hand, they had to think them up before they could do them.

"It's easy for you to say I should tell people all about myself. It's like breathing to you, but it's not to me."

"It's like breathing to your Pops, too. You must have a little of him in you somewhere."

"It's buried then," I said. "I'm my mother's daughter."

"Was she as quiet as you are?"

"Almost."

"And what did other people think about her?"

"They thought she was a snob. That she looked down on them," I said. "I know, I'm making your point for you. She wasn't that way at all, but that's how it seemed to people. I'm sure they would have liked her better if she had been friendly and chatty. She didn't know how and neither do I."

"Yet you talk plenty with me," said Alma Rose.

"You're not the general public. In any case, you don't count. You could probably persuade one of my stone animals to tell you its life story."

1 2

IT WAS INEVITABLE THAT POPS would learn the full truth about Alma Rose's visits. I intended, every day, to tell him, but I kept waiting for a moment when the course of conversation would provide a natural opening. The opening never seemed to come, and the days went by. He and I talked, as always, about the Mercantile, about town affairs and hunting and sports. Our conversations were not the sort that lent themselves to sudden self-revelations.

Someone more daring or less self-conscious than I might have made the arbitrary conversational leap. "Speaking of the basketball team, I thought you should know I'm in love." I could imagine it in my mind, but I couldn't do it out loud. It was not the custom between us. I had never talked to him about Gary Siebenaler, or about Mark, the shipping clerk in Chicago. Nor did he discuss with me how he felt about the ladies he took dancing in Seco Springs. So how could I now suddenly tell him I was in love with Alma Rose?

I suppose it was my just deserts, that he should find out in a way that made for the greatest possible embarrassment for everyone, except for Alma Rose, who was impervious to embarrassment.

From the beginning, Alma Rose had scorned my caution. She liked to flirt with public discovery. It amused her to make me squirm with anxiety, by sliding a hand under my shirt when there was a customer in the next aisle, or by sneaking a kiss when Pops went to the kitchen for a beer.

When she came in the evening, we watched TV with Pops and waited for him to go to bed. Since he hated to miss a moment of her visits, we often had to stay up far into the late night talk shows to outlast him. The three of us would sit there yawning, one after another, bored to death by the cats, eating habits or political views of that night's celebrity, until Pops gave in to weariness and went to bed. The moment he went upstairs, Alma Rose would begin to strip my clothes off.

Eventually a night came when Pops couldn't get to sleep. He came back downstairs to watch some more of the talk show and found us both half-naked on the couch, paying no attention to the discussion of jogging injuries on the television. He tried to back out of the room without our seeing him, but he misjudged the door and instead backed into one of the shelves of porcelain curios that my mother had collected.

The clatter of toppling knick-knacks made Alma Rose and me sit up before we thought. Poor Pops stood there, frozen, shrinking back against the door frame in the face of what must have seemed like an onslaught of bare breasts and navels.

For all of his conspicuous gallantry, he was in fact quite modest about bodies. Certainly I had never seen him naked, and even with just his shirt off, he became a little shy in the presence of females. Nor had he seen me naked, not since I reached school age. Faced by the two of us half-dressed, flushed and sweaty, he was speechless with embarrassment. I was equally immobilized. What could either of us say that would not sound absurd?

Fortunately, Alma Rose was not troubled by personal modesty. She simply reached for her shirt, put it on and buttoned it up, then picked my shirt up off the floor and handed it to me.

"Make yourself decent. We've got company," she said. In picking up my shirt, she had somehow nudged the bras under the couch and out of sight.

Once we had clothes on, Pops seemed to relax a little. His face lost some of its look of shock and he stopped pressing quite so hard against the door jamb behind him.

"Sorry," said Alma Rose. "We shouldn't have sprung this on you."

Pops mumbled something in reply that sounded almost like "It's OK."

He wasn't looking at Alma Rose, though. He was looking at me. He didn't say anything for a minute, but his face began to take on a look of pain mixed with relief, like someone having a difficult bowel movement after a very long and uncomfortable period of constipation.

"So it's just that you're a queer," he said. He did not sound angry. His voice held the same mixture of pain and relief that was in his face. In one sentence, apparently, he had answered a question that had been nagging at him for years.

Until that moment, it had never occurred to me that Pops worried about me, that he perhaps worried about my lack of emotional attachments. He never expressed any worry. He seemed to take my existence for granted and to be content to have me as his housekeeper for the rest of his life. Now, hearing that relief in his voice, a relief that overwhelmed the minor key of disappointment, I realized that he must have worried indeed.

In Pops' eyes I was a queer, but that was better than being an emotional robot. Even that harsh word 'queer' had sounded descriptive rather than derogatory when he spoke it. It was the only word in his vocabulary for what I was. He had never mastered the modern terminology of sensitivity to the disadvantaged. He still used the short, brutally plain words of his own youth—crippled, blind, colored, old, poor, slow, crazy. And queer.

"I suppose I am," I said. I had always been odd. Now I was queer. I laughed, suddenly. The thought had come over me, that now that I was queer, I was no longer odd. Queer was an established category, like old or crippled. I had been odd because the way I was had made no sense, to me or to others. I hadn't fit anywhere. Now I fit somewhere.

Pops turned toward Alma Rose. "You'd better be good to her," he said rather abruptly. This was as close as he could come to the traditional fatherly inquiry into the intentions and prospects of his daughter's admirer.

Then he added, "You won't find a finer girl than Pat anywhere. She's the best."

I heard him with astonishment. He had never said

anything like this to me.

"I know I won't find a better one," said Alma Rose. I noticed she didn't say whether or not she intended to be good to me.

"I guess I'll go upstairs and leave you two alone," Pops said. He was starting to look embarrassed again.

"Stick around, unless you're sleepy," said Alma Rose. "You're not interrupting anything now."

"I can't say as I'm sleepy," said Pops. He perched himself, gingerly, on the edge of an armchair.

"Is anyone here sleepy?" asked Alma Rose, with a laugh.

"Not me," I said.

On the television, the talk show host was now trotting out his well-worn patter of sexual innuendo with a young, pretty sitcom star. Alma Rose grimaced. "This is the first time I've actually listened to this guy," she said.

"I always wondered why you two stayed up to watch this stuff," said Pops. "The guy is a windbag. Puts me to sleep in ten minutes."

"If you got another channel, we'd watch it," said Alma Rose.

"We get Channel 7," said Pops.

"If you call a soundtrack and a few shadows a TV channel, then you get it," said Alma Rose.

"I can make out the picture just fine," he said. "You've been living in a city too long. Your senses have gotten dull."

"Is that all you need good eyesight for nowadays? To squint through the snowstorm on the television?"

Alma Rose joshed Pops for a while longer and he responded in kind. It spared us all the necessity of talking seriously about The Situation. What we needed, or what

Pops and I needed, was a little time for jangled nerves to recover themselves. The last thing either of us wanted was serious talk.

Alma Rose had left long before Pops got up in the morning. He ate his breakfast and left for the store without making any reference to the previous night. In the evening, the closest he came to the subject was to ask when Alma Rose was likely to visit again.

"Why don't you suggest she come on a Friday evening?" he said. "We could close the store early and all go watch the Panthers."

Before I could explain that Alma Rose did not have full control over her schedule, he had launched into a discussion of the chances that the Kilgore Panthers would win the state Class C basketball championship.

One of the changes wrought by the Interstate was that Kilgore High School had shrunk enough to be downgraded from Class B to Class C in athletics. Instead of being one of the smallest schools in Class B, it was now one of the largest schools in Class C, which significantly improved its chances for a state championship. The town had to find compensations where it could.

13

I HAD NOT FORMULATED WHAT I thought would be different once Pops knew about my changed circumstances. I must have expected something, though, because I felt surprise when no change occurred. It was like losing my virginity. It felt like such a watershed in my own mind, I expected the whole world to notice and treat me differently. If Pops was a sample of the whole world, then I must not have changed very much. Either that, or else it was too much bother for him to alter the habits of thought that had been molded to fit and beaten firm by thirty-five years of use.

From his point of view, very little had in fact changed. I still tended the store. I still kept the house tidy and left food prepared for his supper. I still listened to his anecdotes. The only apparent change was that Alma Rose now openly accompanied me to bed, if her visit coincided with bedtime. I suppose one night every few weeks could not overbalance the accumulated weight of daily life.

I could not tell what my neighbors thought, if anything. Since I had not made an announcement in the weekly paper or posted notices on the utility poles, any conclusions that were drawn came from observation, surmise or intuition. Such surmises might be freely exchanged among everyone else, but they were unlikely ever to reach me, except as hints.

Normally I was oblivious to such hints. Now my senses strained to catch them. I noticed every phrase and every nuance of voice and expression. Did I detect a look of curiosity? Was that a faint tone of sneering? For all my hypersensitivity, I never caught any hint so definite that it could not have been my imagination. Perhaps people were less observant than I thought. More likely there was a tacit agreement that as long as I said nothing, they would say nothing, too.

At my post at the Mercantile, I sat right at the center of the gossip network in Kilgore. So long as I was not the topic, people told me just about everything worth telling. The staples of trade were news items about who had broken whose nose in a bar brawl, or whose pickup had been seen in whose driveway well after midnight, or whose son had been suspended from school, or who had bought a brand-new four wheel drive truck that he could certainly not afford. The first time an unmarried couple had set up housekeeping together, the network had hummed for months. Now such arrangements were commonplace enough, even in Kilgore, that they warranted only a short mention. The network went back to its reliable workhorses: adultery, money, sickness or injury, disputes between neighbors and troubles with the law or one's children.

Possibly my love affair with Alma Rose did not strike most people close enough to home for them to react strongly. After years of listening to town gossip, I had concluded that people were the most outraged when someone else committed one of the sins toward which they were most tempted themselves. When a person had sacrificed a pleasure in the name of moral purity, he was understandably infuriated by the sight of his neighbor enjoying that same pleasure. The golden rule of the human spleen was not "Do unto others as you would have others do unto you." It was "If I can't do it, then you had better not do it either."

For most of my neighbors, my behavior did not represent a pleasure foregone. If they disapproved, at least their disapproval was not fueled by the high octane indignation of virtuous self-denial. As long as I kept my doings to myself, perhaps they would continue to keep their opinions to themselves.

Had Alma Rose lived in Kilgore and not just passed through, this sort of discretion would have become a struggle. Her nature was one of strong flavors and distinct textures. A cautious, subtle seasoning like discretion had no place in it. She abhorred secrets. She liked to shake people up.

"You need to take a few risks," she said. "You're as slow and cautious as a ninety-year-old lady on an icy sidewalk. What do you think would happen if people knew?"

"I have no idea," I said. "I don't see why it's anyone's business, though. They don't march up to me and tell me all about their sex lives. Why should I tell them about mine?"

"They get married. That's a public announcement about their sex life."

"If you ever decide to marry me, then I'll make a public announcement," I said. "And then leave town the next morning."

"Chicken!" she said. "How will people ever change their attitude if we all go along in this conspiracy of minding our own business?"

"I'm not interested in changing people's attitudes," I said. "I'm interested in living my own life."

I had no sooner spoken than I wondered myself what I meant. Did living my own life just mean surviving until I died? Muddling along, fending off the worst of unhappiness? I saw myself, suddenly, as one of the low-growing, nondescript bushes that sprouted here and there in the dry hills—an object whose tenacious endurance of a hostile environment is impressive, but whose reason for being there is not apparent.

Alma Rose's thoughts had tracked my own. With uncomfortably accurate aim, she said, "Is it your definition of living your own life, to be a quiet little storekeeper in a tiny town miles from anywhere? To live so that you never have to worry that something unexpected will happen, and you never have to talk to anyone you haven't known since childhood?"

"If that's how you see me, as a quiet little store clerk, then why do you bother coming back?" I asked.

"Because I think you're a whole lot of other things, too."

"What if you're wrong? What if I'm exactly the person you first see?"

"I already know you're not," she said.

"What's different?"

She laughed, then. "For starters, when I first met you, you

carried your body as if it were a lump of inanimate matter that it was one of life's burdens to drag around with you. Now you carry yourself like someone who knows she's fun in bed."

I blushed. "Are you serious? Do I flaunt myself or something?"

"You don't in the least flaunt yourself. But you have an air of liking your body, instead of being oblivious to it. If you're not careful, you might find more people than me sniffing around you."

"I don't want anyone else to come sniffing around," I said.

Alma Rose instantly heard the overtone of long-term commitment in my words. She dodged away, as she always did.

"It might be someone cute, smart and rich," she said. "You shouldn't pass up any chances."

"If it's someone cute, smart and rich, I certainly won't pass her up," I said. I knew better than to say what I was really thinking.

When I was honest with myself, I could see as clearly as she did that we could not have a future together. What did I propose? That she come live in Kilgore? She would be as bored as a monkey in a cage, and anyway there were no decent jobs. Should I move to where she lived? I did not know where that was. She referred to it as the City, and I knew only that it was on the West Coast. If I moved there I would be in a strange place, knowing no one except her, and in a city, which I hated. I would be a dead weight tied around her neck, and on top of that, she would be on the road more than she was home. It did not sound promising, no matter how much we loved each other.

For all I knew, she was not speaking the truth when she

said she lived alone. Maybe she had a husband, or children, or a girlfriend, or all three. Maybe she had a lover at every stop on her route and made rounds, like the mailman, being charming, winsome and provocative to each one in turn. I did not believe it, though.

I had no evidence, except for what she told me and my own judgment of her character. She told me that she lived alone, that she had many friends but only one lover, me. I believed her. I thought it was quite possible that she could juggle a dozen different lovers at once, but I did not think she could lie about it. She was changeable, self-doubting and in many ways difficult, but she was not deceitful. She was too transparent. Everything she felt appeared in her face. Everything she thought came leaping out in speech.

She kept only one secret, where she lived, and she had told me frankly that she did not want me to know. If I knew where she lived, it would be a kind of tie, and she did not intend to be tied. I could easily have found out her address, by opening her purse and looking at her driver's license. She made no effort to prevent it. The purse lay on my bureau, inviting curiosity. I think she was as certain I wouldn't sneak a look as I was certain she wouldn't lie.

Though I had no alternative to suggest, I still felt a nagging frustration at the present arrangement. Her visits were too brief, and there were too many long, interminably long, hours in between. In those hours, the bulk of my life, nothing had changed, except that my impatience made the familiar routine irksome.

My brain felt as though it had been condemned to a kind of futuristic torture. Its sentence was to process an infinite sequence of pieces of paper and columns of numbers, debits and credits, inventories, shipping forms, product lists, order forms, tax forms, cash register slips, charge slips, an unvarying mountainous growth of paper that renewed itself from the bottom as rapidly and steadily as I removed material from the top. When my brain took a rest, my body went to work, receiving deliveries, rearranging and unpacking boxes, stocking shelves, stamping prices, tidying, cleaning and hauling out quantities of trash. All of it was work I had done for years and not minded. Now I could not set to work at the smallest task without my brain involuntarily starting to multiply out the number of days and years still ahead of me in which I would be doing that same task over and over again.

I began to seek the distraction of talk. The customers were the only part of my job that offered any variety and their companionship became a refuge from my thoughts.

It was not new for people to talk to me when they came in. People had always talked, if not about the latest gossip, then about the weather or the basketball team, about politics or the cattle markets. I had served as a filing cabinet. I took everything in, without comment, and stored it in its proper slot, from which it could be retrieved if someone asked.

Occasionally, someone did ask. Marge Gorzalka and Peggy Treadwell had once gotten into a fierce argument about whether it had been Debbie or Donna McNeil who had won the state debate tournament eleven years ago, and whether it had been the same sister, or the other one, who had had a baby out of wedlock two years later. They agreed that it was Donna who had the baby, but Peggy insisted she could not also have won the tournament. They came to me to resolve the issue. I told them it had been Donna, the younger one, in both cases. My memory about such things was trusted to the point that people would rely on it to settle a cash bet, if necessary. I probably would not have recognized Donna McNeil if she came back to Kilgore, but I remembered the facts of the case.

These days I was no longer content to listen and store information. Opinions and stories pushed themselves forward, demanding to be spoken.

At first, my neighbors were almost as startled as they would have been if a manila file folder had offered an opinion about an addition to its contents. They were accustomed to a free and unthinking airing of their views. It threw them off balance to have me answer, and sometimes contradict what they had said. No, I did not think hunting season should be extended by a week. Yes, I agreed that Mrs. Chase's hip replacement was a marvel of medical technology. No, I did not agree that we needed another missile base to bolster the state's economy. Yes, I had heard that the Danzigers were putting an addition on their house.

"Actually, I've seen the plans," I added.

"You have?" said Peggy Treadwell. "I thought they only decided on the addition last week."

"They only told people last week," I said. "Joe said they've been thinking about it for a long time."

"What is it going to look like? How big is it?" Peggy demanded. She obviously resented that I had been in on such a scoop ahead of her. The truth was, I had often been in on scoops ahead of her, and ahead of many people, but I had never let on. Now, suddenly, the things I knew came rushing out almost before I thought.

"Two bedrooms and a bathroom," I said.

"I don't see how they can afford it, on a teacher's salary,

and with all those children," said Peggy. "And their lot's hardly big enough to plant a juniper bush by the back door. Do you think Mrs. Chase knows about it? Their house is almost going to touch hers."

I shrugged. "I've told you what I know." I was not going to be sucked into Peggy Treadwell's habitual handwringing over the wrong-headedness of her neighbors. Joe Danziger had been as excited as a little boy with his drawings. I'd have been excited, too, if I'd been living with a wife and five children in a tiny three bedroom house. Evidently they had found room on their lot and a way to pay. How they had done it was not my concern. It was, however, Peggy Treadwell's concern.

"I think I'll stop by and visit with Mrs. Chase. I want to be sure she isn't taken advantage of, being so elderly and hard of hearing. She has rights in this business, too."

"I suspect Mrs. Chase knows every one of her rights," I said. "She was my counselor in high school, and she never had any trouble heading people down the track she thought was right. Elderly or no, she's sharper than most of us."

I saw Mrs. Chase only rarely, but Pops saw her twice a week, like clockwork, on Monday and Thursday morning, about an hour after the produce truck made its delivery, and about three minutes after the morning stock clerk finished laying all the new produce out in the display cases. I did not think the Danzigers or anyone else were likely to slip something past Mrs. Chase.

She had lost none of her memory, I knew that. Even now, seventeen years later, she would sigh and shake her head when she passed me on the street. I was one of her few failures. She had seen my path laid out for me as wide and straight as the Interstate, and in a fit of adolescent stubbornness I had refused to take it. Though her flesh had shriveled and her stature shrunk, she could still cast a look of withering disapproval.

"Have you heard about the Danzigers' new addition?"

Peggy Treadwell had seized on the next person to walk into the store, who happened to be Lyle Gardner. Lyle looked a little puzzled and only half-interested in Peggy's news.

"I didn't know they were expecting," he said. "Poor Joe. What's that make, six or seven?"

"It's not a baby," said Peggy. "They're putting a new addition on their house."

"Is that right?" Lyle looked a little more interested. "Who have they hired to build it?"

"I have no idea," said Peggy. "But Pat says it's two bedrooms and a bath."

"Gary Pilcher, I think," I said, answering Lyle's question.

"He's a good man," said Lyle. "Built a calving shed for the McNeils after their old one burned down."

"I don't see how they can afford it," said Peggy. "They're barely getting by as it is."

"Guess they must have found a way. Is the foundation in yet?"

"How could it be?" said Peggy. "I only heard about the whole thing for the first time today." She sounded cross at the obtuseness of men.

"They're still looking for someone to do the excavation," I said.

"The reason I ask is, the county's hired a fellow with a backhoe to put in some culverts," said Lyle. "His name's Gillis. If the Danzigers caught him quick, he might dig out their foundation while he's over this way. Save them the cost of transport."

"I'm sure they'd be glad to save money," said Peggy. "What did you say the name was?"

"Gillis. Duane Gillis."

Peggy wrote the name on a slip of paper and put it in her purse. "I'll just stop by on my way home and pass on the name," she said. Apparently her allegiance had shifted, now that she held in her hand a tangible means of championing the Danzigers' cause. She picked up her groceries and bustled out of the store. It seemed to me the cowbell jingled with particular vigor behind her.

"About time the Danzigers got a bigger house," said Lyle. "I've got sixteen dollars in gas and I need some bolts, three-eighths by an inch and a half. You still carry those?"

"We should." I led the way to the dusty shelves at the back of the store. One rack held a few dozen bins of nails, screws and bolts. He found the size he wanted and bought four. With nuts and washers, they came to $1.16.

"I sure am glad you still sell these things," he said. "It would have been an aggravation to drive two and a half hours to get four bolts, but I have to have them. I must have had every other size in the shop, but not this size."

"What's broke?" I asked.

"The swather. It's almost always the swather."

"And all it needed was bolts?" I asked.

"Nah. I've already been to Seco once, to pick up a couple of parts. They gave me the wrong size bolts, and I didn't notice until I got to the ranch and tried to put everything back together. I figured I'd stop by here, before I drove all the way back to town again. They aren't painted red to match, but I guess they'll work all right."

I handed him the slip to sign.

"I don't get to the store much these days," he said. "Usually Gladys comes. She said you were looking well, and I guess you are. It seems to me you women get prettier and prettier the older you get."

"Depends how pretty we are to start with," I said, smiling. "Some of us start out with plenty of room for improvement."

"Don't give me that," said Lyle. "You're just angling for another compliment."

"Could be. I'll listen to compliments all day, if you want to stay here and make them up."

"I wish I had the time." He picked up the small paper bag with his bolts. He paused for a moment and looked at me curiously. "Have you cut your hair different or something?"

"It's the same as it's been since high school," I said.

He shook his head. "Something looks different."

"Maybe it's turning gray."

He shook his head again. "I can't put a finger on it."

"I hope the swather works," I said, as he headed out the door.

I thought, the thing he can't put his finger on is Alma Rose. She was in my head now, all the time, almost as if some sprig of her had escaped and taken root there. It was definitely not me who had joked and bantered and made a near approach to flirtation with Lyle Gardner, whose oldest daughter had been just two years behind me in school.

14

"YOU SHOULD BUILD YOURSELF A
house of your own out here," said Alma Rose.

We were sitting on my rock outcrop. It was late September, and all the small, unobtrusive bushes had turned russet-colored, making bright splotches against the tan and dusty green background of grass and sage. The sky was the clear, bottomless blue peculiar to autumn.

"There used to be a house here, didn't there?" She leaned forward to look down the slope toward the old foundation.

"You're not supposed to move," I said. I had brought my sketch pad and Alma Rose had agreed to sit still long enough for me to draw her.

I had drawn her once already, but she had been asleep then and did not have to be reminded repeatedly to stay still. In that first sketch, she was naked, lying half on her side, half on her stomach, with one knee bent, and her arms curled

116

around the pillow on which her head lay. She had wanted me to pin the drawing up on the wall of my room, but I refused. I kept it tucked away in the back of my sketchpad, perhaps out of some irrational worry that Peggy Treadwell would someday lead an invasion of church ladies into my bedroom.

Alma Rose shifted back into an approximation of her original position, leaning against the rock, with the open country falling away behind her.

"There was a house here, wasn't there?" she asked again.

"Yes, years ago. It burned down."

"It's a beautiful spot for a house," she said.

"I'm not sure I could leave Pops living alone. He's never lived alone and he's getting on."

"He's not even sixty," said Alma Rose. "Maybe if you moved out, he would finally make up his mind and marry one of that flock of eligible ladies he has hovering around."

"Do you think he would?"

"I'd bet money on it. I'll bet he'd have the wedding invitations printed before you had finished unpacking."

I sketched for a minute in silence, digesting the idea. The possibility had occurred to me before now, but I had always dismissed it as impractical. Why keep two households when it was cheaper and simpler to keep one?

Now, given free rein, my mind needed about thirty seconds to build a whole house, small, light and airy, with wide windows opening out onto the valley to the southwest, with Navajo rugs on the floor, sketches and art prints on the walls, my mother's piano in one corner, and a small, tidy kitchen with no dishes casually dumped into the sink and no empty beer bottles collecting on the counter. I could hear the tiny nighttime sounds, the hum and chirp of insects in the grass, the sigh of wind through the pines on the hill above, no longer lost in the drone of the television and the noise of trucks from the Interstate.

Would I miss Pops? I couldn't tell. Sometimes I liked the sound of a human voice, filling the air, and Pops did keep the air well filled. At other times, though, his presence frayed my nerves. For Pops, the concept of companionable silence did not exist. If I was in the room with him, he would talk to me. If I made it clear enough that I was busy and couldn't listen, he turned on the television to keep him company. There were times when I craved a span of solitude, not a few hours here or there, but weeks of it, or months.

Mornings were my refuge, when the house was my own. That's how it was supposed to be, anyway. In fact, even when he was not physically present, Pops spilled himself over into my life. He invaded my hours of solitude in the form of inanimate detritus, his laundry, his magazines and papers scattered about, his dirty dishes, his supper to be prepared, and all the human sheddings of dust, hair and grime that settle on indoor surfaces like a steady fallout of volcanic ash.

Every morning began with his breakfast dishes. He piled them in the sink when he left for the store. I knew he would wash them eventually, if I left them there. I also knew he would not do it until he had run out of clean plates in the cupboard. The same was true of the whole house. Eventually he would pick up his beer bottles, and possibly he might even have vacuumed and cleaned the bathroom. But by the time things got to such a point of filth and disorder that he noticed, my own nerves would have been shot.

He was not deliberately trying to avoid work. It was simply

that his view of the range of possible human activity did not include housework. He did not know how to manage a house, nor was he even aware that this constituted a gap in his knowledge.

"Do I have to stay still when you're daydreaming instead of drawing?" Alma Rose asked.

"I'm sorry. I was thinking about whether I would like living without Pops in the house."

"And would you?"

"I'm not sure. Since I do live with him, what I notice most is how much he encroaches on me. He's a very outward person. Everything he thinks or says or does demands some kind of response from the outside world, and often the outside world is me."

"In other words, he's exhausting."

"Sometimes. On the other hand, I'd probably miss him if he weren't there. And I'd worry. His house would probably start looking like a refugee camp."

"He'd only be right down the road. What is it, ten minutes into town?"

"I know. But it would be a big change, nevertheless."

"Are you going to draw or not? My neck's getting stiff."

I picked up my pencil hastily. I had been lost in visions again, visions of solitude and a place of my own, living my own habits and surrounded by objects of my own choosing. The allure was so powerful, it half frightened me.

"It wouldn't be practical, financially," I argued. "It would cost a lot more to keep up two houses."

I kept drawing, but only on the periphery of clothing and landscape, because I couldn't concentrate on it.

"What's the good of dying rich?" asked Alma Rose. "You

don't have any kids. How much money do you have saved for a down payment?"

"I've got about forty-one thousand dollars."

"Forty-one thousand dollars! Sweet Jesus. That's not a down payment. That's a whole house. How on earth have you saved up so much money? I can't save a cent."

"There's nothing here to spend it on," I said.

"Just being alive costs money."

"Not very much, if you live the way I do. Pops won't take any rent, now that he's paid off the mortgage, and except for books, there's not much I care about buying. The pickup's eleven years old but it runs fine. There's no entertainment, and I don't like gadgets. So the money just goes into the bank."

Alma Rose shook her head. "I must make twice as much as you, and every penny of it goes somewhere."

"What do you spend it on?"

"I don't know. It just goes. My car is two years old, not eleven. I like nice clothes. I have to get a permanent every so often or my hair would look like a dishrag draped over a faucet. Lots of other little things. My vacuum cleaner hose isn't patched with duct tape the way yours is. My blender isn't a one-speed made of surplus cast iron from World War II. I don't share your aversion to any appliance new enough to have a digital display."

She paused for a moment, then added, "On the other hand, I don't have the money in the bank to build myself a nice little cabin in the country and own it free and clear."

"A nice little cabin that you vacuum with a hose wrapped in duct tape," I said.

Though I didn't realize it at that precise moment, the

decision was made. I was to have a house.

With Alma Rose giving the impetus, things moved fast. By Thanksgiving I had a building permit, a well, a septic system and a foundation. By Christmas, I had a roof and four walls and all the rough plumbing, wiring and insulation. After New Year's, Gary Pilcher settled himself in to complete the finicky interior detail.

The house looked a lot like the one I had made in my head in that first thirty seconds. It was tiny, just a bedroom, a bathroom and an L-shaped great room with the kitchen in the smaller leg. Picture windows on the south and west looked out on the creek bottom and the hills beyond. Behind the house, to the east and north, rose my own high ridge of rock, like a looming fortification. Alma Rose had added a porch to my original design, all along the west side facing the road.

"Every house should have a porch," she said, so definitely that it sounded like a natural law. "It's antisocial not to have a porch. You can sit on it in the summer, and your neighbors can see you and wave, or stop by to visit."

"The nearest neighbor is half a mile down the road," I pointed out.

"They drive by, don't they?"

"Yes."

"So there you are. They wave, you wave back, and good relations are cemented more solidly in place. If you are inside, behind the windows looking out, all they see is a blank housefront and reflections off the glass."

15

I HAD HOPED THAT POPS WOULD
take the news about the house as calmly as he had taken the
news about Alma Rose. I was wrong.

The moment I had made up my own mind, I told him.

"What do you want to go and do something like that for?"
he said. "What's wrong with this house? It's a foolish waste of
money to build a house of your own. Paying double taxes,
double utilities. Are you saying you don't want me around
anymore?"

"I'm not saying that at all," I protested. "I just want a
place of my own."

"What for? There's nothing you could do in a place of
your own that you can't do here. I've never said a word about
your goings on with Alma Rose. They're your own business
and I wouldn't try to stop you."

"It's not because of Alma Rose."

"Is she going to move in with you out there?"

"She's not going to move in with me anywhere."

"But she's the one pushing you to do it."

"No one is pushing me to do it."

"So it's just you that doesn't want me around. You'll be happier once I kick the bucket."

"I will not be happier once you kick the bucket. I've never said I don't want you around."

"You're thinking it."

"I am not thinking it. I just need a place of my own. You can visit as often as you want."

I felt like a cow being backed in circles by a pack of terriers nipping at her nose. What the cow wants to do is turn around and give one of them a good belt with a hind hoof. Something stops her, partly confusion, partly the knowledge that for all their noisy bravado and peskiness, the terriers are frightened, vulnerable little creatures. A full force blow from her hind hoof could easily be mortal.

So I kept on backing in circles. My powers of argument had been reduced to the level of a playground squabble, "Tis so," "Tis not," but I couldn't find a way out.

I could have told Pops the full truth, that his constant need for interaction exhausted me and left too little light and air for my slower-growing, more meditative self to exist. I did not think he would see any distinction between that explanation and a desire for him to "kick the bucket." He would not understand that wanting to live separately was not the same as not loving him or wanting him dead. To him, it would simply be that mortally painful blow, and I couldn't bring myself to strike it.

The alternative was to turn tail and flee, with no

explanation at all. I couldn't do that either.

I stuck stubbornly to my repeated half-truth, that I wanted a place of my own and it had nothing to do with him. "I'll be right down the road," I said. "You can visit anytime. It's not as if I'm leaving the country."

"If you were leaving the country, I could understand it better," he said. "As it is, I can't see any reason at all, except that you're sick of having me around."

"It's part of being grown up, to have your own place. Can't you understand that? You and Mom wanted your own place. You didn't live with Granddad and Grandma Lloyd."

"If you were getting married, it would make sense. You wouldn't be alone then. It's normal for a married couple to want to set up their own household. They have each other and they'll be having kids. But you won't have no one out there. Alma Rose isn't going to keep coming back forever. One of these days she won't show up, and then you'll be out on that place by yourself. I can't see any reason you'd want that, except that you don't want me around."

I didn't answer. A whole flock of doubts had started up in my head. Was some devious corner of me trying to lure Alma Rose into settling here? Was I perhaps hoping that, over time, the house, the hills, the peaceful, independent life would entice her away from her nomadic habits?

I tried to imagine true solitude, without the prospect of visits from Alma Rose. Did I really want that? I couldn't tell. Her presence was too deeply embedded in my thoughts for me to imagine her nonexistence. I could imagine the grief I would feel if she were to die, but I could not imagine what day-to-day life would feel like without her there. It was like trying to imagine what I would feel like after I died.

Pops took my silence for stubborn determination and decided to try a new tack.

"It's a fine way to repay me for having let you live here rent-free all these years," he said. "You wouldn't even have the money to build a house if you had been paying rent for this one."

This time the terrier had caught the nose and I kicked out.

"If you'd been paying me fair wages for all the housekeeping I've done for the last seventeen years, I'd have twice as much money to buy a house," I said. "I'm getting a place of my own. There's not a damn thing you can do about it. You can fire me if you want. You can disinherit me if you want. It's up to you. If you make me find another job, I'll find another job. If nothing else, your firing me would give the town something to talk about for a good long time to come."

I stomped out of the house.

"I just might do that," I heard Pops shout after me. "You're an ungrateful daughter. Everything you have I've given you."

I let the dogs out of their yard and they and I jumped into my truck to go for a drive. I didn't know where I was going, but I headed out onto the Interstate.

It was a moonless, overcast night. The darkness closed the world down to just my headlights and the white lines of the highway. After about fifteen miles I thought, why did I head this direction? Then I thought, if I go another sixty miles, and then get off the Interstate and go forty-five miles south, I'll get to the oil town where Chuck lives.

For a few miles I clung to that thought. Maybe Chuck could help me sort out the mess in my head. He had had raging battles with his own father for as long as Bert Eiseley was alive. Maybe Chuck couldn't sort me out, but maybe talking to him would lift the lead weight pressing on my gut.

After another twenty miles or so, it occurred to me that it would be one in the morning by the time I arrived. Chuck now had a wife and children. His wife might very well not understand his receiving a middle of the night visit from a distraught woman.

I drove a few more miles, slowly. I was beginning to think a little more clearly. It was nearly five years since I had last seen Chuck. We did not correspond, so he did not even know of Alma Rose's existence. I had wanted to tell him, but not by letter. I had been waiting until I saw him face to face. Since we never wrote letters, to send him one now, out of the blue, with an announcement about Alma Rose, would make the whole thing far too dramatic. I had just as well launch a flaming arrow with a note in Gothic script impaled on the shaft.

Or alternatively, I could do what I had been planning to do until a minute ago—burst in on him in the middle of the night in a frenzy, having had a blowup with Pops that could not be explained without also explaining about Alma Rose.

At the next U-turn for authorized vehicles only, I turned the truck around and headed back toward Kilgore. As the miles of distance between Chuck and me reeled themselves back out again, I felt an aching pull. Here was a loss I could measure right now. There had been a time when I could have explained it all to Chuck and he would have understood exactly what I was feeling.

His response would not have been brilliantly articulate. Probably he'd have said something like, "A person's folks can be an awful pain." His intuitions and sympathies were rough-hewn and definitely not verbal. I trusted them totally. He offered the same kind of comfort as a southfacing boulder on a winter day, nobby against your back as you lean against it, but solid and warm.

I was cut off from that comfort. Every mile took me further away. It wasn't the miles that mattered, though. What mattered were our two selves and the changes that had come with age. It was an action of adolescence, to burst through someone's door at 2 A.M. in an agony of despair, ignoring schedules, conventions and bodily needs like sleep. In adolescence, all rules could be suspended by an immediacy of feeling. One could demand, and be granted, an all night heart-to-heart talk, even on the night before final examinations or a championship basketball game. That was the nature of friendship. Friendship had not yet been dented and dulled by plodding adult responsibilities, the need to earn a living, to keep appointments, to cook breakfast and supper for one's children and make sure they caught the school bus.

I began to smile at the sight of myself, a mature, solidly built woman, pounding on a door in the middle of the night, wailing because I had had a fight with my father.

For three days, Pops and I hardly saw each other. He did not stay around the store in the afternoon, and he went to bed very early. Each evening, I came home to a house that was dark and silent. I was so used to seeing all lights ablaze and hearing the sound of the television when I came in, it seemed eerie to walk up to a black silhouette, and to hear nothing but the hum of the refrigerator when I came through the door. Pops was gone before I got up in the morning, and he barely paused to greet me when I came in for my shift at the store.

On the following Sunday, there was no convenient way

for us to avoid each other. He did go to church, for the first time in months, but after he came back we were both in the house. It was a gray, raw fall day, so the outdoors offered no escape. Even if the bars had been open, Pops would not have gone there at eleven on a Sunday morning.

For a while we sat in the living room, not saying anything. I was reading and Pops was trying to watch TV. The only things on television were an evangelist and a public affairs talk show, both of which were heavy going for Pops. He sat in his easy chair, half watching and thumbing through the already-read magazines on the coffee table.

In a war of silence, I knew who would win. Silence was a clumsy weapon in Pops' hands. It was the weapon of devious, patient and inward people, and he was none of those things. Already he was chafing. I, on the other hand, could have read my book for hours, not happily, but at least with concentration.

Instead I put it down on my lap.

"What did Reverend Kinley preach about today?" I asked. I wasn't offering a truce, exactly, but I was offering a change in the terms of conflict.

"He preached about giving thanks to God for the harvest. With cattle prices the way they are, I don't know as most people feel much call to give thanks. He talked a lot about the Oktoberfest in Germany, so maybe he meant the German harvest."

"Were many people there?"

"Quite a few."

It was a good season for church attendance, in between summer and hunting season, with the roads clear and dry.

"Even the McNeils came all the way in," said Pops. "Their

service let out the same time as ours today and I visited a little with Fred. He said his folks got a letter from Donna and she's going to come for Christmas."

"I thought they wouldn't have anything to do with her after she wouldn't marry the father of the baby."

"I'm not sure which of them it was that wouldn't have anything to do with the other," said Pops. "I remember you could hear the fight from forty miles away. Donna was dead set against marrying the boy, and her mom was just as dead set that she had to."

"So she lit out on her own," I said.

"She didn't even stay around to have the baby," said Pops. "Her parents didn't hear anything from her for years. She didn't come home for holidays. Didn't call, either. But I don't know whose idea that all was, hers or her folks'."

Both of us were silent for a minute.

"I'll still cook you a turkey for Christmas, you know," I said.

"I just don't understand why you have to get away from me. I'm not trying to make you marry anybody."

"You can come out and sit on my porch. The view's going to be a lot nicer than the front of the Hanfords' house, especially now that they've painted it coral pink to match the birdbath."

For a second I thought Pops almost smiled. Then he said, "You wouldn't ever have thought of this if it weren't for Alma Rose. You shouldn't plan around her so much. She's the kind who does what she pleases and it isn't always going to please her to come back here."

I persisted in my own argument. "Things aren't going to change that much. I'll still be at the store every day. That is, if I still have a job."

"Of course you still have a job. What the hell else am I going to do with the Mercantile if you don't keep on with it?" He shifted around in his chair, looked at the television and said, crossly, "Do you think these guys are ever going to get done yakking about the drug problem? They ought to mix a little arsenic in with the cocaine and that would take care of it for good. They could give a little to the politicians while they're at it."

Except for an occasional brief and involuntary eruption of hurt feelings, Pops made no further mention of my folly and ingratitude.

16

ALMA ROSE HAD GUESSED RIGHT
about Pops. I moved into my house in April. By the end of
June, he was remarried. His choice surprised even me.

Marge Gorzalka was probably the only single woman in
Kilgore that Pops had never taken out to Seco Springs for a
steak dinner at the Longhorn and a night of dancing at the
American Legion hall. Yet it was Marge that he asked to
marry him, and to my greater surprise, she said yes. On the
scale of Kilgore happenings, their wedding was like a major
corporate merger. It brought the ownership of the two oldest
businesses together under one roof.

Pops wanted to get married in the church, but Marge
refused.

"A big fancy church wedding is meant for launching a
young couple off in life," she said. "Or I should say, it's for
putting a bridle and harness onto a couple of young things so

they don't run wild in all directions. We're not being launched in life, and neither Smoky nor I needs a bridle to keep us from running wild. Anyhow I'd feel silly walking down the aisle to be handed over to him when I've known him for fifty years."

They got married in Marge's living room, with just Reverend Kinley and me and Marge's family, her two sons, her grandchildren, her sister and niece, who had driven in from three different states to be there. It was impossible to invite anyone else. No matter who Pops and Marge invited or didn't invite, someone would be offended, and they couldn't fit the whole of Kilgore into Marge's living room. Instead, the whole of Kilgore was invited to the reception, along with the whole of a twenty or thirty mile radius around.

The only place big enough to hold everyone was the school gymnasium. A lot of people pitched in to help set up tables and drape pink and yellow festoons among the black and orange banners that proclaimed Kilgore's small handful of athletic triumphs. Marge and several other ladies cooked for days ahead of time. Pops bought cases of liquor and hired a band composed of a fiddle, an accordion, a bass and assorted percussion.

It turned out to be a party to remember. Pops' buddies poured liquor with a liberal hand, and the band tried its skill at anything anyone requested, polkas, reels, waltzes, Western swing, or the Rolling Stones. The crowd abandoned itself to a mood of carousing that began with Pops, and then, fueled by whiskey and punch, spread like flame through everyone else. Even with the canvas down to protect it, the floor thundered and shook under the pounding of cowboy boots. The air almost steamed from the warmth of bodies. Catching the mood of the dancers, the musicians played with furious enthusiasm, stamping their feet, and grinning at one another as each strove to outdo the others' flashy improvisations. Pops did his best to dance with every woman in the room, and to keep things fair, the men elbowed one another to dance with Marge.

Pops had originally hired the band for two hours. When two hours had passed, no one seemed inclined to stop, least of all Pops. He stepped aside, negotiated with the fiddler for a minute, and the music went on. Every hour or so after that, he and the fiddler put their heads together. The party lasted until one in the morning. Marge sailed through it all, not with wild delight, but with the calm contentment of someone who knows herself well and trusts her own decisions without weaving illusions around them.

The next day Pops and Marge set off on a ten-day circuit of National Parks and monuments, Glacier, Yellowstone, the Grand Tetons, Rocky Mountain Park, Mesa Verde, the Black Hills and the Badlands. It sounded to me as though they would spend all their time in the car, but Pops wanted to see everything.

I was working both shifts at the store. The Donut Hole was closed, with a big sign on the door, "Gone on a Honeymoon." Pops had painted the sign himself and insisted on hanging it there despite Marge's protests.

"That was a heck of a wedding," people said to me for days afterwards.

"Smoky sure knows how to throw a party."

"I hope Marge can keep up with him."

"I hope I'm that full of go when I'm that age."

Such were the comments. The wedding was the topic of

the hour, and Pops the object of everyone's admiration. I could still see him myself, a small, skinny whirlwind, his tie askew, his face bright pink, the bald patch on his head glistening with sweat, gallant and grinning as he seized one lady after another and swept her onto the dance floor. I had been the second lady so swept, after Marge, and I had felt the current of energy in him. He was like a charged electromagnet, charging all the magnets around him, until every dip and spin and leap he made set all the others dipping and spinning and leaping.

"I wish I could have been here to see it," said Alma Rose.

She had come the Friday after, so Pops and Marge had been gone almost a week. It was late, but we stayed up talking, sitting out on the porch of my new house, on a couch I had found at a yard sale.

"He looked as happy as I've ever seen him," I said. "Euphoric, in fact."

"It's a good thing Marge is a tough cookie."

"Why do you say that?" I asked.

"Because otherwise your Pops would gobble her right up. He's what I call a feeder."

"A feeder?"

"All that energy comes from somewhere. He can charm you and make you laugh. He can galvanize a whole room full of people. But somebody somewhere is having the life blood sucked right out of them to feed that energy."

"Don't you think everyone feeds on other people?"

"Sure they do, but it's supposed to be a two-way pipeline. Some people only go one way. Some of them feed, like your Pops. Some of them just lay back and let themselves be sucked dry. Like you."

"I don't think I give out all that much," I said. "I'm not a generous sort of person, the way Pops is. It's been my own choice that I've stayed here."

"I don't think you even know what your own choice is," she said.

A light breeze rustled the leaves of the cottonwoods around the house. The night sky was thick with stars, a billion pinpricks of light flung lavishly across perfect blackness. I felt Alma Rose's hand, absentmindedly playing with my hair, and the warmth of her body, sitting close to me on the porch. I thought, right at this moment I don't care whose choice this is.

I was every bit as happy as Pops was that summer. Being rational, I knew I was spending just as many hours of tedium at the store as ever, but it didn't seem like it. It seemed like a summer of cool evenings sitting in the darkness on my porch, and long peaceful mornings in bed, with the sun pouring in, and lazy rambles with the dogs across the miles of neighboring pastures, exploring the pine-filled gullies, the creeks winding through cottonwoods, and the high windy hilltops. Even the gods seemed to be in a good mood. The days were mild, sunny and crystal clear. Every so often an afternoon rainstorm soaked the ground and brought the grass up thicker than it had been in years.

Since the mood of Kilgore could almost be measured by the height of the grass in the pastures, it was truly a smiling summer. The Donut Hole was suddenly busy when I went there at lunch time, and the sound there was a buzzing murmur of contentment.

Marge moved into Pops' house and rented out her own house to a young couple who had gotten married in June also. She still had the look of serenity she had had at her wedding. If Pops was feeding on her, it was not apparent.

Pops calmed down, gradually. For the first weeks after their return he was in a state of high excitement, accepting congratulations, trading stories about the wedding reception and describing every mountain peak, geyser, mudpot and waterfall they had seen on their trip, as well as every person they had met along the way.

None of the natural wonders had made nearly as big an impression as had a human one, the town of Wall, South Dakota, and the Wall Drug. He couldn't get over it. Again and again, he shook his head and said, "There's nothing in that town except a store full of curios and a million billboards advertising it, but you should have seen all the cars. License plates from every state. We counted almost as many states there as we did at Old Faithful. And all just because of the billboards."

Then, after he'd done describing the tourist sights, he made sure to throw out a few innuendoes about how much better the entertainment had been after dark than it was in the daytime.

He did look younger, a fact that was pointed out to me, smilingly, a dozen times a day. I had noticed it myself, and I was glad. Among other things, it relieved me of any lingering guilt about having moved out. Pops was happier. I was happier. All was right with the world.

17

IN AUGUST ALMA ROSE TOOK A week of vacation and came for a visit. I told Pops I was leaving the store in his hands.

"Fair enough," he said. "I owe you for my honeymoon."

It wouldn't have mattered what he had said. I'd have left the shelves unstocked and the cash register untended before I gave up that week with Alma Rose.

It was a wallow in luxury for me, though we did nothing out of the ordinary. The luxury was not that of dining on rare cuisine or soaking in a hot tub or being tended by soft-treading uniformed servants. We stayed at home and did nothing in particular, and it was the ordinariness of it that was so luxurious. To have dinner, to go to bed at night, and then to get up in the morning and have breakfast together, all felt better to me than a sultan's pleasures. For once we were free of the compulsion to make the best possible use of scarce moments together—by making love, or conversing intensely, or sharing a meal of our favorite foods, or gazing at splendid landscapes and at each other. It was exhausting, to try to wring an emotional peak out of every one of our few short hours. During her visits, I became resentful of trivial necessities, like brushing my teeth and feeding the dogs, because they robbed me of time with her.

Now, knowing she would be there later that day, and the following day, too, I could feed the dogs in peace and even spend time scratching their ears and bellies. I could keep floors swept and dishes washed, instead of postponing chores until the empty gloomy hour after she left.

The only flaw in my contentment was my longing for this to be my everyday life and not a week's holiday. That longing was a constant echo in my mind, like the bittersweet two-note song of a chickadee in midwinter, reminding me of the existence of spring.

I spent many hours drawing Alma Rose. She had decided she liked to pose, provided I sketched quickly. I filled a whole pad with drawings, her face, her body nude and clothed, the whole of her, now sprawled on the ground with the collies, now leaning back in a chair with her tooled cowboy boots propped on the porch rail. She persuaded me to tack some of them up on my wall, though I still refused to display the nudes.

"Why so prudish?" she asked me, teasing.

I shrugged. "I don't know. It feels strange to have nude pictures of someone you know in the living room."

"You prefer to look at a starving cow?" She gestured toward one of my C.M. Russell prints.

"I suppose I do. You'll notice I didn't hang that one over the dining room table, though."

She laughed and looked to see what picture I had hung over the table. It was an impressionist print of the French farm landscape, full of vivid greens and mist-softened blues that evoked lushness, moisture, burgeoning growth, a scene both alien and tantalizing to someone raised where the soil, air and vegetation were all equally brittle and dry.

Of all the drawings I made of Alma Rose, I still liked the first one best, perhaps because I had caught her unaware. The slight smile on her lips came from within, and not from the consciousness of being looked at. When she posed deliberately, she was inclined to strut a little, or to grin mockingly, and something of that air could be felt in every drawing. Her expression was one that simultaneously invited approach and denied entry. Like her charm in person, it first enticed one to come close and then drew a line around her inner self that could not be crossed. When she fell asleep, the intentionally dazzling personality fell away and left behind the plain beauty of her face and body.

In passing an uninterrupted week in one another's company, neither of us could sustain a state of perfect delight. Inevitably, our everyday moods and habits began to surface. Released from the mold of joyous coming-together, our two selves relaxed and spread themselves into wider, more changeable shapes.

We had time to grow grumpy, and then to grow cheerful again. We talked, laughed, quarreled, became silent, apologized, talked some more. She did a load of laundry. I changed the oil in the truck and clipped the dogs' toenails. She arranged herself on the couch on the porch and I sketched her. When a car went by, we both waved. I was content.

After she had left, our conversations wove themselves

together into a single rambling one in my head.

"Did I ever tell you about . . . ?" she often began, and then she spun out one of her tales, about her landlady, about the jazz player she had met while her truck was in the shop in Louisiana, or her track coach in high school, or the home-made Danish pastry she had discovered at a little diner in Indiana.

"Did I ever tell you about the time in high school when my best friend dared me to shoplift a volleyball from a depart-ment store?"

"Did you do it?" I asked.

"Of course I did. How could I resist?"

She went on to describe how she had made herself look pregnant with a big salad bowl and some towels, and smuggled the ball out underneath the bowl.

"By the end, I felt guilty, because everyone was so nice to me. But I was terrified, too, that someone would come up and put their hand on my stomach, and I'd be found out."

"But you got away with it," I said.

"Yeah." She laughed. "I've gotten away with a lot of things. I've been given four warnings for speeding, but no tickets. You should see how contrite I can look."

In an instant, her smile vanished and her face assumed a look of surprise, apology and remorse.

I laughed. "You're incorrigible."

"I know."

She leaned close and kissed my neck. Then she pulled me up off the couch and walked me into the bedroom, unbut-toning clothing all the way. For some reason, being told she was incorrigible, impossible, unredeemable, always made her think of sex.

Actually it took very little to make her think of sex. Had our bones not grown stiff from lying down, she might happily have stayed in bed all day, dozing and making love and dozing again. By eleven o'clock, I needed to move my joints and the dogs needed a walk. I would shower and dress and take the dogs out, and then make coffee. Around noon, she would appear, reluctantly, to eat the breakfast I had prepared.

"You should get a microwave," she said one morning, as we lingered at the breakfast table.

"Why?"

"It would save you time."

"Time for what?" I asked.

"Time for things that are more fun than cooking."

"I like cooking."

"Day in and day out?" she asked.

"Sure," I said.

"I don't believe you. People who say they like cooking always mean they like putting together a gourmet display once in a while. They don't mean they like frying hamburgers and mixing up spaghetti sauce day after day after day."

"I do."

"Then why did you always grouse about making supper for your dad?"

"Because I felt like his housekeeper. Too much of my time went into looking after him when he was an adult, too."

"If you really liked cooking, it wouldn't have felt like a burden to do it. I think you've decided in your head that you like cooking, and you won't admit what you really feel. Even if you groan at the thought of going into the kitchen, you'll stay convinced you like cooking. You decide everything with your head."

I didn't answer for a while. Had all of this come out of my not wanting a microwave? Was it true? Was I a chilly, cerebral android who refused to feel anything my head had not first approved as rational? I sat looking at my half-full cup of coffee, which was now lukewarm. If I had a microwave, I could pop it in and heat it up, so that the distress of hearing her criticism would not be compounded by cold coffee. Then again, maybe I wanted my distress to be accompanied by the sour dregs of cold coffee.

"That's another thing," said Alma Rose. "When you're upset, you clam up. I feel completely shut out. How am I supposed to know what you're feeling if you don't tell me?"

I didn't know where to start. What was I feeling right then? The only thing I was aware of was a pressing weight in my gut, like the one I had felt the night I argued with Pops and went tearing off to look for comfort from Chuck.

"I don't know what I feel right now," I said.

"So what was going on in your head? What were you thinking just then?"

"I was thinking about whether I would want to have hot coffee or cold coffee to drink when I was feeling rotten. I was wondering whether the cold coffee might not be more appropriate even though the hot coffee would taste better."

"I can't believe it. You're sitting there feeling rotten and instead of saying 'I feel rotten,' you step back like a movie director and try to decide whether hot coffee or cold coffee would suit the scene better."

"I can't help what goes on in my mind. The thoughts come and I can't not think them."

"But you set your brain up on a bench, like a judge, deciding which parts of you are permissible and which ones aren't.

You're just like my dad. You've got that judge up there making sure you always do the admirable thing, instead of being honest about the parts of you that aren't so perfect. You're both out to prove that you're better than the rest of the human race."

Her tone was biting.

"I don't understand. I've never claimed to be better."

I was starting to cry and that made me madder than anything. The effort to keep back the tears twisted my face into the grimace of a squalling infant, even though I was not making any sound. I bent low over the table and turned my face away from her.

"I'm sorry, Pat." Alma Rose knelt by my chair and put her arms around me. She stroked my hair and murmured soothing things.

"Something bites me sometimes," she said. "I don't know why. I feel like such a useless person. What have I got to show for my life? A nowhere job and a divorce and a family I can't talk to. Whereas you, you've worked hard, you've saved money, you've got your own house. Your dad is nuts about you. I feel like nothing compared to you."

My throat had unconstricted. Now, instead of her stroking my hair and murmuring in soothing tones, I was stroking her hair and trying to reassure her. "You're not a useless person. You're beautiful and funny and people like you. You could do anything."

"But I don't, that's the whole point. I'm in a dead-end job, and I've got no excuse."

We sat like that for a while, with me stroking her hair and telling her how wonderful she was, and her kneeling beside me insisting that she was no such thing.

It was something I still couldn't understand, how a person so vibrant and appealing could be in such need of reassurance. I truly believed what I'd said, that she could do anything. Yet something stopped her. She seemed pinned by some kind of energy field invisible to the outside observer, a particle held on its course by a web of magnetic repulsions.

More than once I had asked her if she ever thought about other kinds of jobs.

"All the time," she said. "How do you think I occupy myself while I'm staring at those white lines ahead of me? I've considered just about every job there is. Teaching, medicine, social work, journalism, you name it. I even considered law, for about five minutes. That would make my family happy. But I tried to picture myself fussing over the wording of a contract and I knew I couldn't do it. It's the same way with everything. Nothing fits. All the things I like doing don't pay."

"Can't you find something tolerable and use your free time for the things you like?"

"But it's such a waste!" she protested. "It's too much of life to spend on something 'tolerable.' Work ought to be something important. Something you love and believe in."

"So what do you love and believe in?" I asked.

"That's just the trouble. I don't know."

She jumped up from the table and walked around the room. Talk about jobs made her restless.

"I think the only reason I keep driving is that I know I could quit anytime I wanted," she said. "I may not believe in it, but at least I'm not trapped in it."

She began to gather up the dinner dishes, closing the subject. "I'll wash, you rinse," she said. "Since you're so picky about how the drainer is stacked."

It was true. It irritated me to watch someone stack the dishes any which way, so that two plates, one bowl and a saucepan filled the entire drainer, when I could have fit dinner service for eight plus all the cooking pots.

Alma Rose was a casual stacker, and a casual washer, also. She liked to talk while she worked, and gave only a fraction of her attention to the dishes. I, on the other hand, gave only a part of my attention to the conversation, because I was checking each dish for bits of food she had missed in her washing. It crossed my mind that if her stay were ever to be longer than a week, we would have to come to some kind of accommodation in this matter.

"Probably I'm the same way about a lover as I am about work," she said one evening. We were not washing dishes at the time, because my attention was fully engaged by what she said.

"In what way?" I asked.

"I doubt I will ever get married again. I couldn't bring myself to swear to fidelity and eternity, because I would immediately panic. But I have this notion that maybe when I'm old, I'll be sitting in my easy chair, and someone else will be sitting in another easy chair, and I'll look across and think, 'I guess this was the person, because somehow the days have added up and now it's forty years.' No promises. No plans. Just the days adding up."

"Do you think that can happen, that two people can go on choosing to be together every day for forty years? Don't you think there are times for every couple when things get so hard they only stay together because they promised they would?"

"Maybe they shouldn't stay together, if it's only because of a promise," said Alma Rose. "I think people know in their gut if a marriage is worth the struggle. The promise won't mean anything if the gut doesn't agree."

"And I think my gut is a very unreliable organ a lot of the time. Sometimes I don't know until months later what it has been telling me."

That was as close as we had ever come to discussing our own future. I didn't try to ask straight out if we had a future together. I knew what her answer would be. We would have to wait forty years, and then, if we looked across the room and there we still were, we would know we had had a future.

The trouble was, I wanted a plan. I didn't need a detailed blueprint, down to the pipes and wires, but I wanted a preliminary sketch, some hint at the exterior style. I needed some small bit of solidity to use as a foundation for daydreams. As it was, my daydreams floated in midair, at one moment threatening to overinflate and detach from earth's gravity completely, at the next moment threatening to deflate and crash to the ground.

Until now I had never minded that my thoughts floated in a separate realm. They were just daydreams and could be as fanciful as I wished, rising into the stratosphere of Nobel prizes and movie stars if I wanted. I had not minded, because I had had the sense never to launch very much of my real self off in such insubstantial vessels. I sent my imagination, but not my heart and soul. Now, suddenly, the whole of me, heart, soul, mind, body, everything, was up there in midair, suspended among a fragile balance of forces which might shift catastrophically at any moment. If I looked down, or up, or anywhere except straight at Alma Rose, here and now, I felt terror.

I kept looking hard at Alma Rose, the one in front of me, not the one I hoped I would still be looking at when our bones began to shrink and our skin to slacken into wrinkles. I thought, maybe if I kept my gaze focused right here and did not think about the other one, the days would pile themselves up month by month without my noticing until the time came when we were old and shrunk and sagging and still loved each other.

Part Three

18

"I HAVEN'T SEEN ALMA ROSE lately. What's become of her?" Marge asked. She set my turkey sandwich on the counter and refilled my coffee cup.

"She's been on a different route this month," I said. "She called a few weeks ago and said her schedule had been changed temporarily."

"Any chance she'll be here for Christmas? Your Pops and I were hoping for a family gathering, since it's our first Christmas together."

"I don't know. I'll ask her, if she calls again." Even as I said it, I felt cold inside.

It was the week before Thanksgiving. I hated this time of year. Everything was shades of gray, the hills, the bare cottonwoods, the leafless bushes. All the vegetation was dried up and hollow, shut down for the winter. The sky, too, was flat gray, with no shades of light and dark. Now and then it spat a few flakes of snow.

We kept all the lights in the store on all the time now. Otherwise, the place took on the atmosphere of an abandoned warehouse, even at noonday. In the summer, it might feel like a cool welcoming cave. In the dark season before snowfall, it felt gloomy.

Out in the street, the timeworn silver and red tinsel garlands, six of them, had been draped from streetlight to streetlight, spanning Main Street. If it snowed before Christmas, they would look festive. In the meantime, surrounded by grayness, they sagged between the lamp posts like the backbone of an ancient cow. A steady chill wind raised swirls of dust and litter around the feet of the lamp posts. The garlands swayed, making a monotonous rhythmic squeak of wire against wood.

Only nighttime brought relief. The wind died into silence, the gray landscape vanished into darkness, and the town glowed with multicolor Christmas lights, in bright defiance of the approach of winter.

I had felt terror, anticipating the day when my dreams would shatter themselves against unyielding earth. I had imagined, and tried not to, the words "I'm not coming back." What I had not anticipated was an indefinite freefall, through darkness, toward a collision with earth that never came.

She had called me on October 23. I remembered the date without writing it on the calendar. It was the kind of thing I did remember.

"A couple of drivers quit," she had said. "They've shifted my route temporarily. It's back to Louisiana for a while."

"OK," I said.

"I hope it's not for long. You're not too upset are you?"

"No, it's all right. I'll miss you, but it's OK."

"I'll miss you, too. Don't you run off with the first pretty woman who walks through the door."

"Not likely," I said.

"I'll call," she said.

She hung up. I had wanted to howl, it's not OK, I can't bear it, tell them you won't go. I didn't do it though. She'd have fought that claim on her like a mustang fighting a lasso around its neck, and maybe she'd have broken loose for good. Instead I was in freefall, hearing her promise to call and beginning not to believe it anymore.

For Thanksgiving, Pops and Marge went to Utah to visit one of Marge's sons. They invited me to come, but I said no. I did not want to be around someone else's happy family right then. I did not want cheerful noise and grandchildren racing through the house slamming doors and the warm smell of sweet things in the oven baking. I'm not sure what I did want, maybe to dig out one of my baggy brown shirts from high school and put it on and go for a long solitary walk with the cold wind blowing my hair into my eyes; maybe to sit on a rock somewhere staring at dead vegetation, shivering in the cold and trying to feel like the heroine of a romantic tragedy.

In fact, what I did do on Thanksgiving was to lie on the couch and eat an entire bag of potato chips and watch a meaningless football game between Detroit and Tampa Bay, mostly because I had a tiny hope that Alma Rose might call and I didn't want to leave the house. At eleven-thirty at night, I finally gave up and took the dogs out for a walk, up to the outcrop. It was very cold, down near zero, and clear. The grass felt crackly under my feet. There was no moon. The stars looked like sharp slivers of ice against an absolute and brittle blackness.

I stood. It was too cold to sit on the rocks. I looked down the valley toward Kilgore and a small stretch of Interstate I could see through a gap in the hills. Now and then a set of lights went by, sometimes just a pair, white in front, red behind, sometimes a whole rig ablaze in white and orange and red, as if one of the houses in Kilgore had set off down the highway to show off its Christmas display. I kept wishing one of those rigs would slow down, put on its blinker and come down the exit ramp, and then disappear behind the shoulder of hill that hid the town from my view, and then reappear a few minutes later around another hill, winding its way up the road toward my house. While I was watching, two of them did come down the ramp and disappear into Kilgore, but they didn't reappear on my road.

The dogs were whining, so I turned to go back down the slope to my house.

"You can see that outcrop from the highway, you know," Alma Rose had told me one day.

"You can? I've never looked for it. I'd have thought that gap in the hills would go by too quick for you to pick it out."

"No, you can see it, if you know what you're looking for. Just for a moment. It appears from behind a hill, and slides by, and disappears behind another hill. You wouldn't notice it, unless you were trying to see it. It's become a kind of welcome beacon for me. One part of it looks just like your rump when you're lying down."

"I doubt that," I said.

"Sure it does. To my eye, anyway."

I had bought her a Christmas present back in early

November, back when her phone call was still a recent event. It was a bracelet of silver and turquoise, made by the Navajos, slender enough to suit her slender bones, but conspicuous enough to suit her personality. It sat on top of my dresser in a small white box. I scowled at it every night, after another day had crawled by and the daytime had lost another minute or two to the darkness, and I still had no word from her.

I refused to put it away out of sight, even though the conviction was growing in me, as silently but inexorably as a tumor, that I was never going to hear any word from her. I thought, this must be what it feels like to die by inches, the mass slowly growing in one's core, swelling and pressing outward, while slowly, slowly, a coldness spreads inward from the ends of the limbs, until the coldness and the weight meet each other and clamp the heart between them.

My only solace was to look straight at the truth and not flinch or try to look from the corner of my eye. I kept the box in plain sight to forestall the urge to duck away.

On Christmas Day, I put the gift away in the back of a drawer of my desk. Then I dressed myself in something bright-colored and drove into Kilgore to have turkey with Pops and Marge.

19

"YOU LOOK LIKE YOU'VE LOST A
little weight. Have you been on a diet?" Peggy Treadwell
asked.

"Sort of," I said.

"I don't know how you do it at this time of year. I always
put on five pounds between Thanksgiving and New Years. I
barely squeezed into this skirt this morning, and I've still got
one more party tonight, for New Year's Eve."

Peggy ran her hands down the side of her hips, pointing
out the snugness of the skirt. Her figure had a neat, compact
stoutness, the kind that looks like it's cinched in with girdles
and support hose even when it's not.

"The secret is not to have any friends," I said. "That way,
you don't get invited to parties, and no one gives you candy
and cookies. Or, alternatively, you could get a divorce and
let stress take away your appetite."

Peggy began to look a little nervous, the way the counselor used to look when I was in school.

"You have lots of friends," she said. "You must have been invited to parties." She was trying to sound reassuring, but her words were too hurried. She sounded instead like someone who is trying to extricate herself from a conversation before the other person starts talking about cutting her wrists.

I decided to make an effort to be more pleasant. "I did go to some parties," I said. "But for once, I didn't overeat. Not that there wasn't plenty of food." I didn't add that my stomach had gone into knots every time I faced another platter of celery sticks gobbed with dip, or butter cookies sprinkled with red and green sugar crystals.

Like Peggy, I still had one party left. Pops and Marge were holding one of the many New Year's Eve celebrations at their house, and I had promised to go. The party turned out to be almost a replay of their wedding, except much smaller and without the band. The liquor was poured freely, and Pops bounced from group to group like a high energy pinball, setting off lights and bells wherever he hit. His fund of funny stories was full to overflowing, and I kept hearing roars of laughter erupting from whichever corner of the room he was in. For my part, I stayed in a chair next to the bar, getting silently and systematically drunk.

At one point, Pops' travels brought him to my end of the room and I listened, half stuporously, as he told about the time Joe Danziger went elk hunting and brought home a trophy saddle horn.

"Joe was just a kid then, all excited about going hunting with his buddies," Pops said, to the circle who were listening. "They rode way back into the mountains, to where they'd heard there were elk. When they started seeing signs, they decided to tie up their horses and hunt on foot. They went stalking through the timber for a while, a little spread out, but all in sight of each other. After quite a while walking, Joe heard a noise, just the snap of a twig. He waved to the others to hold still, and he began to creep forward. He heard another little sound. By now he was getting real excited. He was peering ahead through the trees, and then he saw it, just the head. He was pretty sure it was a head, with antlers. It moved a little bit, so he took aim real quick. He was sure it was going to light out in another moment. He couldn't see the body, so he aimed for the head and pulled the trigger.

"As soon as he fired, they heard this wild whinnying and hoofs galloping off through the timber. So they all ran forward real fast, and Joe was scared to death he must have killed one of the horses, and the others were yelling at him that he was a stupid idiot. When they got to where the horses had been, all they found were the broken reins hanging from the trees, and there on the ground was Joe's saddle horn. That bullet had nipped it off as clean as could be. The horses didn't stop until they got all the way back to camp, so Joe and them had a good long walk back out. His buddies were pretty steamed by the time they got back to camp. But then they saw his saddle with the horn gone. It looked just like something with its head chopped off, you know, and they all got laughing so hard, they couldn't stay mad. One of the other guys, I think it was Pete Hamlin, took that saddle horn to the taxidermist and had him mount it on a big wooden wall plaque, just the way you would with an elk's head. He put a brass plate with the date on it and gave it to Joe. I think Joe still has it on his wall."

Everyone in the room had heard the story before, but they all still laughed, and I laughed a little, too, partly from the bourbon in Pops' New Year's punch, but mostly because we all knew Joe Danziger, who was a quiet, unassuming, awkward man that you couldn't help liking. A lot of the story was a tall tale, but that didn't matter, either. In fact, none of Joe's buddies had thought to save the severed saddle horn at the time. When they got home, Pete Hamlin had dug up an old wrecked saddle from somewhere and sawed the horn off. He didn't take it to the taxidermist, either. He nailed it to a board and wrote the date underneath with a Magic Marker. It was true that Joe still had it on his wall, though.

Pops and his group wandered away. I stayed where I was, drinking steadily, but slowly enough that I wouldn't throw up before my senses were numb. I don't think anyone except Marge noticed that I was drunk. I never said much at parties anyway, so there was nothing remarkable in my spending the evening slouched in an armchair staring bleary-eyed at the hilarity around me.

I stayed sitting even at midnight when Pops cracked open bottles of champagne and everyone gathered in the center of the room to drink loud toasts to the future. My hand was wobbly as I raised my glass to join the toasts. I carried it quickly to my lips so I wouldn't spill. With the glass braced against my lips and chin, and my head in turn braced against the back of the armchair, I managed to keep everything steady long enough to drink the champagne and put the glass down.

Not long after that, Marge quietly came over and helped me stand up. She put her arm around my waist, and laid my arm across her shoulder, and together we lurched out of the living room and up the stairs to my old bedroom.

"I've got to go home and let the dogs out," I mumbled as she straightened my limbs on the bed.

"I'll go and let them out," she said. "You are not going anywhere."

20

IT WAS A NEBULOUS SORT OF bereavement I was suffering, a little like having a loved one vanish while exploring the Amazon jungle. The mind says, be realistic, she's gone forever, but the heart keeps hoping for the miracle. Because there is no absolute proof, no date can be set for a funeral, the neighbors cannot offer condolences, and nothing can be finally settled.

Since my love had no formal standing, either publicly or privately, it did not come to a formal end. Events simply drifted on and left it behind. A few people remarked on Alma Rose's absence, noncommittally. Their comments were neither an offer of sympathy nor a sneer of contempt, merely an observation of fact.

"That lady trucker doesn't come around so much anymore. Did she give up driving?"

"She's been shifted to a different route," I said, as

noncommittal as the questioner.

"Truckers never do stay put for long. Always on to somewhere new. She was a nice gal."

I nodded agreement, packed up their purchases in a bag, nodded again in answer to their goodbye. That was the extent of public acknowledgment of my loss.

Though our reasons were different, neither I nor my neighbors wanted to talk any more specifically than that. I did not want to parade my humiliation and pain. They did not want more definite knowledge of behavior they might feel obliged either to condemn or to defend, if it confronted them explicitly. Either stance would cause them discomfort, condemnation because I was a neighbor they had known all their lives, defense because they, like me, had been brought up to squirm at the thought of homosexuality.

Through January and February, the days were bitterly cold, but no snow fell. The frost went so deep that water lines froze, and ranchers began to talk ominously about the lack of moisture for next summer's growth of grass. Old Mrs. Chase died, very suddenly, of a stroke, and the whole town turned out for her funeral. Leonard Kinley's prayers for her rest and redemption were still fresh in our ears when the high school science teacher, Mr. Carpenter, was arrested for sexual assault on a fourteen-year-old girl, one of his students. People were stunned. Larry Carpenter had grown up outside Kilgore and was well liked. His family owned a substantial ranch, which his father and brother managed. The charge seemed unthinkable, but he had been caught, in the act, by the girl's older sister.

In February, a fire destroyed two mobile homes in the trailer park at the edge of town, the one where Peggy

Treadwell watched her purse so carefully. In typical fashion, Peggy took charge of collecting money and food for the families, while simultaneously spreading the rumor that the fire had started because they were smoking marijuana in bed. In reality, the fire was started by one of the space heaters they were using to keep their pipes from freezing when the temperature hit thirty below.

I wasn't sure if it was indeed a winter of particular disaster, or if I was simply taking more notice of the disasters because they fell in with my own mood. With each new shock, it seemed that the earth must be more and more awobble in its orbit, that the universe itself was out of sorts. I was spiraling deeper and deeper into gloom, and each piece of bad news from the outside world just added overtones to what was already a sustained chord of grief within me.

I sought out remedies, the usual ones. My New Year's Eve drunk became opening night for a prolonged attempt at numbness. For six weeks, I put myself to sleep at night with whiskey and arose, stuporous, at noon, with just enough time to feed and walk the dogs before going to work. If I was asleep, I couldn't think or feel, and that was what I wanted. At the store, I talked only as much as was necessary to transact business. I sought numbness in routine, in columns of numbers and sheets of paper. Anything that disturbed routine set my circulation moving, and with circulation came pain.

Sometime in February, I didn't calculate the alcohol right. Instead of drifting off into a doze on my bed, I spent half the night retching over the toilet. The next night, I looked at the bottle of whiskey and couldn't make myself drink any. I lay awake, wide awake, staring into the darkness. My eyes burned from staring at nothing. If I closed them, I saw Alma

Rose smiling at me. I felt her arm lying across my body, her hand stroking my neck. I couldn't bear it. I opened my eyes again. The empty blackness was better than the mirages in my head.

Why had I ever let myself believe that she loved me? How could someone so plain and ordinary expect to hold the interest of a quicksilver spirit like Alma Rose?

At dawn, I fell asleep for an hour or two. I awoke disoriented, not recognizing my new house. For an instant, I didn't remember that Alma Rose existed. I was back in an earlier self and I couldn't figure out where I was. Then I looked across the room at the wall full of my drawings and memory awoke. I leapt out of bed and began ripping the drawings off the wall.

"You goddamned coward. You could have had the decency to call," I shouted. I crumpled the drawings into a ball and hurled them against the far wall.

I looked at the window curtains, cheerful bright blues and yellows that Alma Rose had persuaded me would look nice, colors far brighter than any I would have dared choose for myself.

"You sneaky, selfish coward. You could have put a note in the mail, if you didn't want to talk to me."

I grabbed the curtains and yanked. Instead of tearing them, I just pulled out the flimsy nails that held the curtain rods in place. One end of the rod came loose and fell with a clatter. Curtains and rod dangled askew across the window.

"Hell!" Tears were streaming down my face. I sat down on the end of the bed and wept. Around me the house was silent, clean and white, unscarred by use. Every detail of it mocked me, the porch Alma Rose had insisted I needed, the windows whose placement we had debated for hours, even the faucet handles which Alma Rose had found for me in the City, wherever it was.

I had to get out of there for a while. I dressed hastily, put on a winter jacket and hat, called the dogs and set off at a run up the hill to the outcrop. At least the land had been there before Alma Rose existed. The yucca and bunchgrass did not bear the stamp of her opinions. The wind did not blow in and out with her breath.

I sat on my rock and watched the tiny trucks and cars going by on the Interstate. For a moment, I felt almost peaceful. Alma Rose and her rig became a tiny toy, with tiny rubber wheels, rolling across the vastness of land. I, too, was a tiny creature, whose troubles did not cause so much as a ripple in the calm of the universe. It was very restful, to feel so insignificant.

Old Lulu leaned herself against me and pushed her head into my lap, asking for notice and kindness. I rubbed her ears and she pressed closer, wagging her tail. The tears came again, part gratitude for her dumb devotion, part an agonized wish for someone to give me notice and kindness, someone in whose lap I could lay my own head and know she would not push me away.

Then I thought, when am I ever going to stop feeling sorry for myself?

Drugs had not worked. I decided to try the next obvious remedy, sex. Maybe I needed a quick meaningless affair with someone to help me bridge the gap from grief back to normal life.

It was easy to hit upon the idea, but more difficult to carry it out. Sex was not procured quite so easily as alcohol, at least not in Kilgore and not by me. Perhaps for some people a quick, meaningless affair could be arranged as easily as an appointment with the hairdresser. I did not have any idea how to go about it.

In high school, there had been a supply of boys eager to paw any girl who showed herself willing, provided the room was dimly lit and we were all a little drunk. Now almost every man my age was married, and I was not likely to find myself in a dimly lit room with the few who weren't. I didn't even consider seeking out a woman. There was no one in Kilgore I thought would be interested.

The first place to try was a bar, which did offer dim light and alcohol. Late one night I steeled myself and walked into the Rainbow, the fractionally better class bar of the two in Kilgore. The interior was dingy and thick with cigarette smoke, and smelled like stale beer. The walls were covered with Kilgore memorabilia, mostly photographs of athletic teams and local citizens posing with a trophy elk or a rainbow trout. Besides the waitresses, the only other women I saw were two girls barely of legal age, clinging to the elbows of two cowboys from the Quarter Circle T, and Cora Eastman, who was there with her husband. There were about a dozen men in the bar, maybe half of them single.

I lasted forty-five minutes. The problem was not the atmosphere, unappealing though it was. Nor was it the lack of other women. The problem was that I knew every single person there, and they all knew me. Though they all said hello in a friendly way, they were all clearly wondering what I was doing there late at night and unescorted. They seemed embarrassed by this departure from my normal character.

I realized very quickly that even if the men recognized my

purpose in being there, they would not make any advance. They had known me for too long a time in a context entirely unromantic. Nor could I make the approach myself. I was far too shy, and even if I had not been, whom would I approach? I tried to imagine myself flirting with Elroy Weiss, the rather slow-witted man who ran a grader for the county, or with Mike Hanford, the jumpy, pointy-faced manager of the branch office of the First Citizens Bank, or with Dwight Barbula, with his handlebar mustache, six-foot-five-inch frame, and don't-mess-with-me scowl. Imagination failed me. I sat sipping my beer, trying to look nonchalant as I shriveled up with self-consciousness. When a decent interval of time had passed, I slunk out of the bar and went home.

The only other possibility was the truck stop. It was not dimly lit, but at least most of the men there did not know me. Two nights after my foray into the Rainbow, I drove over to the truck stop. At that moment I was driven by the frantic determination of an outnumbered army, which is battling its own doubts as much as it is battling the enemy. If I delayed and began to think, the doubts would overwhelm the determination.

The truck stop was clean and brightly lit. The color scheme was orange, including everything from the vinyl seats and plastic menus to the trim around the plate glass windows. Dark and seductive it was not. I sat down at the counter, looked for a moment at the menu, then took a quick, discreet glance at the other clientele. There were plenty of men, certainly, all ages, most of them unaccompanied by women, and some of them not bad looking. Just down the counter from me, a prospect was munching on a platter of cheeseburger and fries. He was a little younger than me, dark, with a small mustache and a muscular build that threatened to burst the seams of his form-fitting blue jeans.

"Hi, Pat. What brings you here on such a cold night?"

The waitress was Wendy Corcoran. Her mother had been head cheerleader two classes ahead of me in high school.

"Nothing in particular," I muttered.

Wendy poured my coffee and I asked for a piece of blueberry pie.

"Don't see you so much now that that friend of yours doesn't stop in here anymore. She's driving for Gulf Coast Pacific now, huh?"

"I guess so."

"That's what one of the fellows said, anyhow. That she just up and quit, and went to work for another company. Is it true?"

I nodded, hoping she wouldn't ask me for details, since she apparently expected me to know all about it.

"I guess it doesn't matter whether they're a lady or a man. These truckers always keep moving. Right, Ronnie?" She smiled a dazzling, inviting smile at the handsome young man down the counter from me.

"You can bet on it, sugar pie," he said, with a grin at her. She moved down and leaned her elbows on the counter right across from him so that they were eye to eye.

He said something in a voice too low for me to hear. Wendy leaned a little closer and said something back, giggling. They continued to exchange confidential banter for a minute or two. Wendy giggled all the while and their two heads moved closer and closer together.

Now how did she do that, I wondered. If she wanted to go to bed with him, she could no doubt arrange it then and there.

I looked down the counter in the other direction. A skinny, middle-aged man was alternating between methodical bites of a hot turkey sandwich and perusal of a newspaper. What did one say to launch a flirtation? How did one even catch his attention in the first place? I couldn't ask him to pass the sugar, since it was right in front of me.

I waited and watched, surreptitiously. Finally, he paused from the sandwich and the newspaper long enough to take a swallow of coffee.

"How are the Nuggets doing this year?" I asked abruptly. To me, my voice sounded loud enough to catch the attention of the whole restaurant, but it must not have been. I had to repeat my question before he realized I was talking to him. My face felt hot.

"The Nuggets?" he said, vaguely. "Oh, you mean basketball. I didn't look. Here, you can have the whole sports section. I'm done with it."

He slid the section of the newspaper down the counter and went back to the sandwich.

At least now I had something to read. I opened it and began to scan the scoreboard. Wendy was still engaged with the young man. I began to wonder if I was ever going to get my pie.

A tall, burly man settled onto the stool next to me. His weight made the stool squeak with every move, and his bulk was such that Wendy could not ignore him, enthralled though she was. She brought a cup and the coffee pot and asked him what he wanted.

"Two cinnamon doughnuts," he said.

Along with his doughnuts, she brought my pie. I pushed the newspaper aside and began to eat.

"How did the Nuggets do last night?" the big man asked.

I looked at him, startled. The headline was blazoned across the page right in front of him on the counter, Cavs Crunch Nuggets 123–106.

"They lost," I said.

"They're no darn good this year anyhow," he said. "Do you follow basketball?"

"A little."

"I haven't known many ladies who liked sports," he said. "My wife doesn't know a free throw from a three-point shot."

"I know that much," I said.

There couldn't be much promise of intrigue in a man who mentioned his wife in the first three sentences.

"My ex-wife, I should say," he added. "We're divorced."

This called for second thought. Even as he spoke, I saw his eyes travel toward my left hand, which was resting on the counter, bare of rings.

At that moment I felt as though I had become two people. One of the two was sitting at the counter, feeling awkward and wondering how to reply to someone who had just announced that he was divorced. What did one say? "I'm sorry." "Was it because of basketball?"

The other one of me was standing ten feet away watching and thinking, "Is it my imagination or is he working his way toward making a pass? And stranger still, is that woman going along with it, right here on these orange vinyl stools, in front of a waitress whose birth announcement she read when she was in high school?"

The big man did not wait for a reply.

"I wish more women took an interest in things like sports," he said. "It would give us more to talk about together.

Do you like football, too?"

"A little. I usually check the score of the Broncos' games."

"So you know the difference between a pass and a fumble."

"I hope so." In my present state of hair-trigger awareness, it occurred to me to wonder if he was still talking about football.

"Do you watch football with your husband?" he asked.

"I don't have a husband."

"With your boyfriend, then?"

He leaned a fraction of an inch closer to me as he spoke, and that small movement awoke my more usual caution. Instead of saying I didn't have a boyfriend, I said, "No," and left him to guess whether that meant I didn't have a boyfriend or had one but didn't watch football with him.

"I'm not that big a fan, really," I said, trying to sound a little less abrupt.

"Enough of one to read the sports page," he said.

I glanced past the big man toward the skinny, middle-aged one, who was now chewing his way through a piece of chocolate cake. He was not reading anymore, and I wondered if he was listening to this long interchange about the section of newspaper I had so clumsily acquired from him.

"You live around here, or just passing through?" the big man asked.

"I live here. My dad and I run . . . " I paused. Caution took hold again. "I grew up here. I've lived with my dad most of my life. You're just passing through, aren't you? Otherwise I'd know you."

"That's right. I've got my own rig. I come through here every so often. I haven't seen you here before, though."

"I don't eat here very often."

"It's too bad you don't. This place has way too many men and not nearly enough ladies. Especially not good-looking ones like you."

That shut me up. It called for some sort of coy, flirtatious response that was completely beyond me.

"Now I've made you blush," he said. "You shouldn't have to blush because a man thinks you're good-looking."

The skinny man had stopped chewing. He didn't look our way, but he was staring down at nothing with the kind of unmoving attentiveness that meant he was listening. Now I did begin to blush.

"My name is Tiny, by the way," the big man said. "I was Greg until high school. Then I kinda grew and the guys started calling me Tiny and I've been that ever since. What's your name?"

"Pat," I said.

"I've got a niece named that, but we call her Patty. She's only four. Dark hair, just like you. Cute as a button. She'll have the little boys eating out of her hand in no time. My wife and I never had no kids. We were only married three years." He looked wistful. "I sure would like to have kids someday. First, I've got to find a woman who will marry me. Not many women want a husband who's on the road a lot. They need their man to be home, kind of the way a tomato plant needs a stake."

I didn't say anything for a while. For the first time, I forgot my own position long enough to take a real look at him, and I began to feel a little queasy. Tiny had a big square friendly face that went with his big square body. Physically he reminded me of Chuck. From the direction his conversation was going, it seemed he was about as ready to propose marriage as he was to have a one-night stand. If the woman were willing, he might move from the one to the other in a step.

Was I seriously intending to have a quick sexual encounter with someone like Tiny? He was a decent-seeming, pleasant fellow, who behaved with the same jovial and unconscious condescension toward women as a lot of the men in Kilgore. If I had not had sex on my mind, if he had come into the Mercantile on any ordinary day of the week, we would have exchanged friendly relaxed chitchat and nothing either of us said would have caused me discomfort. Instead, my state of mind had led us into an exchange of innuendo and meaningful looks.

Now I had to contemplate, unblinkingly, what had previously been an abstraction in my head, a 'quick, meaningless affair.' I didn't know Tiny. He would be a simple physical object. So how did I feel about him as a simple physical object? Could I imagine kissing that square pink face? Could I imagine unbuttoning that red and gray plaid shirt? Could I imagine those broad fleshy hands sliding under my blouse to caress my breast?

I nearly jumped off my stool.

"There must be women out there who like solitude and independence," I said. I was trying to work the conversation back around to friendly chitchat, unladen with hidden meanings. "There must be women who would like having the house to themselves."

"Do you think so?" he asked.

"I'm sure there are lots, somewhere."

"You don't happen to know any, do you?" he said, with a pointed look that made it an approach.

"Not here in Kilgore," I said. "It's not a very big town. Most of the women are married. I was thinking of a city, if you live in a city."

I tried to assume a tone of friendly detachment, as if all along I had only been taking a sisterly interest and it had never occurred to me that the conversation could have any reference to me personally. I felt weaselly, but I couldn't see any other way out. He looked puzzled for a moment, then fell into step with the beat I had indicated.

"Do I look like a big city boy?" he asked, jokingly. "My town's not a whole lot bigger than Kilgore, and I've pretty well struck out there."

"You stop in a lot of other towns, don't you?" I said.

"I guess I do. But the kind of lady I'm looking for doesn't generally hang out at a truck stop."

"I suppose not."

My pie was long since gone. I drained the last swallow of room-temperature coffee from my cup, paid the check, and slunk out of the truck stop, in much the same way as I had slunk out of the Rainbow Bar.

When I got home I stripped off all my clothes and took a long shower. I felt as if I had embraced something unclean. The uncleanness was not Tiny. He was just an ordinary man, making the ordinary attempt to obtain a woman, for sex or for marriage, as chance dictated.

The unclean thing was me. If I had been overcome by lust and had gone off in search of an anonymous body to satisfy it, that at least would have been an honest, animal thing to do. But I had not felt lust. I had felt only a wish to blot out feeling. I had been proposing to have sex, not only with no emotional attachment, but without even any physical desire. Faced with an actual man, and a rather solid, likable one, what had been a plausible abstraction became a repellent reality.

I scrubbed away with my unscented soap, washing and rinsing, washing and rinsing. Then, as I stood under the gradually cooling spray of water and looked at the white wrinkled skin of my fingertips, I thought about Lady Macbeth and began to laugh. So I had wanted to engage in a meaningless, passionless, mechanical act of sex. It was not exactly blood on my hands. A million people around the world were probably doing the same thing at this very moment—to stave off boredom, to pay for food, to satisfy curiosity or prove manhood or relieve loneliness, or simply from force of habit. My act could have been joined to theirs and what difference would it have made? Perhaps it was too bad that my nature had rebelled.

The shower was quite cool by now. I stepped out of it and began to rub myself dry, vigorously. My mind was wide awake and felt abnormally clear and swift, as it often did when I awoke in the middle of the night and could not get back to sleep. I put on a bathrobe and sat down cross-legged on the living room couch, in the dark, looking out through the windows at the moonlit landscape. Cold white light gleamed off fenceposts, and the bare cottonwoods, and the hood of my pickup. Further away rose the black silhouettes of the hills. There was not a hint of color or warmth anywhere, only a cold purity of light and shadow, bonechillingly serene.

For that moment, I could think of Alma Rose and not feel a wrench. I felt only a stillness of detachment, as if the two of us were floating in the colorless, absolute zero vacuum of outer space.

"She's gone. There is nothing I can do. So be it," I said to myself with Hindu calm.

I sat motionless, holding the mood, willing my mind to blankness, my body to stillness. My eyes fixed themselves on the twin trunks of a cottonwood, focused there as if I could, with perfect concentration, make my self dissolve into the universe and then the universe also disappear, leaving nothing but that tree.

The self refused to dissolve. The mind refused to stay blank. Quite suddenly, from nowhere, a thought intruded, a thought so overwhelming and so obvious, it obliterated tree and universe both.

Maybe she doesn't know. Maybe she thinks I don't care.

My eyes still stared at the tree, but I didn't see it. I didn't see anything. I only heard our two voices on the telephone, first hers, "My route's been changed. I won't be there for a few weeks," then mine, so impassive, so calm, "OK." She had said, "I'll call." I had said, "OK," and then, much too feebly, "I'll miss you." I had not screamed out the anguish I felt. I had not cried out, "Make them change it back. I can't bear it." I had said, "OK," because she was a free agent and I was a free agent, and I would not cling or make demands.

So maybe she thought I was indifferent, that it didn't matter to me whether she came back or not. She had always said she couldn't tell what I was feeling. So maybe she didn't know. I had to make her know, somehow. In the space of seconds, the need took hold of me with the compulsion of the animal need to survive. I had to let her know.

But how? I didn't know where she lived. Perhaps I could call information for every city on the West Coast until I found her.

I was halfway to the phone when I thought, even if I find her number, I can't call her up. She had made it clear that that part of her life was off limits. She did not want me to track her down in this way. To do so would not further my cause.

So what could I do? For the moment, I was stuck.

Then I remembered what she had said about my rock outcrop, that she could see it from the Interstate and that she had always looked for it as a beacon of welcome. Maybe she still passed by on the Interstate now and then. Maybe from habit she glanced to see if she could pick out the outcrop.

I knew what I wanted to do. The idea was there in my brain, whole and round. She had told me I should do something crazy sometime. Well, I would do something crazy and maybe she would see it and know how much she was loved, and maybe she would come back.

I went to my bedroom and searched through my pads of drawings until I found the first one, the one I liked the best. I brought it out to the living room and sat for a long time on the couch, gazing at it. Then I took out a drawing pad and began to make other sketches, like the exercises I had done for drafting in high school. Here is an object. What does it look like from the back? From the side? From the top?

Before long, I had a collection of sketches of Alma Rose asleep, as seen from all different vantage points. I took them into my bedroom and tacked them up on the wall where the other drawings had been, before I ripped them down. I crawled into bed, turned out the light, and within five minutes I was asleep.

21

IN THE MORNING, EARLY, I CALLED
Chuck.

He sounded as solid as ever and a lot more cheerful than he used to when we were teenagers.

"It's great to hear from you, Pat. It's been years. So what bug got in your ear that you decided to call?"

"Do you know anyone who could teach me how to use dynamite?" I asked.

"Dynamite? What have you got in mind? Are you mad at somebody?"

"Not exactly. I want to make a big sculpture out of rock. I want to find out if I can use dynamite to do the first rough shaping. Do you know anyone, maybe from a highway crew or from the mines?"

"How big is this thing going to be?" Chuck asked.

"Very big."

"How big is very big?"

"I'm not sure. Maybe a hundred feet long. Fifteen or twenty feet high. Something like that."

"What's it a sculpture of?"

"You'll have to wait and see. It would take a long time to explain."

"I know a couple of guys who are good with explosives," Chuck said. "The one who's better is a little weird. His name is Clay Shipley."

"I don't mind weird. You know that. Unless by weird you mean that he likes to see how short he can make the fuse and still get to cover."

"No, he's not like that. I don't know how to explain. I guess you'll find out. You've got to tell me when you've made this thing. I want to see it."

Over the phone Clay Shipley was cautious and taciturn, but normal enough. He said he had better come look at the site before he gave any opinions. He was free the Saturday after next.

In my present mood, ten days seemed like an eternity to wait. I had a whole hill of rock to move and I wanted to get started. Since I couldn't sit still, I bought some cans of paint and a hundred foot tape measure and set about marking the outcrop with big splashes of red and blue, here the top of the head, here the shoulder, here the curve of the hip, here the knee, the ankle and the toes. I had made drawings of the outcrop, as close to scale as I could, and then superimposed the drawings of Alma Rose, shifting them back and forth until I found the position where body and outcrop fit each other most closely, and, more important, where the rock did not have any hollows in places where the sculpture demanded protrusions. Working from the drawings, I measured and marked the outcrop, then scrambled down the slope to see how the proportions looked, then climbed back up again to measure and mark some more.

The days were typical of March, very windy, sometimes raw, sometimes alluringly mild, with occasional flurries of snow or quick windblown showers of rain. The weather did not bother me. My body stayed warm, racing up and down the hill. The dogs were delighted to spend so many hours running free out of doors. They poked their noses under bushes and into crevices, and cocked their heads to catch every sound and scent carried by the gusts of wind.

On the Saturday morning, I was up early, waiting with the coffee pot on and all my drawings organized. Clay Shipley appeared exactly when he said he would, at eight o'clock. He drove up to the house in a big square van. It looked like a UPS delivery van repainted battleship gray, with warnings about explosives painted on the sides and rear. The door of the van slid open, and a figure clambered out, a tall gawky figure that somehow made the act of stepping out of a vehicle suggest the movement of a long-legged, many-jointed crab scuttling out from under a rock. His body still seemed to move crabwise even when he was walking straight across the yard toward me.

He didn't say who he was or stick out his hand to be shaken.

"I take it that's the rock," he said, with a jerky sideways gesture of the head in the direction of the outcrop. His tone was not brusque, just preoccupied, as if he were already absorbed in calculating the placement of the dynamite charges.

For a moment I didn't answer. I was taking in his appearance. He had a long oval face with sagging jowls. The top of his head was totally bald, but he had a generous growth of whiskers and beard, slightly graying. He shaved the face itself, down to the jawline, leaving the beard as a fringe from his ears down under his chin. The result was that he looked as if his head was upside down, or at least his hair had been installed upside down.

"That's the rock," I said. "Do you want to see the draw-ings of what I'm planning?"

"I guess I'd better," he said. His eyes kept traveling off to the side, pulled by the rock. The look in his eye was familiar. I tried to think where I had seen it, that intentness, that fixity, as if the rock exercised some irresistible fascination. Suddenly I knew where I had seen it. It was the look that came into the eyes of the collies when they were working sheep.

I'd only been in his company for two minutes, but already I knew that Clay Shipley lived to blast rock. It was not a question of enjoying it. He might or might not enjoy it. It was a calling, something that ran in the blood, and he was evidently one of the lucky people who figure out what their calling is early enough to make a career of it.

I led him inside to look at the drawings. He declined my offer of coffee, scanned the drawings quickly and then went back outside and stood for a long time scrutinizing the out-crop. The marks of paint did not trace the complete outline of a figure, only a few significant points, like the stars of a constellation. Only if I filled the gaps with my imagination could I see a woman's body.

"Lotta work you're taking on, you know," said Clay.

"Is it possible to do it?"

"Anything's possible if you want to take the time."

"I'm a patient person."

He glanced at me and I think recognized a potential fellow fanatic.

"I want to look closer, make sure that rock is what I think it is," he said.

We climbed up to the outcrop, and he clambered around on it, rubbing the rock with his fingers, chipping at it with a chisel.

"You do realize that anything you carve out of this is going to erode away and be unrecognizable in a hundred, maybe two hundred years," he said.

"That's long enough," I said. "I'll be gone myself long before that."

"It won't take so long to carve as marble, anyhow."

"Can I do any of it with dynamite?"

"The rough shape can be made with explosives. The dynamite doesn't just vaporize the rock, though. You'll have a lot of broken rock to clear away."

"How long will it take you to teach me?" I asked.

"A lot longer than it's going to take me to do it myself," he said. "It takes extreme precision for dynamite to be any use for what you're doing. Unless you know exactly how to place the charges, you have to be overcautious so that you don't blow away too much. Then you're left with so much rock to break with a pick, the dynamite was hardly worth the bother. It takes years of practice to learn that precision."

"So how much is it going to cost if you do it?"

He grinned suddenly. "A lot less than it would if you were the Glenville Coal Company," he said. "I've never had the chance to do something like this." His eyes were bright with that feverish collie eagerness.

"When can you do it?" I asked.

"I'll be done with the job I'm on at the end of April. I could fit it in then. If I can get the permits before that, I might come over on a Saturday and do some of the first stage big blasts. That way you'll have enough rock to haul that you won't go jumping out of your skin with impatience."

True to his word, he reappeared two weeks later, on another Saturday.

"You're sure you want me to do this?" he asked one last time.

I nodded.

"Let me see those drawings again."

I handed him the drawings and explained how the marks of paint corresponded to the marks I had made on the sketches.

"Well, here goes," he said. He swung open the back doors of his van.

I looked inside and thought, this must be what it looks like inside a spaceship or a submarine. Every inch of space was filled, except for a path wide enough for a human body. A large part of the area was taken up by crates of explosives, stacked in specially constructed carrier racks and well lashed down. On one wall, an array of tools hung in orderly ranks, beside equally orderly rows of shelves and bins filled with supplies. In the far corner stood a machine that looked like a pump or compressor with long coils of hose. Beside it lay a collection of electronic gear. Everything was polished, immaculate and organized with military efficiency, a display of technological splendor compressed into a tiny space.

"What a beautiful setup," I said.

Clay didn't answer, but a flicker of pleasure crossed his face.

"Could I watch you work?" I asked.

"I'd rather you didn't," he said. "It makes me nervous. I get distracted and my instincts don't work properly."

"I feel the same way when I'm drawing," I said. "I'll stay out of your way."

I left him bent over his tiny workbench, totally absorbed. The moment he stopped speaking to me and turned to sort out the tools and materials he needed, my existence was forgotten. Probably I could have stayed and watched for quite a while before he noticed I was still there.

Out of superstition, I didn't once look out the windows on that side of the house. For a while I paced around the living room, waiting for the first explosion and unable to sit still until it came. But it didn't come and didn't come, and the silence began to feel like a physical presence, like the heavy stillness of the air before a thunderstorm. At intervals, I heard a grinding whine, but for the most part there was only silence. Finally, I gave up waiting and sat down with a book. The dogs had paced with me, filled with anxiety. Now, relieved, they lay down to sleep.

The blast, when it came, ejected me from my chair and terrified the dogs, who clustered around me whining. I patted them and explained that the noise was harmless, but the dishware and pots were still rattling in the kitchen and my voice lacked conviction. After a small interval, the second explosion came, then, after similar pauses, three more. Then the silence settled in again.

I wanted to rush to the window to look, but I made myself stay where I was. If I waited, I might see a visible result. Even when I got into my pickup to leave for work, I avoided looking behind me at the outcrop. I would look in the morning and see the whole day's progress.

"Are you prospecting for gold out there on your place?" Gladys Gardner asked me, later that day.

I shook my head and smiled. "I'm making something."

"What kind of something?"

"A sculpture."

"You mean you're going to make that whole hilltop into a sculpture?"

I nodded.

"Land sakes. That's something neither one of us guessed. We were listening to the blasts all morning. Lyle thought maybe they were doing seismographic testing to look for oil. I thought they must be working on the highway. Then I came into town past your place and it looked like the top of the hill had been blown to pieces. I couldn't imagine what you were doing. A sculpture. What's it a sculpture of?"

I almost couldn't answer, because I was choking in panic. The top of the hill had been blown to pieces? What was I doing? Why had I turned a complete stranger loose on my rock with a van full of dynamite? Maybe he was a madman. Maybe he would blast and blast for the sheer joy of noisy destruction until my outcrop was a pile of rubble. Why had I let superstition rule me, to the point that I didn't even oversee his work?

"Pat, are you OK?" said Gladys.

"It's going to be a sculpture of a person," I said quickly.

"Like Mount Rushmore, you mean?"

"Nothing so grand as that. Maybe the equivalent of Thomas Jefferson's nose," I said. "It's a person sleeping."

"Whatever put the idea in your head?"

I shrugged. That I couldn't tell her. "I wanted something to keep me busy," I said.

Gladys was shaking her head and laughing. "You're quite something, Pat. Most of us would crochet a bedspread or plant a garden if we needed to keep busy. Won't it take years to make?"

"I don't have any idea. I've never done it before."

Word was spreading fast, in that subterranean way that important news always did spread in Kilgore. Everyone in town had heard the blasting. Half of those who came into the store asked if I knew what it was. The other half had already heard some version or another of an explanation, and came furnished with questions and opinions. I mostly kept quiet and listened to what people had to tell me about my project.

It was going to be Sleeping Beauty. Would it have the prince, too? It was going to be a swami meditating. It was going to be a naked woman; a naked man; a naked woman and man, performing an indecency. It was going to be an abstract conglomeration of slabs and cubes, representing mankind's alienation from God. It was going to be a miniature copy of Mount Rushmore. It was a wanton destruction of natural beauty so it didn't matter what it was going to be in the end. It was never going to be finished anyway.

I had little to say in explanation or defense. I was still in the grip of the horrifying vision that Gladys Gardner's description had raised in my head. I had an urge to tell people it was going to be a lifesize sculpture of a mountain climber buried under a rockslide.

To those who asked, straight out, I repeated what I had

said to Gladys, that it would be a person sleeping. If they asked why I was doing it, I said the same thing, too, that I wanted something to keep me busy.

"You'll be busy, all right," said Peggy Treadwell. She sounded as if she thought I could equally well be kept busy cutting out paper snowflakes in a mental institution. "What exactly is the subject?" she added.

"It's a person asleep," I repeated.

"What sort of person, a man or a woman?"

"A woman."

"What does she look like? Does she have clothes on?"

"Probably you won't be able to tell whether she does or not."

"What do you mean? Is this going to be one of those abstract things with four eyes?"

"No, I mean that I'm not a very good sculptor. I'll be glad if you can tell it's a woman when I'm done. I doubt I'll be carving details like buttons and collar ruffles."

Or nipples and navels, I thought.

Peggy began to look a little less like a bloodhound on the scent of impropriety. I hoped she was picturing a young lady in crinoline skirts napping decorously on a bank of daisies, with a chaperone keeping a watchful eye from just outside the edge of the artist's view.

I was not speaking deceitfully when I said she might not be able to tell if the woman was clothed. At this point I had no idea if I could create an object recognizable as human. I didn't see any reason to tell her, or anyone, that I was making a sculpture of my lover in the nude, when they might never see anything more than a rearranged heap of rocks. If it turned out I had skill enough to make my sculpture scandalous, I would figure out how to weather Peggy Treadwell's outrage.

"It seems like a foolish waste of energy to me," Peggy said. "If you're going to put all that effort into something, you could be helping to find permanent homes for the Pisarciks and the Wilkinses."

It was true, I could. How could I justify spending all my free time making a sculpture, when there were people in immediate and obvious need of help? For a while my panic at the devastation Clay Shipley might have wrought was replaced by a pang of guilt that I was not bending my efforts toward some goal of more benefit to humanity.

On all sides of me the needs cried out, and not just the need for shelter for the Pisarciks and the Wilkinses. Fifty miles to the north, alcoholism and poverty were laying waste to the communities on the Indian reservation. Seventy miles to the west, the lumber companies were laying waste to the National Forests. Seventy-five miles to the southeast, the coal mines were stripping rangeland bare. In all directions, ranchers were squeezed between low prices and high debt. Kilgore itself was slowly withering away, as business was sucked away down the Interstate to Seco Springs. In the state capitol, legislators dithered for three months about the crisis in education and then went home. In Washington, the government was on a gigantic credit card spending spree. There was terrorism in the Middle East, famine in Africa, civil war in Latin America, and injustice nearly everywhere. So what was I doing weeping over something so small and private as the loss of a lover?

"What's this I hear about you carving a Buddha out of that hill of yours?" Pops was grinning as if he thought the idea sounded like a terrific lark.

"Where did you hear that I was carving a Buddha?" I asked.

"I was just down at the Rainbow. Hank Eastman said that the blasting we've been hearing all day was coming from your place. He said you were going to carve a giant statue of a Buddha, meditating."

"Did he really say that?"

"Well, he said you were going to make a statue of a person meditating. That sounded like a Buddha to me. Is it true?"

"It's true I'm making a statue, but not a Buddha. It's a woman sleeping. At least that's what I'm going to try to make. Since I've never done it before, I don't know if I'll succeed."

"Sure you will," Pops said. "You're clever enough. You can do anything you set your mind to."

"Do you think so?"

"I'm sure so."

I knew his confidence in me was fortified by a few beers at the Rainbow, but it felt good nevertheless.

Just before closing, Marge came into the store. Pops had carried the news with him when he went home for supper, and she must have left to come talk to me the moment the supper dishes were done.

"I hear you're aiming to carve the biggest tombstone in the state," she said.

"What do you mean? Is that what Pops told you?" I asked.

"No, he told me you're going to turn your hilltop into a statue of a sleeping woman. He's tickled pink at the whole notion. He says it sounds like something he might have done when he was young."

"But you're not tickled at the notion, I can tell."

"I'm not just sure. It's a statue of Alma Rose, isn't it?"

"Yes."

"So it sounds to me like you're planning to set up the biggest tombstone a person could imagine. I think you'd be better off forgetting all about her, instead of setting up a ten times life size reminder right outside your window."

I was silent. I knew her advice was sound. Marge was sensible and kindhearted, though her tongue was sharp. Her advice was in no way self-serving. Still, I felt myself digging in to resist.

"I can't forget just by telling myself I should," I said.

"I know you can't force it, Pat. But you can try not to keep fretting the wound, like a dog that keeps licking a sore. After a while, time will pass and it won't gall you so much, and maybe you'll find someone else."

"Who the hell am I going to find in Kilgore?" I said.

"Well, maybe you won't find someone else, but a statue of Alma Rose isn't going to be any more good to you than nobody. It won't love you back and it won't keep you warm at night. All it will do is keep on hurting you and hurting you. I lived alone for twenty years after Pete died. There are a lot worse things that can happen than to live alone."

She was right, but 'right' wasn't what I wanted.

Driving home, I peered ahead to see if I could see anything of the outcrop. The sky was cloudy and I could only dimly distinguish its silhouette against the lesser blackness of the sky. I would have to wait until morning.

I couldn't sleep. Too many people were talking. Peggy Treadwell had donned a Salvation Army uniform and was telling me to make myself socially useful. Pops was dancing drunkenly on a bar counter and telling me to do whatever I pleased, so long as I stayed in Kilgore. Marge was standing next to an examination table at the veterinary clinic and telling me I was exhibiting "self-traumatizing behavior" and might need tranquilizing drugs. The rest of Kilgore was gathered in conversational clusters, murmuring about yogis and indecency and the desecration of natural beauty.

22

WHEN I FINALLY DID SLEEP, I
slept as if drugged. I was awakened by the telephone. I felt as
if I had to thrash my way out from under an encumbering
weight of blankets before I could open my eyes and find the
phone. The early morning sun was shining in my window,
making bright squares on the wall across from my bed.

"So what do you think?" the voice said, in answer to my
croaked hello. It was Clay Shipley.

"I haven't looked yet," I said.

"Go and look, then. I'll hold on."

I padded over to the window and looked out. At first the
sun was too bright, shining in my face and throwing long
shadows across the face of the outcrop. When my eyes adjusted, I saw piles of broken rubble and surfaces of fresh rock
face, blasted into exposure to light and air. The new rock
made bright jagged gashes of clear color among the duller,

weatherbeaten surfaces of the old rock. Those clean, unscarred surfaces reminded me of the clean white faces of the newborn calves, before time and dirt and sunlight dulled the brilliant white into everyday almost-white.

My eyes adjusted again so that I could see beyond the startling newness of the rock to take in the shape of the whole. My focus widened, blurred a little, and I saw a human form emerge from the patterns of light and shadow. For a moment I stopped breathing and gazed.

It was only the bare suggestion of a human form, like the vague outline made by a body sleeping beneath a thick quilt. It could easily be something else. Nevertheless, the form was there. My eye superimposed my drawing, and I could see every contour there in the rock, the top of the head, then the elbow and knee making parallel protrusions with a deep hollow between, and then another hollow behind the bent knee, and then the feet, tapering almost to blend with the cliff. She was lying up to her belly button in loose rock, but she was there.

"You're a wizard!" I said to Clay.

"I thought she looked pretty good," he said, and I could hear in his voice that he was grinning.

"I hope I can do half that good a job when it's my turn."

"I don't see why you won't. You did those three-dimensional projections in good shape."

"How much more can you do with blasting?" I asked.

"A lot. I only did the crudest part yesterday. The rest will go a lot slower. In the meantime, you've got yourself a little rock to move."

I dressed and walked up to look at the job I had ahead of me. Up close, the heaps of broken rock looked huge. The blasts had sent masses of rock sliding down the slope, but masses more still remained to be cleared away by hand. The slope was too steep to bring a bulldozer to do the work, so my own labor would have to suffice.

Experimentally, I picked a rock off the pile and tossed it away, down the hill. It bounced and rolled with a satisfying clatter and finally lodged itself somewhere in the rockslide below. I tossed another rock and watched it ricochet in a wide arc, like the flying body of a dummy falling from a cliff on the movie screen. I threw a few more, watching the path of bounces each rock made and thinking it was no wonder that small boys had such a passion for hurling objects.

After a while, I grew bored. Also, I was hungry. I had not yet eaten breakfast. I looked at my watch and discovered I had been throwing rocks for more than an hour. The pile had not diminished visibly. I decided to work for a while longer before going down for breakfast. It was going to be a long task. It could not be more boring than the paperwork at the store, however.

"How have you stood it all these years?" Alma Rose had asked me once. It was eight-thirty and I was closing out the cash register.

"Stood what?" I asked.

"Doing a job that uses only a fraction of your brain, when you have such a considerable brain."

Absentmindedly, my considerable brain did a thumbnail calculation of the number of times I had closed out the cash register. Six times a week times fifty-two weeks made about three hundred times a year, times eighteen years, made five thousand four hundred times. If I made change forty times a shift then I had made change two hundred sixteen thousand times.

"I'm used to it," I said. "I don't think about it."

"What do you think about?"

"This evening I've been thinking about botany."

"Botany?"

"I'm reading a book about plant structures. When I'm not helping a customer, I think about how pine trees transport water sixty feet into the air, when a pump that works by atmospheric pressure could only raise it thirty-two feet."

I stopped pitching rocks for a moment and looked down the hill at my sparse struggling population of pine trees, none of which was close to sixty feet high. I pictured the roots boring their way through the bone-dry soil, sucking up the imperceptible traces of moisture in their path, almost molecule by molecule, and then compelling the reluctant molecules from cell to cell, up through the weathered trunk and branches to the tender growing tip of green. Biology was a conjurer who played tricks with the laws of physics and chemistry and made matter do things that appeared to be impossible.

Alma Rose had not been interested in hearing about miracles wrought out of capillary action and osmotic pressure.

"You have a whole world there inside your head, don't you?" she had said. "Do you even notice the actual world around you? I don't understand how you can ignore the reality of something you do for forty-five hours a week. I'd go nuts if I'd spent eighteen years working in a store."

For sure, Alma Rose would be going nuts doing what I was doing now. All my free time was spent moving rocks. I was becoming more efficient. I no longer paused to watch where they landed. I tossed them, steadily and mechanically, so that the sound of them bouncing down the hill was an unbroken clatter. I paused only when I came to a rock too large to move by hand. Then I took a five foot pry bar and rolled it, inch by inch, until a final shove pushed it over the edge and it thumped heavily down the slope.

I tried once bringing a radio out for company. The only stations within range played either easy listening or country western music, both of which became more tedious than the silence after a few hours. After that one try, I left the radio in the house.

Instead I had Alma Rose for company. Our conversations came back to me now, the way they had when I was awaiting her next visit. Through the short days of winter, my thoughts had been too muddled by despair and alcohol to think clearly about her. She had returned only in the form of agonized stabs of longing. Now, working outdoors in the cool spring air, feeling the ache of fatigue in my muscles and their slowly growing strength, I began to remember details of our time together. The obscuring veil of pain became less opaque. Memories began to emerge, like mountain peaks when the low-hanging clouds drift away or dissipate in the daytime warmth.

"Why didn't you finish college?" I had asked her.

"Because I didn't know what I wanted to do with the education. College seemed a waste, when I had no definite purpose."

"What about learning just so you know things?"

"That's an idealistic notion. When you're busting your butt taking exams, it's hard to appreciate knowledge for its own sake. A lot of the stuff was silly anyway. One of my economics professors would fill the whole blackboard with formulas, and then he would turn around and say, 'Remember, this isn't calculus. These formulas don't always work.'"

I laughed and she added, "Maybe the real reason I quit college is that I like being someone who makes the formulas not work. My parents always assumed I was going to college. They never even asked me whether I wanted to go. They only asked which college. So I went. I just wish I hadn't wasted three and a half years figuring out I didn't belong there."

"You dropped out after three and a half years?"

"I sure did, and man did it feel good, calling and telling them I wasn't going to finish. I was terrified at how angry they would be, but once I conquered that fear and did it, I had such a feeling of freedom and power. They couldn't believe it. They kept saying, it's only five more months, just stick it out. They didn't see that that was the whole point, that it was so unreasonable."

She grinned. "Maybe the only thing you can be sure of is that I won't do what other people expect."

Remembering that comment, I looked around at the raw gashes of blasted rock on all sides of me. I thought, this might be the first thing I've ever done that no one expected. Then I looked at the piles of stones still to be moved and thought, maybe the reason no one expected it is that it's a lunatic idea.

I bent over and began tossing stones again.

"I think my Aunt Rose might have understood," Alma Rose had said. "She was a sweet, gentle person, but underneath I think she felt that same urge to chart her own course. The most important thing was to choose for yourself, even if you made false starts and wrong turns."

At the time, I had said nothing.

Now I thought, your aunt chose to kill herself. That's an awfully big wrong turn.

I wondered how far Alma Rose might go in trying to prove to herself that she was making her own choices. And then again, if all of her efforts were bent on defying other people's expectations, wasn't she as much shaped and controlled by those expectations as she would be if she sought to conform to them?

23

THE HILLS WERE SHADING GREEN
when I finished moving the rock from the first round of blasting. In this climate, the green did not burst forth lavishly. It
crept across the landscape like the subtle flicker of expression that crosses the face of a card player when he draws a
good hand.

The change caused a lifting of spirits in all of us. Even if I
had not been working out in the hills, even if I had never left
the counter of the Mercantile, I would have known that the
hills were turning green. People moved and talked with a
restless air of anticipation that marked the change.

Two successive soaking rains put everyone into a particularly happy frame of mind. The dryness of the winter had
brought the everpresent worry about drought closer to the
surface. In two days, more than an inch of rain fell and the
worry subsided for the moment.

The store was busy on rainy days, as people were forced to pause from the springtime rush of outdoor jobs and rushed instead to do the errands they had been postponing.

"It's a good thing we got this moisture," said Fred McNeil. "We were supposed to be branding this week, but I guess we don't mind waiting." He was smiling.

"My peas are three inches high," Peggy Treadwell announced triumphantly. She turned toward Fred's wife Alice and asked, "How big are yours?"

"My seeds are still in the bag," said Alice. "I don't ever get much planting done before Memorial Day."

Peggy shook her head disapprovingly. "You can't wait until Memorial Day to plant peas," she said. "It gets too hot before they mature. They won't have good flavor. Have you planted yours yet, Pat?"

Before I could answer, she went on, "That's right. I forgot. You don't plant a garden. Such a shame."

"What's a shame?" asked Mrs. Kinley as she stepped into line behind Peggy.

"That Pat doesn't grow a garden. Her mother used to grow the most beautiful garden. I'm sure Pat must have the touch, if she would ever use it." It was a certainty I heard repeated every spring.

"I'd say you have enough to do, if you're really going to make that hilltop into a statue," Mrs. Kinley said to me.

"When do you start cutting the stone?" Joe Danziger asked. He had come in for a roll of masking tape.

"Soon," I said. "Clay Shipley is going to do some more blasting. Once I've cleared the rubble, I start carving."

He shook his head. "Better you than me. It's taken two years just to do the finish work in our little addition. If I'd known, I'd have had Gary do the whole job."

"How is it coming?" I asked.

His face brightened and he held up the masking tape. "We're painting the last room now. Cheryl has been camped out in the unfinished room for a year now. I don't know how the time disappears the way it does. Kids, I guess."

As I counted out his change, he added, "Speaking of kids, you ought to see if Coach Peters would send the boys on the football team out to help you move rocks. It would be good for their arm strength."

When the weather dried out, Clay came back to my place.

"Now the fun starts," he said in greeting. "I've been looking forward to this all month."

He took out one of my sketches. "I'm going to start with the legs. They're the least complicated. I'm learning as I go along, I hope you know."

"So am I," I said.

"So how big a mess do you think we can make, between us?" he said with a grin.

I looked up toward the rock. "Pretty big."

Returning to business, Clay began to explain his plan. "I figure we'll have to do it in four stages, working from the top down. The top relative to earth, I mean, not from head to foot. I'll blast out down to here, say . . . " He sketched a faint pencil line, horizontally, about a quarter the way down the figure. "Then you'll carve that much. Then I'll blast the next level, and so forth."

I looked at the sketch and saw his reasoning. "That way I'll have a place to stand while I work," I said. "I had been envisioning scaffolds and ropes."

"You got it," he said. "I'll leave you a little ledge to stand on. Not quite as nice as an easy chair, but almost."

Once again the house rattled from explosions, although these sounded much smaller. Once again I left for work without turning around to look at the outcrop. This time I had no worry that I had left my hill in the hands of a madman. He might be a fanatic and a perfectionist, but not a madman.

It took him three days to finish this stage. The morning after he finished, I rose early and went out to look. The ledge he left for me traced a rough contour line across the face of the rock. Below the line, the human form was still only a suggestion. Above the line, the form emerged quite definitely, roughly hacked, but recognizable, a rounded mass of head, a point of shoulder, a long, dipping curve of back, a rising curve of hip and buttock, and the start of the deep hollow between the nearer, bent leg and the far one, almost straight.

I gazed at it for a long time. It looked like something the earth was heaving up out of itself, as if some slow, gigantic force from below were pushing a human form up and out of the surrounding rock and soil.

After breakfast, I let the dogs out and nearly ran up the slope to begin clearing the debris. In a couple of weeks, I thought, I could begin the real work with pick and chisels.

Even though I wore gloves, my hands had grown calloused from the hours of moving stones. I could feel the muscles of my arms and shoulders growing more massive and solid. The work no longer left me exhausted, only pleasantly tired.

That day, as I clambered about over the rough shapes of rock, I began to see them as an ankle or a hip, Alma Rose's ankle and hip. I thought about the two of us twining our bodies together in bed, and about me, now, like a tiny beetle scuttling across Alma Rose's limbs. If those limbs could feel, would it be pleasant, a light, tantalizing massage, or would it tickle and be torment? I laughed, and began clearing the rubble from around her ankles.

"I don't know how people survive celibacy," Alma Rose had said once. "Didn't it bother you?"

"I didn't know what I was missing," I said.

"Weren't you curious?"

"I'd tried sex. It was nice enough, but not a deep compulsion. So I figured I didn't have a strong appetite. And I didn't seem to fall in love with anyone, either. I came to the conclusion I must be missing a faculty that other people had. Some people have weak eyesight. Some people aren't very smart. I didn't fall in love."

"You never fell in love with a woman before me?" she asked.

"Looking with hindsight, I suppose I did. I would have stormed a fortress and died happily in a hail of shrapnel if I had thought it would please my tenth grade geometry teacher, Miss Odegard. Only I didn't call it love. I called it hero worship. The wildest extent of my fantasies were that she would invite me to a movie, or tell me all about herself over tea. It didn't enter my head to think about touching her body."

"Why not?"

"Because that was something you did with boys. There were two compartments in my head. In one compartment there was kissing and love, which you did with boys and which didn't appeal all that much. In the other compartment was the way I felt about Miss Odegard, which didn't have a name or an existence in the world outside. I never connected the two. There was a wire missing."

"You'd never heard the word lesbian, then."

"Of course I'd heard it. I knew they existed somewhere, in big, dark, corrupt cities, I suppose. But lesbians were weird, and so everything they did and felt must be weird. I don't know why I was so sure of that. It was one of those beliefs that seems to come out of the air, because everyone believes it even though no one talks about it. But the way I felt about Miss Odegard didn't feel weird. It didn't feel dark or perverse. It felt like an urge to do brilliant proofs on the blackboard so that she would smile and tell me how clever I was. And then it felt like resentment when she went off and got married and left me to learn trigonometry from a stocky, middle-aged man with a crew cut, who was of no interest whatsoever."

"I can't believe you didn't figure it out until you were thirty-four years old." Alma Rose was laughing.

"A person can't be brilliant about everything," I said.

"I know, but sex is so basic. It's like not discovering food until you're thirty-four. It's like spending thirty-four years subsisting on boiled cabbage and rice."

"It wasn't quite that bad."

"It would have been for me. Sex has always been the one thing I could count on to make me feel good."

At the time I said, "Maybe that's why people are so attracted to you. That you like it so much."

At the time, I had thought only of her freedom and sensuousness, which I envied. Now, with my beetle self tickling her stone feet, I wondered if she had truly meant it when she said that sex was the only thing she could count on to make her feel good. What about everything else?

What about Pops, sweeping me onto the dance floor with a whoop? What about a shaft of sunlight, piercing the dark roiling thunderheads to set a hilltop ablaze in shimmering light? What about Lucy, belly to the ground, watching the sheep and listening for my whistle, a small natural miracle that she should bend her instincts to my command? What about Lyle Gardner saved time and frustration by a handful of bolts? Without these occasional gifts of grace, I would be in despair, with or without sex.

Could she truly have meant it? She had said it, and I had not thought to question her. Now she was not around to ask. I wondered if I would ever learn to register things at the time they happened, instead of six months or six years later.

Then I wondered, might I have a chance in the future to ask her? Might she indeed see the sculpture and come back, at some moment when I least expected it?

I did not allow myself to dwell on that thought. The hope was too ready to leap into life and grow with a wild jungle abandon that would overwhelm its surroundings. I would not cultivate it, because I could not bear the disappointment if it grew to magnificence only to be cut down.

24

A COUPLE OF NIGHTS LATER, I came home from the Mercantile and found a note tacked to the front door.

"I put the boys to work for a while. They were glad to get off school grounds. I hope you don't mind."

It was signed by Coach Peters.

In the morning, I found that the ledge was clear of rocks. The rocks were strewn far down the slope, scattered farther and wider than the ones I and the dynamite had thrown.

I went back down to the house to call Coach Peters and thank him.

"No trouble," he said. "It's good for them. Builds their arms."

Off the phone, I panicked. Now I had to go to work for real. I had to take my pick and start chipping away the rock, and hope I had the skill to make my tools follow the design

I had made on paper.

First I took my tape measure and paint and marked off my intentions with fresh splashes of blue and red. Then there was no more postponing. I hefted the pick. It was brand new, the head still glossy with green paint, the handle clean blond wood. I swung it, tentatively, against the face of stone. The metal rang and a chip flew off, about half an inch across. I swung it again. Another half inch chip flew off. At this pace, my statue would take longer than the pyramids. I swung the pick, hard, and this time a satisfying chunk came loose.

In an hour, most of the glossy green paint was gone and my back and shoulders were aching. There was a heap of loose stone around my feet, but the larger rock did not look much different. From the house, when I walked back down to shower before work, the patch I had cleared with the pick looked like a small dimple on the leg.

I wondered how many years the project might take. I was glad I was not working two hundred feet underground, breathing deadly black coal dust.

For a while, when the word went round that I had actually begun work, some of my neighbors drove out to check on my progress. They climbed up the hill, I paused from my work to chat for a moment, and then they settled in to watch. They soon discovered that there was little to see, just chunks of rock flying loose from a bigger mass of rock, according to a design that was obscure to any eye but mine.

I think they felt a little embarrassed for me. Some of them may even have worried about my sanity. There were days when I worried myself. In mid-June, we hit a patch of rainy weather, and my hair hung dripping in my eyes and my drenched clothing stuck to my skin. In July, the air became heavy and still and the thermometer hung over ninety. The sweat dripped stinging into my eyes, and my clothing was again drenched, although the sky was cloudless.

By the end of July, half a human form had emerged, the half from buttocks down. It still lay deeply buried in rock, but above the line of ledge that Clay had left rose a rounded curve of hip and thigh, and the angular bend of heel and ankle bone, no longer roughly hacked, but clear and definite.

I had long since abandoned the pick for hammers and chisels. The work progressed in half inch chips and small scrapings, wearing away the roughness of new rock to create an illusion of human softness. When I first began, chips had sometimes sheared off in unexpected directions, as the blows of the chisel revealed the fracture lines inherent in the rock. I quickly learned that I had to bend my work in accordance with those lines. I gave up the idea of transforming rock into the perfect smoothness of human skin. Only wind and water could do that. Instead, the curves of the human form were approximated by a multitude of planes, the planes the rock allowed. From a distance, the eye was fooled and saw curves. The illusion of softness could almost be believed. Up close, the curves resolved themselves into innumerable small flatnesses, almost a visual catalog of the innumerable chisel strokes that had made them.

Most of my neighbors had lost interest. The changes happened too slowly to be seen.

"A person could just as well sit and watch the grass grow," Pops said, after he came one day and watched me for an hour. "Are you coming to the rodeo with us next week?"

"I guess I will," I said. "I can't work every day."

Superstition, which never died, made me hope that my

absence for a day might cause Alma Rose to appear, as she had that first summer. This year, though, the rodeo took place in its more accustomed weather, baking sunshine, and there was no note waiting for me when I returned home.

"The only thing you can count on is that I won't do what you expect." That was her creed.

What did I expect? Did I really expect her to see my sculpture from the highway and be pulled down the off-ramp, as if she were under a spell?

Now and then, I went out to the truck stop for coffee after work. I was not in search of a man. I was hoping to hear some word about Alma Rose. I chatted with some of the drivers, comfortably now, since my motives had nothing to do with the men personally.

In October, I finally did hear word.

"Seems that Alma Rose has decided to settle down," one of the men said. The speaker was a driver Alma Rose had talked about sometimes, a young man named Wayne with a wife and three kids in Illinois. He had always flirted with Alma Rose when he saw her, and she had flirted with him, and afterwards she said to me, "Wayne likes to talk, but he'd spy for the Russians before he'd cheat on his wife."

I tried not to show my excessive interest in his news. "Where's she settling?" I said, casually.

"She met some fellow out in California," Wayne said. "He's in advertising or radio or something like that. She's moving in with him. Surprised me to hear it. I didn't think anyone was ever going to reel her in."

"Did she quit her job?" the waitress asked, as she cleared away Wayne's dishes, with businesslike efficiency.

Wendy Corcoran had moved away, and her place had been

taken by Cheryl Danziger, who was friendly enough, but had none of Wendy's talent for romantic teasing. Cheryl went straight to the practical, maybe because a large part of her sixteen years had been spent changing diapers and sharing a tiny living space with an ever-multiplying crowd of younger siblings.

"I think she's still driving, but I don't know how long that will last," Wayne said. "The fellow makes plenty of money, from what I heard."

"Are they getting married?" Cheryl asked.

"I haven't heard anything about marriage," said Wayne. "I think just moving in is a big step for Alma Rose. That first husband left her a little gun-shy."

I was beginning to feel queasy. I paid my bill and left. I had been telling myself for ten months that Alma Rose was not coming back, but telling myself was not the same as hearing the fact plainly stated by a disinterested third person.

When I got home, I climbed the hill and perched myself on the shoulder of the sculpture, Alma Rose's shoulder. The first tier was finished to that point. The head and neck were still an undifferentiated mass. I was chipping away at the hair, but it was complicated and very slow.

Though there was no moon, the stars were bright enough to cast a silvery sheen across the undulations of stone that stretched away from where I sat. Looking at it in the faint light of nighttime, it occurred to me for the first time that this object, so mistakenly conceived, might turn out to be beautiful. Until now, I had only been concerned that it be recognizable as human, so that I would not be humiliated by a gigantically public display of ineptitude.

I sat and simply looked at it, without straining to see the

shapes still buried in rock, without planning where the pick would strike next. What I saw was a series of graceful curves that, as pure form, were quite pleasing. It should not have been a surprise. I had often lain in bed and gazed at the same arrangement of lines, and thought how simple and lovely the human body was. We could have been given the shape of an oil derrick, or a propane tank, or a sheet-metal Quonset barn. Instead we were given the delicate crease of the spine, the fullness of the calf, the gentle angularity of ankle bone and collar bone, and the fanlike tendons on the back of the hand.

I had wanted to bring the pick with me when I climbed up here, but I had decided against it. I had been afraid I might swing away with it in fury and then regret the damage in the morning. After sitting still and looking for a while, I no longer felt any urge to wield the pick as a weapon.

"The hell with you," I said. "I'll finish her anyway, even if you never do see her."

25

THE BACK OF THE HEAD TOOK
two months. Each day I carved out one curl of hair. On
cold days, my hands hurt from the pounding. Twice, when
it didn't get above ten degrees at noon, I had to stop work
because my hands became too stiff to control my tools
accurately.

Finished, the hair lay in an unruly tangle around the
prominence of shoulder, like water flowing around a boulder
in a creek bed. The design was complete. She was a whole
human, still three quarters buried in rock, but whole.

A warm spell came, early in December. With sunshine
and a strong south wind, the frozen ground quickly thawed
and the earth exhaled the moist scent of spring. Such false
arrivals of spring came often in this climate, a thousand miles
from any buffering ocean to temper the overnight swings from
one season to another. One day, the pulse quickened with

awakening growth. The next day might bring arctic air sweeping down from the Canadian plains to petrify every growing thing and turn the ground back to iron.

With the warmth, an opportunity to be seized, Clay Shipley returned to do the next round of blasting. I had talked with him on the phone a few times, to let him know how I progressed, but he had not come to see.

"I feel the way you did," he had said, when I invited him to come look. "I want to wait until you're finished, so I don't fret over how slow it's going."

When I went to greet him, beside his van, I found him scowling.

"Now you've got me worried," he said, before I even said hello.

"What's the matter? Have I ruined it?"

"Just the opposite. You've got me worried that I might ruin it. She's really something, just the way she is. I don't want to miscalculate and blow a big hole in her side."

He stood looking up at the hill. "It's crazy, you know," he said. "All you can see is her hip and her shoulder and the back of her head, but you can tell she's a pretty woman."

Perhaps because he was nervous, it took him longer to finish this stage. The blasts came at wider intervals and sounded much smaller, more like fireworks than dynamite. When I took the dogs out in the morning, I saw each day's progress, five steps, from feet to head.

"My wife is jealous," he said, on the last day. "I told her how beautiful this thing is, and she wanted to know who the model is. I think she was picturing a woman posing for me while I work."

I laughed and he added, "I told her I work from drawings.

So then she thought I was crazy for sure, because I had fallen in love with a drawing."

"Have you?"

He grinned. "I'm not that crazy. I mean, I might be in love with her, but I'm not expecting her to marry me or anything."

"What if you met the original?"

"Met her how? On the street to shake hands, or lying naked on a bed, like this?" He gestured with his head toward the sculpture.

"Either way," I said.

He paused. "It wouldn't be the same, I'm sure. She might have bad breath or talk in a screechy voice. Or if she was perfect, then what would she want with an ugly old guy like me?"

The blasting roused a brief flare of curiosity in Kilgore. It reminded people of my endeavor, which had largely been forgotten, pushed out of people's minds by their own daily routines.

In the days after Clay finished his work, several people drove out to see the result.

"It's starting to look like a person." Such was the summary of their comments, though each one phrased it differently.

Peggy Treadwell squinted hard, looking for buttons and collar ruffles I was sure. From below, it was not yet obvious that Alma Rose was naked.

"She's lying on her stomach, is that right?" Peggy asked. "Am I seeing it right?"

"That's right. Not flat on her stomach. A little to one side. But mostly on her stomach."

"It's hard to see very much yet," Peggy said. "The hair is very nice. Quite realistic. When will it be finished?"

"I don't know. It might be a couple of years."

"Hmmm."

She walked a few paces closer, as if that gave her a better view.

"It's not going to be obscene, is it?" she asked abruptly.

"What do you mean by obscene?"

"Surely that's obvious."

"It's not my intent to be obscene," I said. "It's just a person sleeping. She's not doing anything obscene."

Would Peggy Treadwell pin diapers over the phallic art of the Greeks and Egyptians, and drape polyester maternity dresses over the round pregnant bellies of ancient African fertility goddesses? Probably.

"I hope you realize you have a responsibility to the community," she said. "This is a very public object. The children can see it when they go by on the school bus. Anyone who visits and drives by can see it. We do not want to become notorious for having a giant piece of obscenity on display."

"It will not be a giant piece of obscenity, I guarantee that."

When Leonard Kinley came to see it, he cast his concerns in more practical terms. As a minister, he must have felt a responsibility to take some kind of a stand. I was not worried about what he might say. Neither his theology nor his ethics were rooted in large abstractions. He lived on the same street with his congregation and his preaching had to be palatable to all the orphan Baptists, Methodists, Lutherans, Episcopalians and Presbyterians who took shelter under his church's generic Protestantism. His dogma could be described as Applied Christianity, the simplest of

Christian principles shaped to fit the needs of people he knew personally.

"I suppose she won't have any clothes on," he began.

"No," I said.

"You could calm some people's worries if you'd just blur some of the details a little," he said. "I'm not bothered by nude sculptures myself, not if they're tasteful, but some folks aren't entirely comfortable with the idea. It might help if you didn't put in every detail."

I smiled. "You mean, don't carve every curl of pubic hair the way I've carved the hair on her head."

He looked startled. Then he smiled a little, too. "And don't talk to people in general about pubic hair," he said.

"I know better than that."

He looked up at the rock. "I shouldn't think those details are necessary to the overall effect."

"Most of those 'details' don't show anyway, because of the way she is lying," I said. "Anyway, that rock has a mind of its own. It can't be shaped into a lifelike human replica, the way marble can. So she'll be blurred whether I like it or not."

"She's quite extraordinary," he said. "Even now, when most of her still has to be imagined."

Now I was the one to be startled, at how grateful I felt for his admiration, how grateful for an eye that could see beyond what was actually there to the prospective whole.

After he left, I considered what he had said about people's worries. It had crossed my mind long before now that some of my neighbors might object to a giant nude. I had waited, a little anxiously, for hate mail or scathing remarks or some other kind of attack. Very little had happened. I had received two letters, handwritten but unsigned, to the effect that people like me did not belong in a god-fearing community. Apart from that, nothing had been said. I was puzzled, because I knew enough about my neighbors to know that some of them must find the statue objectionable.

Gradually, I realized that for all of its size and publicness, the statue was in some ways an elusive target for attack. For one thing, to attack it meant attacking a conviction as deep rooted as any standard of sexual morality, the belief that people could do as they pleased with their own time and money on their own private property. If they objected to my carving the rock on my own land, they might find me objecting to the quantity of old rusty machinery they chose to collect in their back yard.

More than that, the sheer scope of the project protected me. If the sculpture had sprung upon them one morning, huge and whole and gloriously naked, they could have reacted instantaneously with outrage. As it was, she was taking shape so slowly that there was no one moment when she could hit them in the eye as an obscenity. At what moment did she cease to be a vaguely defined shape in the rock and become something offensive to the sensibilities? By the time there was even any indication that she was naked, they had already been living with her for months.

Of all the people who took an interest, Pops was by far the most eager and impatient.

"When do you suppose she'll be finished?" he asked me time and time again. His impatience seemed to me inordinate, considering how little the work had to do with him.

"It's going to be a year or two, anyway," I said.

"Who ever would have thought my quiet little Pat would tackle such a crazy project?" Pops announced to the world at large, which in this case meant whatever customers happened to be in the Mercantile at that moment. "She's something, isn't she?"

The only people in the store right then were Fred McNeil and a woman and a boy I didn't recognize. The woman looked faintly familiar. Since she had come in with Fred, I assumed she must be his sister Donna. I had heard she was back in town again with her son Jordan, whom she had kept and raised.

Fred grunted a vague acknowledgment that he had heard what Pops said. He was standing in front of the rack of rental videos that we had installed beside the checkout counter. He held a video box in each hand, trying to decide between a sweaty, muscular man with an automatic rifle and a sinister, hawk-nosed man with a switchblade.

"You can't ever be sure what someone might do," the woman said. She didn't say it in a pointed way. If anything, she seemed to be talking to the air or to herself.

Hearing her speak, Pops became conscious of a social necessity. "Pat, you remember Donna McNeil, don't you? She's decided to move back here for good. Went all over the country and couldn't find a better place to live, am I right, Donna?"

He spoke with satisfaction, as if every person who moved away from Kilgore were an insult to the town, and every person who stayed or came back were somehow a victory.

"I don't know as I'd say that," she said. She had a slow way of talking, not like someone who was dull-witted, but like someone who had spent a long time hurrying and found it didn't get her anywhere.

"The place you grew up is inside you whether you like it or not," she added. "I guess half of us are trying to get away from that place and the other half are trying to get back to it."

"Your boy has grown up good-looking," said Pops.

"He looks like Fred," she said, and smiled. Smiling, she didn't look as old as she did serious, but either way she looked much older than she was, thirty or thirty-one.

When Fred finally made up his mind in favor of the sinister man with a switchblade, the three of them left. In the doorway, they passed Marge coming in.

"Donna looks like she's been through a wringer," Pops said, when the door had closed behind them.

"She probably has been," said Marge.

"What's her story? Where has she been living all this time?" I asked.

"I don't know," said Pops. "She's only been back a week, and she's mostly kept quiet about herself. About all I know is that she's got some kind of computer job in Seco Springs. It's funny. She sure wasn't one you'd have bet would get herself pregnant. She didn't run around with the boys, and she was a good student. She just turned up pregnant one winter and no one knew who the boy was. Donna wouldn't say, except that he was someone at the university. Fred Sr. was ready to drag the boy out by the collar and escort him to the altar, but it kind of stumped him when Donna wouldn't say who it was and swore she wouldn't marry him anyway. They had the priest out to talk to her, and about half a dozen of her teachers from high school. Donna wasn't having any of it."

Marge put in, "It's the way teenagers are. They moon around and sigh and moan, and can't decide anything, but then when they do get their mind set on something, they're like an elephant who's decided to lie down. There's not a thing you can do about it, unless you want to take a gun and shoot them."

After a minute, she added, "I'd almost think you were a teenager again, Pat, with that statue of yours. I've never seen someone get set on an idea so quick. It seemed like one morning you thought of it and the next morning your dynamite friend had blown up half your hill."

"It wasn't quite that quick," I said.

"It seemed so to us, since you never said a word to anybody until you'd started blasting."

"You would have tried to talk me out of it."

"Darn right I would have," said Marge. "Do you think it's going to make you happy to have Alma Rose staring in your window for the rest of your life? She'd give me the heebie-jeebies."

"Her eyes are closed," I said.

"Then she probably snores. And there's another thing, too . . . "

Marge had to postpone the other thing for a moment, because Gary Pilcher's wife had come in and was hovering in a nearby aisle with barely disguised curiosity about what "other thing" was causing Marge to speak in such an adamant tone. Marge began leafing through a magazine. Finally, Mrs. Pilcher gave up and collected the macaroni, frozen peas and cigarettes she had come to buy.

When she had left, Marge resumed her argument, but in hushed tones, as if Mrs. Pilcher might have planted a bug on her way out. "Suppose you ever do meet someone else," she said, almost in a whisper. "What's that person going to think about someone who keeps a statue of her former lover in the back yard?"

"I have no idea," I said. "I'll worry about it if I'm ever lucky enough to meet someone who cares what I have in my back yard."

"Maybe you'll meet someone on account of her," Pops put in.

"What do you mean?" I asked.

"Maybe some people would be scared away, but maybe other people would be curious and interested. Maybe she's as likely to bring someone as to keep someone away. I've got a notion about her, myself."

"What notion is that?" Marge asked very quickly. I think she was starting to feel nervous about the notions Pops and I might take into our heads.

"It's not anything yet," he said. "I have to wait and see how she turns out first."

Marge tried prodding, but he wouldn't say anything more. "It might all come to nothing," he said. "Pat's still got a lot of work ahead of her. She might get bored and decide she has better things to do."

26

THE WORK WAS BORING, BUT NOT intolerably so, because my thoughts were usually elsewhere. I could stay content for hours chipping away at rock, because I was simultaneously carrying on conversations in my head. Sometimes I came to myself at the end of one of these monologues with no memory of what my tools had been doing for the last hour. Then I worried that in one of these spells I might chip away a whole section of rock that was meant to be there.

It seemed that my automatic guidance systems were functioning, as they did when I drove a car or stamped price stickers on the canned goods. As yet, I had made no large mistakes.

What did bore me was not the endless tap, tap, tap, of the hammer and chisel. It was the endless, automatic repetition of the question, "How's your sculpture coming?" and my endless, automatic repetition of the answer, "It's coming along." Most of my customers saw me just seldom enough that they considered it polite to inquire every time they did see me. Since each of them, individually, only asked the question once or twice a week, they did not realize that, cumulatively, I was asked the question twenty or thirty times a day.

The progress was slow enough in itself. Measured by twenty inquiries a day, it began to seem nonexistent. What could I tell people that would be more exact? "I just finished three feet of her bicep. Tomorrow I'll do another few feet. Pretty soon I'll start on the armpit."

Often the weather was too cold for me to work. My hands grew numb, the chisel slipped, and every blow of the hammer traveled like a jolt of electric current to the center of my bones and joints. On those days, I came back inside and picked up a book from the neglected pile I still accumulated, out of habit, from my book club.

I did not concentrate well. My thoughts kept wandering off to the rock, and my plans for how to shape the next bit. It was an obsession. Probably it was unhealthy, but there it was. I was conscious of only two things that winter, my work at the store, which was so routine it barely required consciousness, and my work on Alma Rose. Day after day, I chipped away at the rock, and carried on conversations in my head. Now and then I thought, maybe I'm losing my mind.

"What was your mother like?" Alma Rose had asked me.

"My mother?"

"Yes, your mother."

"My mother. What was she like?" My thoughts wouldn't focus. My memories of conversations with Alma Rose were growing blurred. Sometimes I wasn't sure if I was remembering an actual conversation or inventing one that might have happened. I concentrated and the conversation came back to me more clearly.

"She was like me," I said.

"In what way?"

"She was an iceberg." I began to laugh. I had only thought of the idea that moment. "Most of her was out of sight. She floated off in her own world and people saw only the little bit that she showed. It looked so cold and uninviting, they didn't explore further."

"Was she cold?"

"Am I cold?" I asked.

Alma Rose considered for a moment. "You're not cold, but you're very well insulated. If your mother was an iceberg, then you're a Thermos bottle. From the outside, a person can't tell if the contents are cold or hot."

"Or lukewarm."

She shook her head. "Definitely not lukewarm," she said. "So, did you think the same thing, that your mother was an iceberg? When you were a kid, I mean."

"Of course not."

"What did you think she was?"

"I didn't think," I said. "She was a given. When you're a little kid, you don't judge your mother. She's the yardstick by which you measure everything else. She's like those standardized kilograms they keep in a sealed chamber. She's the norm and everything else is normal or abnormal according to how it compares to her."

"How did the rest of the world compare, then?"

"I thought the rest of the world was noisy and crude, because she was so quiet and serene and intellectual. It wasn't until I was eleven or twelve that I started to wish she were more like other people's parents."

"My mother was exactly like other people's parents, so when I was twelve, I wished she were different," said Alma Rose. "My parents were so conventional, they could have been the family in an ad for a Chevy station wagon. My dad went off to an office. My mom kept the house and did volunteer work. They packed us all off to college, because that was what people did, but I don't think they seriously expected their daughters to be anything more than someone's well-educated wife."

She smiled, then, a smile twisted by bitterness. "It's funny that they had so many girls. My dad would tell people how delighted he was to have all those daughters, but first he always said how much they'd wanted another son. 'Someone to play with Jack, you know,' he'd say, and then he'd rush to say, 'But, of course we love our daughters, too.' They had two girls and then two miscarriages, and then finally they had Jack. So then they decided to have another one, to even things off, and that was me. Only I didn't even things off, because I was another girl.

"I think before I was born, Dad had this image of Jack in the back yard throwing footballs to his little brother. Jack and I did throw a lot of footballs to each other, but the picture never looked right. I think Dad just blanked out the half of the picture that was me. What he saw was Jack throwing a ball to somewhere out beyond the edge of the frame, and then after a second the ball came back and Jack caught it. It didn't matter what I did, I was always off somewhere outside the picture. My junior year of high school, I was the Minnesota state champion in long jump and two hundred meters and Dad didn't even come to the meet."

She paused once more, and then some new memory made her body shudder involuntarily. "I remember the night of the prom, at the end of that year. I was all dressed up to go out, and my dad looked at me and said, 'Where did this beautiful girl come from?' as if he'd never seen me before, as if I had just walked in off the street. He was trying to make a joke, I know, but it felt as if it were the first time he had really and truly registered my existence.

"And then he said, 'You be careful the boys don't try anything they shouldn't, because they're sure going to want to.' Half of me wanted to scream back at him, 'They won't even have to try, because I've been willing and eager since I was fifteen and they know it.' But the other half of me was feeling sick, because my dad had exactly the same look in his eye that the boys did right before they reached for my tits."

She had hunched forward then, with both arms wrapped tightly around her own torso, and I had watched her, helpless.

Her agony felt like my own, tearing at me, searing my insides. I writhed and then struck out, animal instinct fighting off an attack from something invisible. The pick in my hand swung viciously and blindly, with all my strength behind it.

The force of the blow jarred me into present awareness. I watched a large chunk of rock break loose, and a long crack spread itself down the leg toward the kneecap.

"That was stupid," I said aloud. It was just as well the rock was so big. One angry blow could not scar it too seriously.

I thought about the nights when Alma Rose had lain awake, rigid and sweating, with some demon of memory chasing her brain in circles. I could not help her then, either. She did not want caresses. If I offered them, she turned away with angry emphasis. If I asked what was wrong, she said, dismissively, "Nothing new." So I had lain beside her, with corresponding rigidity, trying not to let my existence impinge on her. She was like a person with a fever, to whom any touch, even a loving one, is painful.

"Don't be so nice to me," she had said once.

"Why not?"

"Because I can't be that nice back. It makes me feel unequal."

"I owe you much more than you owe me," I said.

"What have I ever done for you? What could anyone ever do for you? You don't need anything. You take care of yourself perfectly well, with or without me."

"That's not true!" I cried.

"It is true. You might cry a little if I weren't here, but you'd bob back upright again, just like one of those plastic clowns with a weight in the bottom."

"Do you want me to kill myself every time something goes wrong?"

"No, not that. But once, just once, I'd like to see you throw yourself into something headlong. Put your whole heart and soul into something that might not work out, and that might devastate you if it doesn't."

"Maybe that's not the kind of person I am," I said. "Maybe it's not in my nature."

"Maybe it's not," she had said, and it had sounded like a file folder being closed and put away.

27

MARGE CALLED ME ONE EVENING to suggest that she and Pops and I go to the Elk River Reservoir for a picnic some Sunday. Reluctantly, I said that I would go, but not until after I finished this stage.

"Clay said he could come back next month, if I was ready for him. I can't stop until then."

"It's not healthy to work so hard," Marge said. "Don't you go turning into a kook because of this sculpture."

"I may not have any choice about it," I said.

The truth was, I was finally growing bored, and bored almost to madness. At night, I dreamed about Everest-sized expanses of rock, which I had to carve with a dentist's pick and a fingernail file. My conversations with Alma Rose no longer kept me entertained. They had grown so vague and so often repeated that they circled in my head as monotonously as the tapping of my hammer.

I was out of bed and working as soon as it was light in the morning. I worked every available minute, frantic to be finished. I feared that if I paused for breath or even slackened my pace, the work remaining to be done would start to look too vast and I would give up entirely. I didn't dare picture to myself another year or more chipping rock.

When I finished the second tier, and Clay returned, he admired her with the same enthusiasm as before. This time he sparked no enthusiasm in me. I was no longer excited about the sculpture, merely doggedly determined not to leave her half-finished. I could not tell if she was beautiful or not. I could see only that she did look human, that her proportions were more or less correct.

"Do you realize what an amazing sight she is?" Clay asked.

"Is she?" I said.

"I look at her when I'm driving up here, and I think she's a wonder, curled up there asleep on the top of the hill."

I wished I could join her, curled up asleep. I was sleeping only five or six hours a night. Even though my mind was fuzzy with exhaustion, my eyes flew open at the first sign of light and would not close again.

Clay looked at me and said, "You look like you need a vacation from this. Why don't you take a few days to rest and read some books?"

"I can't take a vacation," I said. "I might decide I liked it, and never go back to work again."

He looked at me intently, frowning with worry, but I think he understood.

The picnic with Pops and Marge was not a great success. My mind was on the work I was not doing and I felt myself to be a weight dragging down the high spirits of my companions.

Pops did his best to whoop and holler and splash around in the tepid lake water. He pulled Marge and me in after him. He tried to start a game of water polo with a beach ball. He flopped himself backwards into the water, as if he were catching a wave. In every way he could, by force of imagination, he tried to make the Elk River Reservoir into a Caribbean resort with white sand, palm trees and a transparent aquamarine sea. My mind stayed stolidly on the bank of the reservoir, too distinctly conscious of the coarse gravel of the manmade beach, the opaque, unmoving, reddish-brown water, safe but not inviting, the skeletons of trees still standing far out in the reservoir where the river bank had once been, and the few scraggly cottonwoods that had taken root on what was now the bank. All around us, the dusty brown hills stood as silent testimony that the presence of so much water in one place was an alien and aberrant phenomenon.

I swam a little, then sat down on the blanket Pops had spread across the gravel. Marge joined me, leaving Pops to paddle around and bat the beach ball by himself.

"Are you all right?" she asked, with unaccustomed gentleness.

"It's not a question of being all right," I said. "I suppose I'm not all right, but I have to do what I'm doing. It might be crazy, it might make me crazy, but I don't have any choice."

Marge shook her head. "I don't understand why you don't have a choice." She wasn't angry or critical, just puzzled. She understood practical compulsions. One had to earn a living. One had to feed a baby and change its diapers. One had to eat and sleep, and maybe one even had to have sex. But to her, a need that arose purely from the murk of a person's state of mind had no more solidity or compelling force than a bubble of swamp gas rising from the muck of putrefying vegetation. Why could I not let it dissipate, harmless, into the air?

I didn't know, and so I couldn't explain.

"I guess you're just different," she said.

I nodded, sliding comfortably into the characterization I had been wearing since I was a child.

I could feel that my determination was flagging. One day, instead of working on the figure itself, I climbed up to a piece of vertical face below the base of the sculpture. There I carved out the letters of the name, Alma Rose. I thought, maybe if it has a title I'll be more likely to finish it. With her name on it, reminding me, maybe I wouldn't give up. Then I went back to begin work on the sloping expanse of her ribcage.

Toward the end of summer, an incident briefly interrupted my routine and broke through my numb concentration enough to make me laugh.

My road was a narrow strip of rough gravel, not leading anywhere a tourist would want to go, only out to a few widely scattered ranches. Followed far enough, it emerged onto a paved road, which led eventually to another town. Now and then an out-of-state car passed by, either a visitor to one of the ranches, or someone who was lost, or someone who looked at road maps and chose to follow the thinnest, faintest gray lines, because they were the most 'interesting.'

Cars were infrequent enough that I always noticed them. They appeared a mile and a half away as a moving cloud of dust. When quite close, the car appeared out of the cloud, and I heard the crackle of spurting gravel, and the car raced past at fifty miles an hour, heedless of potholes and washboard in the need to cover long distances.

This car did not travel fast. The cloud came creeping along, maybe at twenty miles an hour, so it had to be an out-of-state driver. I wondered if someone had relatives visiting, or if it was the occasional stray tourist trying to avoid the beaten track. Then the car did not merely creep, it came to a halt, near the end of my driveway. I kept watching, on the chance that it was someone I knew. But I did not know any-one who would have crept so cautiously over the bumps. Even my aunt and uncle from Great Falls would have bounced cheerily over the washboard and slewed through the loose gravel on the corners without flinching from the gas pedal.

Two people got out of the car, a couple in late middle age, to judge by their bright polyester clothes and graying hair. The man had a video camera propped on his shoulder. I watched them and they watched me. They shuffled about a little, looking uncertain, not daring to cross the cattle guard onto my property. The man waited with his camera, appar-ently hoping I would go back to work, so that he would have live action to show in his video.

Just as well make them happy, I thought. When they ar-rived, I had been working on a fussy detail with the smallest of my chisels. Now I walked over to where my pick was lean-ing against the next stretch of fresh rock. Out of the corner of my eye, I saw the man bend to sight through the camera. I smiled to myself, seized the pick and swung away with it, knocking chunks loose from the gap between the upper arm and the breast.

After a couple of minutes, I abandoned the pick and went back to the chisel. The man was still filming. They stayed a surprisingly long time, walking up and down the road to gaze and point. They must be tourists in search of tiny roads, to have so much leisure. Finally, they returned to the car and as they were climbing in, the woman lifted her hand, tentatively, to wave. I waved back and her own salute became more definite.

I remembered a time, years before, when the same thing had happened. Then, I had been working with the collies. The couple had had the same wide car, the same graying hair and polyester attire. They had not had the video camera, though, which was a pity, because the dogs and the sheep would have made far better action than my painstaking tap-tap with the chisel.

This summer, I did not have any sheep. I had no time to work with the dogs. Lulu had grown too blind and decrepit to work sheep anyway, but I felt occasional pangs of conscience about Lucy. She no longer leapt eagerly to her feet when I headed for the door, because she knew there were no sheep in the pasture.

Usually I took them out with me while I worked. Lulu would immediately seek a patch of shade and lie down. Lucy would explore for a while, half-heartedly, and then lie down, too. She was not a hunting, tracking dog. Mysterious smells did not hold her interest for long. She wanted a live, moving quarry to pursue with eyes and ears. She wanted, also, to win my praise with cleverness. So she nosed about until she grew bored and then lay down, first casting a reproachful look at me to remind me that she was too young a dog to spend her days sleeping in the shade.

"I won't be doing this forever," I said in answer to her look. I was sure she could hear the lack of conviction in my voice. To a dog, three years was almost as good as forever.

It was beginning to feel like forever to me, too. I worked

as steadily as ever, but somehow my progress became slower and slower. I felt as if I had become trapped in Xeno's paradox. I would finish half the task, and then half of what remained, and then half of what remained after that, but I would never reach the end, because however small the remaining half might be, I must divide it down again into halves. Although the halves grew smaller and smaller, they took the same amount of time, so that time began to stretch itself out toward infinity.

I had started with the torso and head on this section, leaving the cruder work of the legs for the cold of winter. As the days shortened into autumn, I reached the face. The cottonwoods blazed golden. The sky was unfathomable blue. My spirits wanted to lift at the sight, but the weight of monotony was too great. I plodded onward, barely looking at the glory of color that surrounded me.

According to my sketch, I must now carve her smile. I stared at that smile. It was not a Mona Lisa smile. Mona Lisa is awake, looking at the world and smiling at her own thoughts, whatever they may be. This smile was the smile of someone who has relaxed into unconsciousness, who is aware of nothing and thinking nothing. It was the smile of nature rather than humanity. It had no kinship with the soaring delight of a symphony, or the warm good humor of a holiday dinner. Its relatives were the cow, lying in the sunshine with closed eyes, chewing her cud, and the crocus, pushed upward by some unseen current of joy to challenge the cold brown mud and catch the April snow in cups of purple and gold.

I could not do it. I did not dare try my hand at that smile. I was hollow and dry inside, like December grass. I feared

that, in my hands, the smile would slacken into chilly in-
difference. I left the mouth a rough face of rock and moved
on to the nose, which does not have such visible moods.

Part Four

28

I DID NOT SEE LUCY WANDER away. I noticed her absence only when I heard a savage, snarling bark, and then, in answer, a high-pitched frightened shout, and the clatter of metal.

I whirled around and saw a confusion in the road below, the quick black and white figure of Lucy dodging and snarling and snapping, a silver bicycle lying in the gravel, and a boy, on the ground, also, shielding his face with one arm and trying to untangle his legs from the bicycle.

"Lucy, no!" I screamed, and blew a futile whistle commanding her down. I began to run, stumbling down the slope toward the fallen boy and my dog turned vicious. Time did indeed stretch toward infinity as the collie dodged in and out and the boy shrieked and the bushes caught at my legs and my feet stumbled over loose rocks and my voice seared my throat as I screamed, uselessly, for her to stop.

She heard me, suddenly, as I reached the driveway. She crouched down, chagrined and afraid. The boy scrambled to his feet, trembling and staring at the dog. He looked to be all blood, his bare legs scraped raw by the gravel, and one leg and one arm scored by long gashes from Lucy's teeth. I grabbed Lucy's collar, to do what I could to calm his terror.

"I'll put her in her kennel," I said. "Come to the house and I'll get you to a doctor."

I did not bother to scold Lucy. There was no scolding possible that could make a dog trustworthy after such an attack. I gripped her collar firmly and led the way back toward the house. The boy picked up his bicycle and followed.

As we approached the house, he saw Lulu picking her way slowly and blindly down the slope toward us. He flinched and moved so that I was between him and Lulu. Tears welled up in my eyes, partly for the boy's fear, but mostly grief that I had brought my dogs to such a state that a boy need be afraid of them. The boy would recover, but might be scarred by fear for life. Lucy would never recover. I had no choice but to kill her. She had not killed the boy, but she might have, if he had been smaller.

I locked her in her kennel, and Lulu, also, and then compelled myself to calm so that I could return to the house and help the boy. Later, I would weep for Lucy, with the childlike anguish one never loses in one's attachment to animals. Right now, I must be an adult, with a child in my care.

In the kitchen, the boy sat quiet, still trembling, while I washed his cuts. The two biggest ones still oozed blood and would need stitches. I gave him pads of gauze to press against them. I did my best to converse while I tended him, hoping that talk would be soothing.

"You're Jordan McNeil, aren't you?" I said.

"Jordy," he said.

"Jordy. Do you ride your bike on this road often?"

He shook his head. "I stayed at a friend's house last night. I was riding home."

"A friend in Kilgore? That's a very long ride on a bicycle."

"Uncle Fred said it's twenty-four and a half miles. I like to ride. It's a mountain bike. It's good on gravel."

When I had done as much as I could with the cuts, I called his mother.

"This is Pat Lloyd. One of my dogs attacked your son," I said, without preamble. "He has some cuts, so I'm taking him to the doctor. I'm very sorry it happened. Do you want to meet us at Dr. Raynik's?"

She was matter-of-fact. "I'll be there in half an hour. Are the cuts serious?"

"Two of them need stitches. They're not life threatening. He was very scared, though. It was a scary situation."

"Yes. Just do what you can to explain to him. He's not timid. He'll understand after a while."

I loaded his bike into the back of the truck, then helped him climb into the cab. All the while I was puzzling over how to explain. I didn't know how to talk to a twelve-year-old. As we started off, I glanced across the cab at him, thinking he looked very small and slight for his age.

"It was my fault, you know, not the dog's," I said. "She wasn't naturally vicious. She was high-strung. She needed a lot of attention and I was too busy to give it to her. Something in her must have changed, from being left alone so much. That's what sometimes happens with dogs like her, if the owner doesn't take proper care."

"What will happen to her?" he asked.

"I'll have to have her killed," I said. The tears were there again, right in the back of my eyes and throat.

He pondered that information in silence for a minute.

"She didn't kill me," he said. "Why do you have to kill her? Can't you just tie her up?"

"She'd be miserable tied up all the time. She'll never be trustworthy now, and being tied up would make her worse."

"Because she'd be so unhappy?" he said.

"Yes. And because dogs don't go back, once they learn to attack in earnest. It's like a tamed animal reverting to wildness. There's nothing you can do."

He still resisted. "I wish you didn't have to kill her," he said.

"I'm the one who should be shot, really. If there were any justice." I only half-succeeded in making my tone joking.

"I don't think anyone should be shot. It's just a few cuts. She hasn't done any real damage. Probably the bicycle scared her."

His mother was right. He was not timid. Now that his reaction of terror had passed, he scorned pain and danger.

"If she had attacked a sheep, she would be shot without question," I said. "This is a lot worse, to attack a person."

"I don't think it's worse," said Jordy. "A sheep is more helpless than a person. Also, unless she was hungry, she couldn't have any reason to attack a sheep, but she might have good reasons to attack a person. I might have been a thief or a murderer."

I remembered suddenly that his mother had gone to the finals of a regional debate tournament. For whatever reason, he had taken up the cause of the dog, and it appeared he was ready to use every resource of logic or illogic to defend her.

He was still arguing when we reached Dr. Raynik's office.

"What solution do you propose, then, so that she doesn't ever do it again?" I asked him as we got out of the truck.

"You'll have to keep her with you all the time and pay close attention, so that she can't attack anybody," he said.

Could there be clearer justice? It was my fault. The remedy should be my total attention and devotion.

Dr. Raynik's office was next door to his house. When a call came like this, on Sunday, he simply slipped on a white coat and stepped across the yard to meet us.

He was a thin, scholarly-looking man, only a little older than me. His manner was reserved and serious, but he had quick intuitions. He knew which of his patients liked the laconic veterinary style, a quick shot of antibiotic and a cheerful "That should fix you up." He knew which ones wanted a voluminous explanation of their case. He knew which ones did not feel safe unless they had been X-rayed, and which ones were sure that an X-ray would give them cancer. As a result, he was a very highly regarded doctor.

"You're Jordan McNeil," he said, as he was scrubbing his hands. "I know your aunts and uncles, but I haven't met your mother yet." His voice was soft and deep-toned, innately soothing. It did not seem to be a cultivated manner. He talked the same way if he came to the Mercantile to buy a piece of hardware.

He stooped down to look at the cuts. "Do they hurt much?"

"Not too bad," said Jordy.

"I'm afraid it's going to hurt more while I clean it up. Can you take it?"

Jordy nodded again, determined.

Dr. Raynik set to work, quietly and quickly. Jordy's jaw was set, but he didn't flinch.

As Dr. Raynik worked, he made verbal notations for Jordy's benefit. "Most of the cuts are superficial. This big one on your calf got into the muscle a bit. It will need a lot of stitches. There's no damage to tendons, though. Nothing that should have any trouble healing."

Jordy's mother arrived just as Dr. Raynik was preparing to stitch the largest cut. He had injected a local anesthetic around it. Now that the area was numb, Jordy was watching the preparations with surprisingly cheerful interest. Perhaps it had dawned on him that he would have something spectacularly gory to show off at school.

Donna scrutinized her son for a moment, saw that he was calm, and said, "Hello, Buckaroo, I hear you had to fight off a pack of wolves."

"It was a small pack," Jordy said, and managed a smile.

She smiled back and gave him a quick hug. "Hang in there," she said.

She came over to where I was standing, as far out of the way as I could get in a small room. She thanked me for bringing him in, and I apologized again for my dog's behavior.

"Had she bitten anyone before?" Donna asked.

"No. But you know border collies. They can be nervy. They need work and I hadn't been working her and something must have gone wrong in her head."

Jordy looked over his shoulder at our low-voiced conference and must have seen us plotting Lucy's fate.

"Mom, you have to make her promise not to kill the dog. I'm hardly hurt at all."

"We'll talk about it after you're fixed up," she said. She

was smiling a little.

"Your son takes after you, I've discovered," I said.

"In what way?"

"He spent the whole drive in here trying to corner me with arguments. His topic was 'Resolved, that dogs should not be punished for the sins of their owners.' If I paused for breath, he came at me with another reason why Lucy should not be shot. He must have inherited your facility for debate."

"He can pin me in a corner with arguments, too. Sometimes I wish we had a referee, so I could call time out." She paused. "I didn't realize that anyone in Kilgore would remember my debating days. I assumed my later feats of notoriety would blot them from memory."

"People in Kilgore don't forget anything," I said. "So few things happen, we remember anything that does."

She laughed. "I should have known that. Mrs. Chase sure never forgot your tearing up your college acceptances. She said to me, 'I hope you're not going to be like Pat Lloyd and throw away your opportunities.' I barely knew about it when it happened, but Mrs. Chase made sure every class after you heard the story and learned a lesson from it."

She turned toward her son and asked, "How are you doing, there, Jord?"

"OK."

"How many stitches so far?"

"Nine."

"Maybe Willie can take you to Show and Tell next week. But I suppose your Aunt Debbie wouldn't like that idea."

Jordy looked over his shoulder again and grinned at her. That conspiratorial look, and their easy familiarity with each other, made me think of every pair of adventurers who ever set off together to take on the world. In that instant, they could have been Don Quixote and Sancho Panza, or Huck Finn and Jim on their raft.

Jordy would not let me leave them until I promised that I would not shoot Lucy without first trying to cure her.

"It's only fair," he said, and in my heart I agreed with him, so I promised.

Once the agreement had been negotiated among the three of us, we turned toward Dr. Raynik, anxiously. If the story became known to the town, all of Jordy's persuasiveness would not turn aside public opinion.

Dr. Raynik answered before we asked. As he spoke, he was looking at me with a sympathetic intentness that seemed to want to convey some message beyond the immediate meaning of his words.

"People don't often come to me expecting gossip," he said. "I don't see why I should go out of my way to spread it."

Until this moment, catching his look, I had not thought much about Dr. Raynik's position in Kilgore. He did not grow up here. He had moved here with his family to take over the practice when old Dr. Wilcox died. Not much was known about his background, but it was thought that his parents had had to make a hasty departure from somewhere in Eastern Europe or the Balkans when he was a child. His speech still had an echo of their accent. People did not know why he had come here. Nor did they know his exact ethnic identity, which could have been Slavic or Greek or even Turkish, or his religion, except that it was one of the sects on the eastern fringe of Christianity.

He was treated with the same nervous awe that people might feel toward a medicine man or a wizard. Though he was trusted implicitly as a doctor, the majority of his patients shied away from meeting him socially. Their children were instructed to treat the Raynik children nicely but not to get too close. It was a strange position he occupied in the town, simultaneously admired, respected and shunned.

The look he gave me was there and then gone, in a moment, but I was sure I had not imagined it. A shutter had opened and closed, casting a light briefly from his life onto mine, and now he was talking again in that deep soothing voice, asking me if my dog had a current rabies shot.

I said, yes, she did. My neglect had not extended that far.

Outside, I helped Donna wedge the bicycle into the back of her small foreign car. The car still had Oregon license plates. It looked nearly as old as my pickup truck, though not yet as scarred by flying gravel.

"Let me know how those cuts do," I said to Jordy.

"May I come visit Lucy?" he asked.

"If you really want to, you can come anytime I'm home."

"Since you've decided to defend the dog, what are you going to tell the kids at school?" Donna asked him. "They'll want to know what happened."

"I've got that all figured out," said Jordy. "I'll tell each person something different. I'll tell one person it was a coyote, and another person it was a raccoon, and another person that it was Reverend Kinley's dachshunds, and another person that a gang attacked me with switchblades outside the bowling alley in Seco Springs. If I tell enough stories, they won't know which one is the true one."

"Someday he is going to be governor," I said.

She smiled. "Until some reporter digs up his birth certificate," she said. There was a twist in her voice.

29

THAT SAME WEEK I BOUGHT SIX
cull ewes from the Paskes, one of the few families in the county
who still ran sheep. In our county, the century-old cattle and
sheep war had been won by the cattle, though it was a hollow victory. The cattlemen had displaced the sheepmen only
to find themselves being displaced by an economy in which
most small ranchers either folded or found a second job in
town.

The Paskes survived on their small spread because they
had no family to support, and because they lived almost as
simply as their immigrant grandfather, who travelled with
his flocks and lived in a tent. There were just the three of
them, the old couple and their bachelor son Karl, who was
nearing fifty. Like the grandfather, they kept to themselves
and they bought their supplies a season at a time. I almost
never saw them. Even though they now traveled in a pickup,

they still viewed a trip to town as an expedition on which one sets out at dawn. By the time my shift began, they would have come and gone.

They were glad to sell me some sheep. They were culling the flock in anticipation of winter, and I gave them a few dollars more than they would have gotten at the commission sale in Seco Springs.

After I unloaded the sheep in my pasture, I came into the house to find Lucy dancing in anticipation.

"Not today, old girl," I said. "The poor sheep have just been bounced over forty miles of gravel road. They deserve a break."

In the morning, I took her out for her test. I watched every move she made, every look, for signs of a predatory interest. I could see nothing different in her behavior, only the normal fanaticism of the collie in the presence of sheep. She responded to my commands as readily as ever. She rounded them up, guided them into the pen, and then sat by the gate looking smug. All seemed normal.

Things were normal, at least, so long as I was there with her. The more severe test was still to come, when she confronted Jordy or some other child, someone who would rouse her fear in a way that the sheep did not.

I thought Jordy might lose interest in the dog when he returned to his own house and his accustomed round of activities. Once again, he surprised me. At seven o'clock on Saturday morning, the phone rang. When I heard his voice, I thought, what kind of a twelve-year-old gets up at seven o'clock on the weekend? I had the impression that boys that age were starting to grow and needed to spend all of Saturday and Sunday morning lying in bed to take the weight off their expanding bones. Maybe that phase started later. My memory of seventh grade was getting vague.

"Can we visit?" Jordy asked immediately.

"Sure. You may find me working, but you're welcome," I said.

Since the dog fracas, I had spent little time on Alma Rose. I was beginning to feel edgy about the delay. Sometimes the project felt like a pregnancy without a fixed gestation length. The creature was growing, with urgent force, toward its eventual emergence into light. Unlike a real pregnancy, though, the process of growth could be slowed or stopped completely by intrusions from the outside world.

What would it be like for a pregnant woman if the fetus stopped growing whenever she took time to do laundry or talk on the phone or go to work? What if the birth date could be pushed forward indefinitely into the future by trivial distractions? She would go mad. She would begin railing at friends, neighbors, household, weather, work, at life itself, for prolonging this state of heavy, uncomfortable and impatient anticipation. If her husband tracked muddy boots across the kitchen floor so that she had to mop, and if she felt the live being inside her grow suddenly still, she might well have an urge to seize a carving knife and cut the uncomprehending husband's throat.

Her sanity is saved by the inexorability of gestation. It makes no difference to the growing creature whether she spends her days scrubbing floors and running errands, or whether she lies on the couch eating bonbons and contemplating the miracle of procreation.

I wished Alma Rose were so inexorable. But she was not a lusty mass of living cells full of the drive for self-perpetuation.

She was an evanescent image flickering in the mind. She could be blotted out in a moment by the need to remember a phone number, by Pops rattling on about the approach of hunting season. Her creation had a 'Pause' button, accessible to every detail of daily life. I sometimes wondered how many times her growth could be suspended before she died and became a rotting object inside me which I must reabsorb or expel.

After Jordy's call, I hastened out to do as much work as I could before they came. I would eat breakfast later. When they arrived, I would offer them a share of my coffee and doughnuts, and thus squeeze hospitality and my own need for food into the same hour of time.

In my hurry, I misjudged a blow with the pick and knocked too large a dent in the side of the nose. I rested the pick on the ground and took a long breath.

"Slow down, you fool." I murmured. "So maybe this rock will take you the rest of your life. So what else were you planning to do?"

With tiny careful taps of the chisel I began to smooth over the damage I had done. After a time, Lucy alerted me to the arrival of my visitors. She ran to the end of her tether, whining, and I turned and saw the car pulling into the driveway. I clipped a leash to Lucy's collar and led her down the hill to meet them.

Jordy looked as if he were braced not to back away as we approached. At my command, Lucy sat down. Slowly and hesitantly, Jordy walked closer to her.

"Say something to her," I said. He looked questioning and I added, "It doesn't matter what you say, as long as your tone is quiet."

"I'm not a burglar, you know," he said to Lucy and took a step closer.

I kept my eyes on the dog, watching for any hint that she was going to snap at him.

"And the bicycle won't bite you, either," he said. He stretched out a hand, slowly. Lucy strained forward against the leash to sniff it. She shifted her body uneasily, trying to move closer to me, although she was already pressed against my legs. Her ears flickered back and forth, forward toward Jordy's voice, then back toward me for reassurance that I was still there. Jordy stroked her head. She looked anxious rather than pleased, but she tolerated it. He babbled nonsense to her, in the way that I often did when no one could hear.

"You probably thought I was an alien on a nuclear pow-ered bicycle," he said. "You probably thought I could fire la-sers from the handlebars. You probably thought I was going to carry your owner off in a spaceship and leave you here all by yourself. It's no wonder you bit me. I'd bite someone if I thought they were going to vaporize Mom."

Lucy did not look happy, but she had relaxed a little un-der the influence of his monotonous stream of talk. Jordy gave her one last pat, then backed away. He looked at her wistfully. What he wanted to do, I was sure, was to kneel down, put his arms around her and give her a squeeze. He had the sense not to push his luck.

With that test over, I offered them the coffee and dough-nuts. Donna accepted the coffee, Jordy the doughnuts.

Between mouthfuls, Jordy asked me, "Why are you carv-ing a naked lady?"

Why was I carving her, in fact? "She was someone I loved," I said. "She isn't around anymore."

"Did she die?"

"No. She just moved on."

"What was she like?"

"She was lively and funny and pretty. She drove a semi."

"Why did she leave?" he asked. He was looking at me unblinkingly, the way children do before they reach puberty and self-consciousness.

"She didn't exactly leave, because she never stayed in the first place. She passed through. And then one day she stopped passing through. I don't think there was ever any chance she would settle here."

"Not many people would want to settle in Kilgore, unless they'd grown up here," Donna said.

"She wouldn't have stayed with me anywhere else, either," I said. "I wasn't the right sort of person."

"What would have been the right sort of person?"

I thought for a moment. "Maybe no one. But definitely not me. I'm too rooted and safe and self-contained. She'd want to be with someone whose nerves were all on the outside of the skin. Someone whose moods leap out like flames. Someone who would wrestle with her emotionally. I didn't want to wrestle. I wanted to be peaceful and happy. I suppose that was boring."

"I've been wrestling for thirteen years," Donna said. "I'd give anything to be boringly happy."

"What were you wrestling with?" I asked.

She laughed. Instead of answering, she asked, "Were you hoping to get some work done on the sculpture today?"

"Yes, but it doesn't matter."

"Telling you what I've been wrestling with would take more time than a cup of coffee. You wouldn't get anything done. Can we come up and watch you work instead?"

I hesitated. I disliked having an audience. On the other hand, I wanted them to stay. Perhaps Donna would answer my question while I was working. I wanted to know her story. I thought I understood what had driven her out of Kilgore, but I wanted to know how she had lived all those years, and why she had come back.

"You can watch if you want," I said.

If she meant to answer my question, she wasn't in any hurry. She and Jordy climbed around on the rock, while I set to work on the nose. I heard them laughing about something as they stood on the crest of the buttock.

When they rejoined me, Donna said, "Jordy thinks you should invite the audience to participate."

"This thing would make a great playground," he said. "You should carve some handholds and footholds, where they wouldn't show too much. It's a kick, running down someone's backbone and shinnying down between their buns."

"There isn't any audience to participate," I said. "And if there were, someone would probably fall and break their neck. I'd have to build a big fence around it."

"You're no fun," he said. "It could be just like North by Northwest, where the good guys and bad guys are all chasing each other across George Washington's face. The hair is good, too. The curls are shaped like those saggy canvas beach chairs. People could sit up here and look at the view. It's too bad she isn't hollow. You could make a tunnel into the inside and make lots of caves inside. Now you're in her stomach, now you're in her lungs, now you're crawling through the intestine. It would be a blast."

For an instant, his excitement and the sheer nuttiness of

it made it sound like a good idea. Then I envisioned myself hunched over inside a tiny dark space, chipping away still more piles of rock. What are you carving? A big intestine.

"I'll be content if I finish the outside," I said. "So you will have to be content with thinking up uses for the outside."

"Why didn't you do her mouth?" he asked.

"I wasn't in the mood," I said. "She's smiling, and I didn't feel like smiling."

"You're smiling now."

"Am I?"

It was true, I was.

Donna had had enough of climbing. "I'm going to sit down," she said to Jordy. "You can go find new body parts to scale, if you want to."

He dashed away, and she sat down on the ledge with her back against Alma Rose's chin. The sun had come around far enough to shine on this side of the outcrop, so the rock was growing warm. Otherwise the autumn air would have been too cold for sitting.

Now that the situation was made for conversation, both of us were silent. I tapped with my chisel. Donna rested her head against the rock and gazed down the valley. The air was still, and nothing seemed to be moving, except for Jordy scrambling about somewhere above and behind us. I stayed busy with the chisel, raising little whitecaps of noise so that a spoken word, if it ever came, would not fall with a conspicuous splash into an unbroken surface of silence.

I could think of a dozen questions I wanted to ask, but they sounded too baldly personal, coming without a preparatory greasing with social chitchat. The chitchat was beyond me. How could I make polite inquiries about her parents' health when I was wondering how she had gotten back on speaking terms with them?

"Are you glad to be back in Kilgore?" I asked finally.

"I'm not sure yet," she said.

"You've been back almost a year, haven't you?"

"Eight months."

"And you're still not sure?"

"I'm still doing research," she said.

"What is there to research?"

She didn't answer right away. She was looking off at something in the distance, or perhaps at nothing.

"Don't jump the fence if I've drawn a wrong conclusion," she said. "This woman was your lover, wasn't she?" She gestured with her head toward the rock behind her. "Jordy was positive, but I'm older and more cautious. People mean a lot of different things when they say they loved someone, and I know for sure you can't judge by the rumors that fly around town. I don't want to make a blunder if she was just a close friend who didn't mind posing in the nude."

"She was my lover," I said. "Why was Jordy so positive?"

She shrugged. "I don't know how kids know things. He knew right away. The moment we left the doctor's office and got into the car, he said, 'They were lovers, I'm sure of it. She and the lady in the statue.' He was very excited. I don't know what it means about his head, but he is fascinated by lesbians. I hope it doesn't mean he will fall in love with them and be frustrated. That would be a new twist on the Oedipus complex."

It took me a moment to digest all of what she said, and to draw my own conclusions in turn. "Do you mean, then, that you're . . . " I paused. The word still stuck in my throat, weighted down by centuries of scorn. I had never heard it spoken publicly, as part of ordinary vocabulary. 'Murder,' 'rape,' 'torture,' 'genocide,' 'famine,' 'plague,' 'injustice,' all might take their place at the dinner table, but 'lesbian' would cause forks to drop and a painfully embarrassed silence to fall.

"A lesbian," she finished for me. "Yes."

In spite of myself, I turned to look at her, as if she might suddenly look different. She saw my look and laughed.

"I never thought . . . " I began. "It never occurred to me. You have a child, so I assumed . . . "

"Luckily for my parents, most people make the same assumption."

"Why for your parents?"

"Because it has taken them almost thirteen years to swallow the idea that their daughter lives in mortal sin. If the whole neighborhood knew about it, I'm not sure they could do it."

"You told them thirteen years ago?"

"Why do you think there was such an explosion? An illegitimate grandchild they'd have swallowed in a few months. They were so relieved I didn't want an abortion, they could almost overlook the sinful sex that started the whole thing. But they couldn't overlook my being a lesbian."

"Are you always so honest?" I asked.

"It wasn't honesty. I was harried into it," she said. "They'd been after me for weeks to marry the father. I said I didn't love him and they said I would learn to, and I said no, I wouldn't, and they said yes, I would. We went around and around that circle until it was beaten into concrete, and finally I said, 'I don't love men. I love women.' When I said that, everything stopped dead. There was just silence. Total, ominous silence."

She paused, and I could hear the kind of silence she meant. It was not the shifty, nervous silence of embarrassment. It was the silence of gathering wrath, the kind that fills a room, stifling, suffocating, as if all the air had been pushed out, and something heavy, unbreathable but invisible, had taken its place. I could feel the squirming anxiety that takes hold, the frantic wish for something, even something cataclysmic, to release the tension.

"My mother just exploded," Donna said. "Her yells would have woke the neighbors, if we'd had any closer than a mile away. She wanted to march me down to Father Sullivan for an emergency confession, for fear a lightning bolt might strike me down before the next Sunday. I told her I couldn't confess, because I wasn't repentant. I said I didn't believe it was a sin, or if it was, then God was the sinner, because God was the one who made me the way I was. That was blasphemy and it really set her off.

"We both started screaming anything that came into our heads. Somewhere along the way I said God must have made the priesthood as the place for homosexuals, since they were both supposed to stay celibate. My mother kept yelling that I was spitting on the church, that I was a piece of filth, and that she never wanted to see me again. I still have nightmares about that fight. I hear Mom screaming that I'm damned beyond hope of redemption and I see her face all twisted with hatred for me."

She grimaced. "Sometimes now I can laugh about things we said, but at the time I thought I was going to split wide open from the pain. I had to choose between two halves of my being. I could deny my parents and their love and my crying need for their love. Or I could deny the whole center of what I was myself. I thought the choice might kill me."

She picked up a chip of rock and flung it down the hill, watching it ricochet off the rubble below.

"Fortunately, people don't die that easily," she said. "These past few years Jordy has started having definite beliefs of his own. It's made me realize that my parents were as much split in two as I was. They had as much need for my love, their religious belief was just as much at the core of their being, and they had to choose between the two. It must have torn them apart as much as it did me."

"What changed?" I asked. "How is it you've been able to come back?"

"Maybe we all softened a little with age," she said. "A couple of years ago I wrote them a letter and said I can't change what I am and I know you can't change what you believe, but I'd like to see you again and Jordy would like to meet his family. They went and talked to Father Paul about what they should do. Father Paul's not as hardline as Father Sullivan was. He told them if I was sinning, it was up to God to punish me, not them. So they invited me for a visit, and when I wanted to come back to stay, they said OK.

"I think my mother may have some idea about retrieving Jordy from my influence. I know that every time she looks at me, she looks grieved." Donna smiled. "It's a strange feeling, to have someone look at you as if you're already dead and lying in your casket."

She leaned back against the rock and closed her eyes. Her face had a look of remembered pain, but her lips still curved in a smile.

I studied her face. In repose, it was rather plain. She did not have what are called good bones. Instead, her face seemed to be a vehicle for expression, and its most habitual expression was one of determination and good humor. I thought she looked like the kind of person who gets chosen to be a squad leader or team captain, someone who inspires respect and trust in close associates but who would never hold a crowd in thrall with charm.

Could I have stood so firmly and stubbornly against a parent's anger? I had never had to find out. Pops had been easy. He was too lazy and affable ever to stand rigid on a matter of principle. He wanted everyone to get along. He was ruled by feelings, not beliefs, and his opinions could always be reshaped if they came into conflict with his affections.

My mother was different. She had serious and deeply felt convictions. She held them inwardly, though, living by them without announcing them to other people. On this subject, I could only guess what her opinion would have been. Sex was not a subject that ever came up in her conversation, and I truly did not know what she would have thought.

I did know that she had loved me with all her soul. If something I did had offended her deepest beliefs, she would have suffered anguish far beyond anything her disease, or the doctors, or the devil himself could have caused. I was overtaken by a thought that horrified me, that perhaps her death, for all the pain it caused me, might also have spared me some pain of a different kind.

"I'm lucky, I suppose," I said. "Not to have had that kind of battle."

"Does your dad know about you?" Donna asked.

"I expect the whole town knows, given this sculpture. But, yes, he knows."

"And he doesn't object?"

"He doesn't like it, but he sees it as a natural anomaly, like being an albino or having a club foot. I'm a freak, but it's not my fault and there's nothing to be done about it."

"I think I could handle being a freak," Donna said.

I smiled. "Given that choice, being a natural freak, or a moral degenerate, I'll be the freak, too. People stare, but they aren't so likely to throw stones."

30

"I HEAR YOUR DOG ATTACKED ONE
of the McNeil children," said Peggy Treadwell.

"That's true," I said. "She bit his leg."

I should have known better than to think the incident could be kept secret. I was sure that neither Jordy nor Dr. Raynik had told anyone, but it didn't matter. In Kilgore, news just spread whether anyone told anyone else or not. Maybe it traveled through the ground water and came up through people's pipes. Turn on the faucet to brush your teeth and suddenly you know, with certainty, that Cora Eastman is having an affair with Dwight Barbula.

"I heard it was much worse than one bite," said Peggy. "Did you have her put to sleep?"

"No."

"She might attack another child at any time, you know."

"I don't ever let her run loose anymore."

"You can't be sure, even so. A child might come up to her where she is tied. A dog that attacks children is a public menace. She should be done away with."

Peggy was gradually building up the head of steam she needed to launch a crusade.

"I'm taking every precaution," I said. "She's not tied. She's in a run with a high wire fence. A child couldn't walk up to her. There are no children within a mile of my place anyway."

I could see, even as I was talking, that Peggy was not listening. She had the blank look on her face of someone who knows what she believes and is not interested in discussion.

"The boy who was bitten does not want her killed," I said. "He wants to make friends with her, so that he won't be afraid of dogs."

"Children have no judgment," Peggy said. "It is not the boy who has already been bitten that concerns me. It is the children who might be bitten in the future."

"I'm taking responsibility for making sure that no one does get bitten."

"You can't hold onto her collar twenty-four hours a day. What about this very moment, while you're here at the store? She might get loose from her pen. Or you might forget sometime and some child's face might be scarred for life. Or worse."

I saw Lucy transformed by Peggy's brain into a gigantic wolf with flaming eyes and slobbering jaws, loping through the countryside in search of children. There was no use explaining that Lucy was a high-strung timid dog who snapped out in fear and might attack viciously in fear, but that she was not a ruthless bone-crunching hunter who would actively search for prey. Peggy was not interested in particular cases. She was interested in general principles.

"Every dog owner swears it won't happen again, and then it does," she said. "If we make an exception for your dog, then every time someone's dog kills a sheep or a calf, the owner will plead for an exception."

I felt my arguments being borne under by the tide of her conviction, a tide that soon swelled with other people's voices in agreement. If I had been sure I was right, I might have stood against it. Instead, I could feel my own inner doubts nibbling away the ground beneath my feet.

"Though I hate to admit it, I think Peggy is right," said Pops. "There might be reasons why not in this case, but we have to stick to the principle or else every case will become an argument. You know yourself, you won't really trust Lucy anymore."

I didn't need to hear his reasons. I had heard them already, a hundred times, inside my own head. On the one side was the principle, clear and absolute, familiar to me for as long as I had been aware of principles. A killer dog must be killed. On the other side I saw Jordy, pleading with all the irrational force of love and fear, and hope that bad things might get better, if given a chance. I felt Lucy, cowering against my legs, racked by fear and by eagerness to do what would please me, forcing her nose forward to sniff Jordy's hand, forcing her head to stay still under his touch. Lucy's psychology did not matter, though, and neither did my good intentions for my future care of her.

For many days I argued my case in the forum of the Mercantile. Perhaps a number of people would have been content to overlook the incident, but now that Peggy was trumpeting her outrage through the town, they had no choice but to take a position. The position was unanimous. Some of them might look their sympathy to my cause, but none would speak it out loud, except to say they knew how tough it was to put a dog to sleep.

Jordy came to see Lucy on weekends, and she had become less afraid of him, though never friendly or playful. Finally, on his fourth visit, I said to him, "It's not going to work. I have to put her down."

I think he knew from the way I said it that there was no more persuasion possible. "She was making progress," he said, plaintively. He stroked her head, and she managed one tentative wag of the tail before fear gripped her again and she backed away to lean against my legs.

"I'm taking her later this morning," I said. "I wanted you to know before I did."

"I want to come," he said immediately.

"Are you sure?"

I glanced at Donna, but she was silent, leaving the decision to her son.

"Yes, I'm sure," he said. "We're in this together."

I took her out for one last time with the sheep and let her put on a show, rounding them up, shifting them from one pen to another, circling, crouching, rushing forward to prod, then back to let the sheep calm down. Her ears were up, listening for commands and for praise. For an hour she was as happy as a dog can be. Then I let the sheep go and whistled her into the back of the truck. Jordy, Donna, and I climbed into the cab to drive to town.

Jordy hung close behind me as I led Lucy into Dr. Fitch's clinic. Even as I boosted her onto the sterile metal table to be killed, one detached corner of my brain was thinking how odd it was that so much of this acquaintance among the three of us was going forward in antiseptic medical examining rooms. I cursed my facility for detachment. I wanted to be in this moment only, with my dog, whom I loved. Instead my brain was wandering off into abstractions.

Lucy was terrified, as she always was at the vet.

"It's a shot, old girl," I said.

I wanted to reassure her, the way I usually did, telling her it wouldn't last a moment, it hurts but then it's over, it will be good for you. I couldn't do it. All I could say was, "I'm awfully sorry, old Lucy girl." I kept one hand on her head, rubbing her ears, while Dr. Fitch stuck in the needle.

It always surprised me, how fast the drugs worked. The phrase 'put to sleep' somehow suggested that the animal slowly dozed off. Lucy did not gently drift off. Within seconds, her body sagged, her legs buckled, and she lay limp on the table. Jordy uttered a small cry, then did what he had been wanting to do all along. He threw his arms around her neck and hugged her, only now he was sobbing.

I didn't cry then, not when it made sense to cry. The tears burned behind my eyes and constricted my throat, but refused to flow. We wrapped Lucy in a blanket, carried her home and buried her. All through the evening, Lulu hovered near me, blind and worried. I thought, what am I going to do with those darned sheep? Without a dog, I couldn't even round them up to load them onto a truck and take them to the commission sale.

I put off the matter of the sheep and went back to work on the sculpture, feeling savage, with my neighbors, with the unshakeable codes of the West, but mostly with myself. I swung the pick wildly, as fast as I could. Strangely, the blows landed true.

At the store, I was silent. People felt awkward, maybe a little guilty some of them, and I made no effort to relieve the awkwardness. I had done my part. I had done my public duty. I was not yet in a mood where I cared about smoothing the path of neighborly relations.

"You did the right thing," said Peggy Treadwell. "I'm sure it must have been hard, but it was the right thing."

"I'm sure it was," I said abruptly. I did not want to talk to Peggy Treadwell about how hard it had been.

About a week later, Leonard Kinley came into the store. He wandered around, randomly picking up and putting down objects from the shelves, until the other two customers in the store had left. Then he came over to the cash register. He fingered a couple of magazines before he finally said, "You probably don't want to think about this yet." He fingered another magazine or two. "Maybe in a little while you will, so I thought I'd let you know. My wife's brother-in-law had a litter a few weeks ago. Not him, I mean, but that bitch you sold him. He's real proud. Eight of them, he said. Anyhow, I thought . . . "

He couldn't finish his thought, because I had burst into tears. Once they started, they came uncontrollably. Reverend Kinley was pinned there, snared by his own kindness. Even if he had pressing engagements, he couldn't walk out and leave me crying. So he stayed, shifting from foot to foot, offering me a handkerchief, trying to find something to say that would dry up the torrent. He probably thought that the idea of trying to replace Lucy had sent me into this spasm of grief. It was not that. I had already resolved to find another dog, since I still had those sheep and something must be done.

What had undone me was the simple kindness of his

gesture, the directness of his sympathy, not the cheap sympathy of saying, "I know how you feel," but the real sympathy of someone who has felt what you feel and tries to do the thing that he knows helped him in the same situation. Leonard had two fat dachshunds, and he had had two fat dachshunds ever since I had known him. Clearly, they had not been the same two dachshunds for twenty-five years.

I thought, maybe for some people the puzzle of mortality was fully answered by Christian theology. They could bury their love under a granite marker and feel sure that it would someday come back to life in an unseen realm. For other people, the ones still bothered by a doubt or two, some more immediate and human solution was needed, so they kept a piece of their love unburied and grafted it onto the new young things coming into the world.

31

PERHAPS BOLSTERED BY HER
victory over Lucy, Peggy Treadwell decided to take up the
matter of my sculpture. Public opinion had been lying dormant through the long slow process of manufacture. Most of
my neighbors were not going to tell me I couldn't do what I
wanted on my own property until they were fairly sure I was
doing something they didn't like. The whole idea of the sculpture was so fantastic, they couldn't tell whether they were
going to like it or not. It was outside all the usual frames of
reference. They could not extrapolate from past experience
to predict how they were going to feel. They had to wait
until there was a solid visible object, and then they could
form an opinion.

That winter, Alma Rose was getting near enough to
completion that people began to form definite opinions. The
majority appeared to be lining up behind Leonard Kinley. In

his opinion, the shapes were crude enough, the stone rough enough, and the pose discreet enough that she was not indecent, even though she was naked. The viewer saw nothing that could not be seen on a woman in a bathing suit. The pubic area was an undifferentiated surface of stone, deep in the shadowy hollow below her torso. The breast lay against the bed beneath her, no nipple showing. Her pose had the relaxation of sleep, not the arched tension of sexuality. And I was not a clever enough sculptor to make the face recognizable as Alma Rose. Her face was a generic woman's face. She had a little of the stylized, crude simplicity of a primitive sculpture. If she was a goddess, however, she could only be the goddess of sleep.

She really was what I had said she would be, a woman sleeping. As a sculpture, she had no particular merit. If she caught and held the eye, it was only because of her great size and because of her situation, perched high among the wild rugged hills.

Though the majority might share Leonard Kinley's view, there was a distinct minority, led by Peggy Treadwell, who did not. They were fewer in number, but far more vehement in their views.

"I don't care whether you see every detail," Peggy said. "It's clear that she's naked, and we don't want a naked lady sitting up there on a hill for all the world to see. What kind of a town will people think this is, with a lady sculptor who carves naked ladies?"

"Would you be happier if I had carved a naked man?" I asked.

"No decent woman would carve anybody naked."

"How about if I add the straps of a bikini? It wouldn't be

hard, just a couple of lines." I had no intention of adding a bikini, but I wanted to see her reaction.

She fidgeted a little. "That isn't the point."

"What is the point, then?"

"You should know," she said, with a look that was meant to wither me. I knew exactly what the point was, but unless she was willing to step out from behind the cover of innuendo and state her case in plain words, I was not going to reply with anything other than stupidly puzzled innocence.

"It's not normal," she said.

"What's not?"

"That you should want to carve a naked lady."

"People have been carving and painting naked ladies since the dawn of time," I said.

"Women haven't."

"Women rarely had the chance to carve or paint much of anything, until recently."

"The point is, she's that lady truck driver."

"So?"

"So how can you go putting a statue of her up in front of the whole town?"

"Why shouldn't I?"

"Because it's not natural. You two weren't natural."

"We weren't? In what way?"

I was smiling a little, remembering Donna McNeil saying, "I could handle being a freak." A freak of nature, but nature made all sorts of oddities. We were the albino horses, the four leaf clovers, the seven-foot basketball centers, the left-handed pitchers, the cretins and the Einsteins, the kangaroos and giraffes, the redheads, the opera singers and the sumo wrestlers. So what?

So what?

Peggy had won the battle over Lucy because at bottom I had believed the same principle she believed. She had turned my own mind against me.

On this issue, I did not believe what she believed. She could not use my mind as the strongest weapon against me. She could not attack and keep herself unscathed, nor cover me in mud without getting the slime on her own hands. To triumph, she must plunge her own self fully into the fray.

And what resources did she have? If she shunned me, I would hardly regret her absence. If others joined her, I would still survive, because the people who mattered to me showed no inclination to join her.

I supposed she could try to dynamite the sculpture, though that was more easily said than done. In the extreme case, I supposed she could haul me into an alley, beat my brains out, and thereby make me a martyr and herself a criminal. It may be small comfort to a martyr to know that the killer is a criminal, but at least it is better than being tricked into wielding the bludgeon upon oneself.

In the meantime, I could look straight back at her and dare her to come into the clear. She was the one calling me unnatural. She was the one who must spell out her meaning. I would grant her "odd." "Unnatural" she must prove.

"In what way?" I asked.

"You know very well."

I shook my head and shrugged. "No, I don't." My tone was amiable.

She paused, stymied for the moment. I could imagine her difficulties. In order to spell out her meaning, she must talk explicitly about sex. Neither she nor anyone else in Kilgore did that with any ease, especially not in the aisle of a store. Also, though she might be convinced in her own mind of my nature, she had no actual proof and so there was a small crack for doubt to enter. The getting of proof, if it came to that, would involve such a gross invasion of privacy that even Peggy Treadwell might hesitate.

Lastly, I think she was beginning to realize that even if she steeled herself and made the accusation in plain words, even if she forced her tongue to form the word lesbian, I was still going to look back at her and say, "So what?"

32

"It's easy for you to say 'So what?'" said Donna.

She was sitting on the ledge, with her knees pulled up against her chest for warmth. Jordy was nearby, tossing chips of stone in the direction of Alma Rose's face, trying to bounce them off the very tip of the nose.

He had used my acquisition of a new puppy as an excuse to continue coming to see me. Their visits had become almost a routine, on Sundays. He and Skipper played together, I worked on the sculpture, and Donna sat, bundled up against the cold, to talk to me. When Jordy and the puppy had worn each other out, the puppy would curl up for a nap next to Donna, and Jordy would hover on the fringe of the conversation, tossing stones or trying his hand with a chisel.

When I told Donna, with a small air of triumph, about my ongoing fencing match with Peggy, she did not enter into the triumph as fully as I had expected.

"Why do you say it's easy for me?" I asked.

"Because you have almost nothing to lose. What can anyone do to hurt you?"

"What makes you think anyone wants to hurt me, apart from a few people like Peggy?"

"Most of them don't. But it doesn't take very many Peggy Treadwells to make your life miserable, if you're vulnerable."

"What do you mean by vulnerable?"

"If you were a schoolteacher, they could get you fired. If you were a politician, they could make a scandal. But what can they do to you? You don't have a landlord to kick you out. They can't turn your family against you, and they can't get you fired, since your boss is your dad. They could boycott the Mercantile, but that's an awful lot of trouble for them when it's the only store in forty miles. Most people aren't that dedicated. They can sneer and snub you socially, but the people who would do that you probably don't care about anyway. So it's easy for you to look those people in the eye and say 'So what?' You don't have a kid who gets beaten up on the playground because of you."

"Does Jordy get beaten up?" I asked.

"He used to, in some of the places we lived. It's not so easy to thumb your nose at the world when the world turns around and pounds on your kid."

"I used to do what Pat does," Jordy said suddenly. "I mean, I'd say to people 'So what?'"

"You did?" She looked at him in astonishment. "Is that why they beat you up?"

He shook his head. "They beat me up long before that. Some big mammoth kid would grab me and say, 'Your mom's a queer,' and I'd say, 'Don't use that word,' and punch him, and then he would pound me into the ground. After a while I got sick of it. So instead of getting mad when they said, 'Your mom's a queer,' I would smile at them and say, 'Thank you. I hear your mom is a really good cook,' as if being a queer was a big compliment."

"Did it work?" Donna asked.

He grinned. "Nah. They'd still pound me into the ground. But they didn't have as much fun doing it."

"You shouldn't have to get beaten up at all. Especially not because of me."

"Aw, Mom, some of those goons would have beaten up on me no matter what. How was I going to stop them? All the time they were hitting me, I'd be thinking, 'Someday I'll go to Japan and learn karate, and then I'll come back and flatten you, you gorilla.' And then I'd think, what if the gorilla goes to Japan and learns karate, too? Then I'll really be in trouble." He shrugged. "I figured if they couldn't make me mad, then I'd won the first round. They might win the last nine, but at least I got one."

Peggy Treadwell did not abandon her crusade merely because I had backed her into an awkward corner in a duel of words. Her next tactic was to try to rouse the parents of the children whose schoolbus passed by my place on its way into Kilgore. Did they want their children to be exposed to such an object every day? she asked. Did they want their children to think that the community approved of such an object? What seeds of iniquity might be planted in fertile young minds, she hinted in dark tones.

It was a time-tested strategy. If people could not be roused to irrational fear on their own behalf, perhaps they could on behalf of their children. It had worked against the Jews, who were portrayed as murdering Christian children in dark alleys in the Middle Ages. It had worked against blacks, who were portrayed as lustful animals eager to ravish the innocent daughters of white slaveowners. It had worked against some great pieces of literature, which were accused of corrupting young minds. Probably it had worked against every variety of racial, religious and ethnic distinction, exposure to which might cause a child to grow up as a less-than-exact replica of his parents.

Two young mothers, more timid than Peggy Treadwell, approached me one evening and asked, very tentatively, if I would consider putting clothes on the statue somehow. Because they were so diffident in asking, I found it much harder to say no.

"Have your children been upset?" I asked.

"No, it's not that. At least, they haven't said anything. But we worry how it might affect them, seeing it every day. As Mrs. Treadwell says, it is reaching their brain, even if they don't say anything about it. We've always tried to teach them to be modest and decent."

"It was never my intention to make an indecent sculpture. Do you think it is so?"

The one who was acting as spokesperson hesitated, then said, "I think maybe it is, yes. She's not wearing any clothes."

I could not argue with these two the way I could with Peggy. There was no spitefulness in them, nor any complicated reasoning either. On their own, they would never have raised the issue. They were far too shy. There was no ground for debate between our positions. They simply thought that a person in public with no clothes on was indecent, regardless of circumstances.

I said, "If you can persuade me that most of the town feels the way you do, then I might do something about the sculpture."

Evidently my answer was relayed promptly back to Peggy Treadwell. The next day she said, "I understand you will be willing to destroy the sculpture if a majority in town think it is indecent and don't want their children to see it."

She smells blood on her quarry, I thought.

"That's not exactly what I said. I said I might do something to change it, if most people in town want me to and come and tell me so to my face."

Lyle Gardner's son Roy had been standing just down the counter from us, picking through the rack of flashlight batteries. "Seems to me you're too late, Peggy," he interjected. "Seems to me every kid in town must have seen the thing already. If they're going to be shocked, they already have been. I don't see how they could be shocked, though. They can see things a lot worse than that on TV any hour of the day, and the TV is right in the living room."

"You can turn off the television. In any case, the town doesn't give its approval to the things on TV."

"You can look the other direction when you drive by Pat's place," Roy said. "And I don't see why you say the town has given its approval, just because we leave it be. You could just as well say the town had given its approval to those cockeyed wind generators out on Bud Donnelly's place, or that we all approved when Gary Siebenaler went out and bought a damned Japanese car."

"Those things don't affect children the same way," said Peggy. "The schoolbus goes right by that statue every day."

"I know it does. My kids are on it. They don't even notice the thing anymore, except that they're all dying to go watch the next time that dynamite man comes to blow up some more rock."

"Maybe you aren't bothered by what your children look at, but I assure you, other people are. They don't want their children looking at a naked lady every day on the way to school."

Roy looked at me and grinned. "I'll bet Pat and me could rig up some curtains for the schoolbus windows. We could string a cord the whole length of the bus and hang the curtains from it, and put the whole business on pulleys. Then the bus driver could pull the curtains closed when the bus came in sight of the statue and pull them open again once it was out of sight. What do you think, Pat?"

"Could be done," I said.

"You think you're on top right now," Peggy said. "You'll find out what this town really thinks before I'm through."

She stomped out of the store and then, to compound her irritation, had to stomp back in again to retrieve the bag of groceries she had left behind on the counter.

"Won't be a boring winter, anyhow," Pops said to me a couple of weeks later. "Some years a person wishes he were a bear and could go to sleep after New Year's and not wake up until April. Not this year, though. That statue of yours has everybody wide awake. Half the town comes in and asks me when my daughter is going to get rid of the sculpture, and then the other half comes in and asks when Peggy Treadwell is ever going to lay off. It's too bad you're not trying to sell the thing. If it were a book, it would be on the bestseller list."

"What do you say to everyone?" I asked.

"I say I'm putting my money on you. Peggy might be fast out of the gate, but you're a stayer."

I did not feel much like a stayer, being at the center of controversy. I knew Pops was having the time of his life. He liked commotion, and he liked to be right in the middle of it. He could talk all day anyhow, and my statue was as good a topic as any.

The ruckus might suit his temperament, but it did not suit mine. It exhausted me, trying over and over again to explain my position, to answer questions and to stay calm in the face of insinuations. Except twice, in anonymous letters, no one went further than insinuations.

My supporters were almost as tiring as my attackers. When I wasn't fending off criticism, I was expressing appreciation to all the people who hastened to reassure me that they were on my side. I was grateful to them, but I sometimes wished they would not reiterate their support so often. I was simply not used to so much conversation with me as the subject.

As the winter wore on, I noticed that Marge's face was showing some of the weariness I thought must be showing in mine. I still ate a sandwich at the Donut Hole before work most days, only now Marge refused to let me pay for it. Once the other customers had departed and the two of us were alone, we both sank gratefully into the silence that was becoming a rare blessing. Then one day her irritation burst out.

"Don't people ever get tired of talking?" she asked crossly. "I must have heard the same arguments a thousand times. No one has anything new to say. By now, anyone who's going to change his mind has already changed it. So why do people have to go on repeating the same thing they said yesterday and the day before? I wish we'd have a darned good blizzard. It would give them something real to worry about."

"Spring will be here before long," I said. "Maybe they'll have more cheerful things to think about."

"They won't have so much time anyhow, once there are lawns to water and gardens to weed, and the ranches start haying," she said. "And who wants to spend their free time debating morals when they could be barbecuing steaks in the back yard?"

The argument had reached a stalemate. As Marge said, anyone who was going to change his mind had already done so. Now the discussion ran in circles, and the track got deeper with every pass. People went on talking about it because there was little else to talk about.

Our most reliable wintertime diversions had failed us. Despite Marge's wish, no blizzards howled down from the Arctic. The weather seemed almost domesticated, just a few gentle snowfalls and many clear still days, and regular chinooks to clear the ground before the next snow.

The basketball team had settled itself like silt at the bottom of the league standings. The town attended the games with customary loyalty, but with a team as bad as this one, that same loyalty discouraged any discussion of the games afterwards. There was nothing kind to be said, and we were not the sort of fans who enjoy dissecting the failings of our team. Basketball became almost a non-topic.

"Panthers lost again. Seemed to me they played a little better defense."

"Not quite so many turnovers, maybe. I heard Joe Danziger's boy is already six feet and only in eighth grade. So maybe next year . . . ."

In other years, the conversation might have gone on for

half an hour, drawing in an eager circle of participants. This year it trailed off, tactfully averting its gaze from a scene of such distress.

No new adulteries were discovered. No disasters befell anyone's livestock. No one new moved into town. A couple of young people did move away, having given up the effort to find decent jobs. Like the basketball team, this was a matter too distressing for more than a passing mention. Also, it was not new. Young people had been moving away, in a small but steady trickle, since I was a teenager. It was never a mass migration, which could be felt as a single catastrophe, like a generation slaughtered by war or the ghost towns of the Depression. Rather it was a slow, monotonous drip, a drying up of the sap, the way an ancient tree withdraws more and more of itself into the tough, scarred trunk and each year puts out fewer and fewer new shoots of green.

No one remarked in any particular way when Leonard Kinley's son Roger decided to move to Phoenix to look for work, or when Wendy Corcoran finished her cosmetology training in California and decided to stay there. Winter was a pulled-in sort of season, anyway, a time when hopes and expectations were as dormant as the vegetation, and disappointments were received with resignation rather than the injured surprise of more ambitious seasons.

This winter was far too calm for my comfort. The absence of other preoccupations left the stage clear for my affairs to fill the whole of it. For almost two years, the sculpture had been my own private obsession. Now it seemed the whole town was infected with it. Probably only two individuals were truly obsessed, myself and Peggy Treadwell. When people are feeling bored and stagnant, any definite force, however small, can be enough to set them in motion. Any definite opinion will carry the day.

In this case, there were two definite opinions, and the randomly drifting particles had divided themselves between the two. My array was much larger, but Peggy's formed a tighter, more disciplined rank behind her. Her slogan was clear. "Save our children from depravity." Her allies could form a solid phalanx behind it.

My side milled about untidily among a collection of nebulous slogans. "Live and let live." "Mind your own business." "It takes all kinds to make a world." "Judge not, lest ye be judged." They might be widely held sentiments, but they have never been much of a rallying cry with which to march an army to its death.

As an offensive force, mine was useless. As a defense, it had its points. It simply had no vital center against which to strike the mortal blow. For Peggy, it was like boxing against a down comforter, or thrusting a sword into a cloud of mosquitoes. My side did not actually have to do anything. They had only to resist Peggy's efforts to make them do something. In this, they were succeeding.

An endlessly circular debate was fine for winter. As the days lengthened, and the ground warmed, the stalemate became more irksome. Peggy's desire for action became more urgent, and so did my own and my supporters' desire to be left alone. No one could see a possible compromise. Either the statue stayed or it went. One side had to lose, and neither side seemed inclined to concede.

As people wished more and more earnestly for a resolution, and no resolution came, tempers began to fray. I heard comments about Peggy that bordered on malicious, and I heard some of the same directed at me. We were becoming a pair. She was the 'self-righteous interfering bitch,' and I was the 'lewd, immoral bitch.'

It seemed to me that Peggy was as obsessed as I was, but she did not have the daily outlet that I did, in my hours with the hammer and chisel. Given no tangible release, her obsession was winding itself into a frenzy. I thought sometimes that she might indeed have gone out one night with dynamite, if she had had any knowledge of how to use it.

More than anything, I wished that spring would not advance with such excruciating slowness. I had hopes that the rush of activity that came with warm weather would draw people away from the debate. The ceaseless, fruitless disagreement was breeding rancor in a community to which rancor did not come naturally. If it had been only the two of us, I knew I could resist her forever. With the whole town involved and angry, I was less sure. I feared that Peggy might win, because she believed in her principles to the point of tearing the town in two, if necessary. My own beliefs sometimes wavered, and I began to doubt whether my individual rights were worth such a price in discord.

At times, I felt that I was becoming two people. A piece of me seemed to have detached itself and to be carrying on a life of its own. That piece had staked out a position in the public forum and spent hours every day defending it. Somehow a piece of me had stumbled onto a soapbox.

The other part of me looked on, and cried, inwardly, that I never wanted to become an issue, that I had not been thinking about issues or morals, that I had only wanted Alma Rose to come back.

As the weeks passed, the inward part of me stood at a

distance and watched that detached piece, that unfamiliar person, Pat Lloyd, manager of the Kilgore Mercantile, Heir Apparent to the Mercantile Fortune, Controversial Sculptress, and Woman of Questionable Virtue. She began to do things that amazed me.

At first she had looked as comfortable on her soapbox as a cricket on a hot stove. Now she was starting to get used to it, and there were moments when she almost seemed to belong there. She could shift her ground from First Amendment protections, to scriptural quotations, and on to the rights of private property, all without interrupting the rapid tap of her fingers on the now-computerized cash register. Her speech was growing more fluid, her face less impassive.

One day, when her cheeks were flushed and her eyes sparkling in eager pursuit of some bit of logic, I suddenly saw Pops, whirling the ladies of Kilgore out onto the dance floor. He was there and then he was gone.

The purchases were packed up, the customer departed, and her face settled back into its customary stolidity.

33

IN LATE APRIL, THE FIRST HINT
of green appeared in the hills. Its arrival brought forth rakes,
and then pruning shears and hot caps, and then Weber grills,
horseshoe stakes and garden hoses. With their appearance,
one by one, the debate began to change. Somehow the issues
of free speech and the preservation of the nuclear family began to get tangled up with the pruning shears and the Weber
grills. No one seemed to be able to keep their thoughts focused anymore. Right in the middle of a duel of Biblical quotations, me from the Gospels, my opponent from St. Paul,
the issue of mulch would intrude, and suddenly the debate
would shift to straw versus black plastic.

I had no opinion about mulch, but someone else in the
store invariably did, possibly several people. Soon half a dozen
voices might be embroiled in the debate. Alliances were
swiftly formed and battle cheerfully joined. The line of

demarcation did not follow the division in the sculpture debate. There was no correlation to be found in one's opinion about personal morals and one's opinion about mulch. The forces of St. Paul were divided between straw and plastic, and so were the forces of the Gospels. In place of the two well-ordered ranks standing face to face, muddled groups ran hither and thither, and there were unseemly bursts of laughter. By the end of May, with the sun high overhead and white puffs of cloud drifting lazily across the sky, most of the combatants seemed inclined to scatter in search of entertainments more suited to the season.

Seeing her army distracted, Peggy chose to make a tactical retreat. "Don't think this matter is over and forgotten," she said. "It's summer, and people lose sight of what's important in the summer. But before long, it will be winter again and then we'll see."

I felt only relief at the mass desertion. The antics of my public spinoff might astonish me, but they also left me exhausted. Work on the sculpture had slowed to a crawl. Too much of the time I desired nothing except to be able to sleep, for hours and hours.

I made myself keep working, as steadily as before, but it did indeed seem that my progress was dividing itself into smaller and smaller increments. In May I finished the third section, but it had taken me a full year, almost twice as long as the other sections.

Sometimes when I worked, I had the sensation that Peggy Treadwell was standing just behind me, waiting for an opportunity to jar my arm so that the chisel would slip and mar the carving. I became more cautious, more painstaking, especially when I went to work on the mouth. I had postponed the mouth all the way through the winter. I felt a superstitious fear that Peggy would somehow manipulate my hand and transform the peaceful smile of sleep into an expression conforming to her own worst imaginings, perhaps an insolent leer, or perhaps the slackly parted lips which, in the visual language of movies and advertising, were shorthand for panting sexuality.

In my cautious avoidance of Peggy Treadwell, I lost a good part of the real smile as well. I achieved a safe, bland mouth, with only a ghost of the blissful serenity caught by the original drawing. Perhaps the cause was simply my lack of facility, and had nothing to do with Peggy. Still, with every tap of the chisel, I had felt my hand choosing the line of caution. That new strange public self, full of bravado, might relish the duel of wits, but the other part, the silent, inward part that felt like home, still sought the safety of unobtrusiveness.

Through the long winter, the visits from Donna and Jordy had become an anchor for me. Donna's understanding and empathy did not rest on principle, nor on ties of family and affection. In this particular struggle, she was my ally by a decree of nature. Her presence was restful in a way that no one else's was, no matter how much they loved me or believed in my cause.

"I never intended to be an issue," I said to her once.

"If you didn't want to be an issue, why did you make a hundred-foot-long statue of your lover?" she asked.

"I didn't think about it."

"How could you not think about it?"

"I mean that I set out to make the sculpture so that Alma Rose would see it. I was thinking about whether she would be able to see it from the Interstate, not about whether the people in Kilgore would see it."

"Can you see it from the Interstate?"

"Yes, if you know where to look."

"I've never noticed it. I almost never drive that stretch of Interstate anyway. It's quicker to go the back way from the ranch to Seco Springs. How does she look from the highway?"

"I think she looks good, especially in late afternoon when the sun lights her up."

"And you really made her so that Alma Rose would see her?" Donna asked.

"That's how I started out to make the thing. I wanted Alma Rose to come back. I don't know if I truly expected it to work." I paused. "It was like the feeling you have when someone dies unexpectedly and you worry they died without knowing how much you loved them. It was a kind of panic. Somehow I had to let her know that I loved her."

"Has she ever seen it?"

"I don't know. She hasn't come back, that's obvious. The last I heard, she was settling down with a man in California."

"And you're still working on the sculpture."

"Yeah." I smiled. "Stupid, huh? I don't expect her to see it now. I want to finish it so that it's finished."

Donna shifted her position and squinted toward the gap in the hills where the Interstate showed itself. A pickup went by, then two semis close together.

"What was she like?" she asked.

"You mean, apart from being smart, pretty, charming and all around desirable?" I said, in a jesting tone that was a cover for uncomfortable feeling.

Donna did not jest in return. She shook her head and repeated, in her slow-spoken way, "What was she like?"

I paused, because images were crowding each other in my brain. I saw Alma Rose leaning against the counter of the Mercantile, smiling her provocative smile. I saw her wince as she told me about throwing footballs to her brother from the limbo outside the frame of her father's awareness. I heard her trading banter with Pops and with other drivers at the truck stop. I felt the lash of her voice, telling me I was unfeeling. I felt her hand caressing my skin. I saw her falling asleep, the tight lines of strain in her face slackening as consciousness departed.

"She was so unhappy," I said.

"Unhappy?" Donna looked surprised. "She didn't sound like someone who would be unhappy."

I was surprised myself at the first word to come out. Why did I think she was particularly unhappy? Didn't everyone suffer?

"She didn't know how to make herself happy," I said. "She could make other people happy, but not herself."

I was puzzled how to explain further. "It was as if her skin didn't fit her," I said. "She kept shifting around trying to make it fit. She couldn't settle into anything, and she always thought it was because she hadn't found the right thing, the right job, the right place to live, the right lover. She'd done a host of different jobs before she started driving a truck. She'd had a host of lovers. She told me all about them. She would talk about almost anything personal, and she wanted everyone else to do the same, including me. She thought people's lives should be laid out for the world to see. We argued about that sometimes. In the Mercantile, she would come up behind Peggy Treadwell and make smooches at me over Peggy's shoulder, and the whole time

I'd be wanting to glance behind me to make sure there wasn't a mirror there."

"I take it there never was," Donna said.

"No," I said. "People liked her. Even Peggy liked her. She could have charmed a rattlesnake out of a prairie dog hole. She could have been queen of the world, but then her skin would start to pinch her. She hadn't lived up to her family. She had wasted her talents. So on and so on. She would writhe around until she got her skin so thoroughly twisted up that she was miserable. She wanted to do something dazzling, and at the same time she was convinced that nothing she did ever could be."

I paused. "Loving her made me ache inside, because there was nothing I could do. No matter how much I loved her, it didn't help. I couldn't make her skin fit."

Donna had listened in silence. She stayed silent now. She was looking down the hill at Jordy, who was throwing sticks for the puppy far below us.

Skipper picked up the stick and dashed about, looking enthusiastic but showing not the faintest notion that he was supposed to bring the stick back to Jordy. I had never had a collie who would learn to retrieve. I thought, the heredity of instincts must be one of the great natural mysteries.

After a while, Donna spoke. "I'm reminded how terrifying it is to be a parent sometimes," she said.

"What reminds you?"

"Your description of Alma Rose. As a parent you have such an awful power, in ways you don't even know. You can never be sure if you are doing something that will make your kid grow up feeling that his skin doesn't fit, as you put it. You have to muddle along as well as you can, because there is never any certainty. Although when is there ever? Even my computers are a little uncertain sometimes."

"At least you don't have to worry that someday they will hate you for the way you programmed them."

She smiled. "No."

"Did you always long to be a computer engineer?"

"Hardly. Originally I planned to change the world."

"What happened to that plan?" I asked.

"I got older," she said.

She stood up and stretched. "We'd better go or you are going to be a lot older before you finish this sculpture. You don't get very much done when you're talking to me."

"I've got my whole life to finish the sculpture," I said. "I'd rather talk to you."

"We should go anyway. Jordy postpones all his homework until Sunday afternoon."

34

DONNA AND JORDY HAD COME
often, through the winter and spring, but had never invited
me to visit them. Donna was living at her parents' house.
She said I would have to wait to visit until my notoriety faded,
or until she moved into her own house, whichever came first.
With the help of Fred and a contractor from Seco Springs,
she was converting an abandoned barn on the ranch into a
house. It would not be done until fall. In the meantime, our
acquaintance went forward with the day's weather over our
heads, the rock looming beside us, and the land stretching
away in all directions.

In winter, the wind had blown my sculpture clear of snow.
Every bush and yucca plant caught a long drift, and the
undulating wind-carved ridges of snow became miniature
copies of the larger geologic landscape. Every hollow was shad-
owed blue, and every surface gleamed with the translucent,

293

lemon-tinted light of the low-hanging winter sun. In March, all the colors turned to the brown of mud and the gray of clouds. Shapes flattened, and textures blended in the dull, diffused light. The air was raw, carrying neither the icy purity of winter nor the warm pulse of spring.

The quickening, when it came, could be felt first in the air. The land was still mud, the colors still flat brown, but one day the air softened. The chill, inanimate gusts of wind gave way to gentle, changeable breezes that touched the skin like puffs of breath, and one knew that the last of the deep buried frost had left the earth. The last of winter's hoard of cold had been spent. If a spring blizzard came, it would not last. Like the thaws of winter, it would be brought by the changeable air, not the inexorable earth and sun.

As the days lengthened, so did the visits. Donna no longer had to brace herself against the cold, and Jordy no longer had to stay in motion to stay warm. Often now, they lingered for hours. It seemed that Jordy's homework had become a less pressing obligation.

Occasionally, reluctantly, Donna agreed to come inside for lunch. She did not like to accept a meal from me when she couldn't reciprocate. It made her feel in my debt, and I had learned that debt was a touchy subject for her.

I asked her once, "Why don't you buy a new car? When you drive a hundred miles a day back and forth to work, you ought to have a decent car."

"I can't afford one," she said.

"I thought computer engineers made a lot of money."

"They do, but I'm up to my eyeballs in debt. If I buy a new car, that's more debt. I have been in debt for my entire adult life, and what I want more than anything is to pay it off."

"Why are you so far in debt?"

"Because if you pile up a bunch of student loans and then get pregnant and drop out of school, you start out in a bit of a hole. I didn't have any money at all when I got to Oregon. All I had was one of those credit cards they used to hand out to students. So for a while, until I could find a job, I lived on the credit card. I got to be like a junkie, a real pro at working the system. It's amazing what you can do with a cash advance. Sometimes I even used one to pay the next installment due on the credit card."

"How did you ever get to be an engineer? You must have gotten your college degree."

"Eventually I did. I had some luck along the way."

"Like what?"

"Well, there was Carolyn. When Jordy came, I had to quit my job and go on welfare. That would have been another sin chalked up to my account, if my parents had known about it. But then I happened to see an ad on a bulletin board, 'Woman with small baby looking for roommate' and that was Carolyn. I moved in with her and we both went back to work, her on days and me on nights, so that we could look after each other's kid."

"Were you lovers?"

Donna laughed. "Definitely not. Carolyn was very religious and very conservative. She was also one of the sweetest-tempered people I've ever known. She was a born-again Christian. If I asked her what she thought about something, say apartheid in South Africa, she wouldn't answer until she had looked in the Bible to see what it said. Her husband had ditched her and she was too broke and too ashamed to go back to her hometown. So there we were, the two of us, like a Jew and an Arab clinging to the same piece of flotsam in a flood. We lived together two and a half years. It's hard to believe, now."

Gradually Donna told me more about her time away from Kilgore, about her years working in the paper mill, tasting the chemicals on her breath at night and dreaming about spinning rolls of paper. Boredom finally drove her to quit and take a lower paying clerical job at a computer software company, where she thought she might have a future. She worked her way into a job programming, began to earn better money, began to take night courses. Then, when Jordy was in school full time, she gathered her courage and quit her job to go to the university in Corvallis.

"So what were a few more loans?" she said with a laugh. "I was an expert on loans."

She talked about herself in a slow, offhand way, almost as if she were telling stories about someone else. For some reason, listening to her, I was reminded of a pack pony I knew, back when Pops and I still went hunting together on the Spear Canyon Ranch. Biscuit was a sturdy, cheerful buckskin, who worked willingly but became as immovable as stone if he thought I was on the wrong trail or trying to lead him somewhere impassable. I learned to trust him, because he was usually right. He also had an air of self-possession and good humor, as if he could always find something amusing or ironic to console himself with on the days when a sudden autumn storm brought icy sleet, and the other horses plodded forward with ears flat back and heads dragged toward the ground by gloom.

"When I went off to college the first time," Donna was saying, "I had dreams about teaching history, or doing research somewhere overseas. This time I took a clear look at my situation, at my debts and at what I wanted for Jordy. It took me about two minutes to decide on computer science.

"After graduation, I went back to Portland and took the highest paying job I was offered. I couldn't believe all that money. I wallowed in it. I bought a car. Secondhand, but still, the first one I'd ever owned. I bought Jordy a good bike. Then, finally, I paid off all my credit cards, and I felt the same kind of jittery euphoria I saw in an alcoholic friend of mine when he finally got off the booze. I still had my student loans but those were on a schedule. Not like a credit card where there's always something more to buy and the interest keeps compounding itself like a rabbit having babies."

"And that's why you won't let me fix you a sandwich," I said. "It might start compounding itself."

She grinned. "Well, you know, one thing kind of leads to another. Next thing you know, you'd be fixing me soup, and then stew, and then roast beef, and then chocolate cake. Before I knew it, I'd be so far behind, I could never get square again."

"I wouldn't expect you to pay me back," I said.

"I know that. I know you're not going to make me sign a promissory note for three peanut butter and jelly sandwiches. It's entirely emotional, so you won't get anywhere with logic."

The Sunday visits had become a routine, yet I felt there was something fragile about them. I never felt that Donna settled in and relaxed. There always seemed to be a kind of wary alertness in her. She talked openly and told me her history in detail, but kept an air of detachment, as if she were guarding some essential part of herself from my view.

For a long time I was frustrated. Then, one day while I

was working in solitude, it struck me that her caution was only a mirror image of my own. I barely acknowledged to myself, and certainly not to her, how much I was coming to rely on her friendship. I talked to her as I talked to no one else. Every Sunday, I counted on the sight of her dusty, sand-colored car barreling down the road toward my cattle guard. Until it appeared, I was distracted by impatience. Once she had arrived and greeted me with her slow smile, and Jordy had said his grinning hello and galloped off with Skipper, I felt a mixture of contentment and exhilaration that they still sought out my friendship.

I was aware of all this, and still I could not imagine saying, "I like you," in plain words. I feared the principle of physics which says that the act of measuring a phenomenon causes the phenomenon to change. Perhaps I feared, too, that a direct statement of liking might feel to her like a kind of debt which she was obligated to repay, and she would shy away from it.

I thought of Alma Rose, who did not believe in tacit arrangements.

"Anything that is unspoken is likely to be misunderstood," Alma Rose had said.

Every level of being must be probed and pulled open and laid out in the clear sunshine. She willingly went first, laying out her most private hopes and sufferings for my inspection. She was like the person who greets a proposal to go skinny-dipping by peeling off her clothes, and in doing so, gives her companions courage to follow suit. She ran the risk, always, that her companions would not follow and she would be left alone in her nakedness while the others did their best to hide their embarrassment.

At one moment her vulnerability made me ache. In the next, I felt fury, that she had led me to strip myself bare and then abandoned me.

And then, instead of the skinny-dippers splashing gleefully in the sparkling water, I saw a person watching from the bank, fully clothed and safe from embarrassment. I saw a person, cool, self-contained and monosyllabic, made invisible by the familiarity of her presence as she counted out change and methodically stamped prices onto cans of Campbell's soup. No one would ever point and laugh, because no one would ever notice she was there.

In that moment, regret and anger left me, and I felt a rush of gratitude. I might now be notorious, but at least I was not invisible.

I stopped my work with the chisel and walked to where I could look at the huge stone face. The eyes were still closed, the mouth expressionless. On an impulse, I stepped forward and began to chisel at the corner of the mouth, extending it into a smile as distinct as the one in the original drawing. I matched the curve of the lip with a curving indentation in the cheek. When I was done, Alma Rose looked like someone whose dreams amuse her.

"I hope someday you see this thing, Alma Rose," I said. "It's the only thanks you'll ever get."

35

"YOU WOULDN'T KNOW ME IF IT
weren't for Alma Rose," I said to Donna. I had persuaded her
to stay for lunch that day. It was hot for May, and clouds
sailed by on a brisk breeze. She and I lounged on my porch,
eating sandwiches and drinking the first sun tea of the season. Jordy had wolfed his sandwich and returned to a project
he had started earlier, trying to turn my bit of creek into a
pond with a dam of rocks and willows.

"I'd still know you," she said. "Everyone knows you."

"You wouldn't be here eating lunch, though."

"Why not?"

"For one thing, Lucy would never have bitten Jordy. But
more than that, I was not the sort of person anyone noticed."

"Alma Rose noticed you."

"She saw me as a challenge," I said. "I was the most bottled
up person she had ever met. She wanted to unbottle me.

Maybe she thought I would explode, like champagne. I think she believed my plain exterior was just a cover, and that inside I would be all fizz and froth."

"Is that what she wanted, fizz and froth?"

"She wanted fireworks. She wanted life to be breathtaking."

Donna was gazing at the ice cubes circling in her glass of tea. "I wonder if she found fireworks with her man in California," she said, musing.

"Probably for a while."

"For a while, yes. It's always 'for a while'."

I hesitated, then asked, "Are you speaking from experience?"

"I suppose so."

I waited without saying anything.

"You want the gruesome details, too?" she asked.

"Of course I do."

"They're not very interesting. No grand passions. Just the ordinary love affairs that end badly. There was Cindy, while I was in Corvallis, and after that, in Portland, there was Rachel."

"And that was all?" I asked.

"Unless you count a few brief experiments in college, before I had Jordy."

"Like Jordy's father."

"Well, yes. He was the last of the experiments. I guess you could say I had collected all the data I could handle for a while. Once Jordy came and I started working nights, I stayed celibate out of sheer exhaustion. I remember I got propositioned once, and all I could think about was how much time it would take and how much I would rather use that time for sleep. I think I may have groaned out loud when the woman suggested we have an affair." She laughed. "Poor Gloria. I tried to explain, but there was no getting around that first groan."

"Were you ever sorry you decided to keep him?"

"Jordy? Are you kidding?" She looked off toward the creek and her son, who could be seen every now and then through gaps in the bushes. Watching him, she laughed again. "He'll never get his dam to hold, not with the spring runoff."

At that moment, Jordy seemed to have come to the same conclusion. He climbed up onto the bank, put on his sneakers and started back toward the house.

"I suppose for the first three or four years I had my doubts," Donna went on. "I was exhausted and poor and strung out and bored, and all the while I was worried that I was doing a terrible job of raising him, because I never had any time or energy." She paused until Jordy had come within hearing, then added, "And you were a little three-year-old hellion, weren't you, Dr. J?"

He grinned at her. "You keep telling me I was. I don't remember what I was like when I was three."

"You have improved immeasurably. We both have. You were a hellion, and I was a bad-tempered tyrant. Now you're the best kid I know, and I'm almost tolerable."

"Almost," he said, still grinning, and she wadded up her napkin and threw it at him. He settled himself at the far end of the couch and took a handful of the Oreos I had put out with lunch.

"It wasn't until Jordy and I were both in school that I had any energy to contemplate a relationship," she said. "That's when I met Cindy."

"One of the ones you say ended badly," I said.

"Yes. Although Cindy and I didn't actually end all that badly. We knew we were headed in different directions from the start, so we just had a good time. But Rachel . . . " Her face looked somber and she shook herself, as if the memory were stinging her.

"Rachel was so pragmatic about it," Donna said. "I was ready to jump off a cliff for her, and she was busy calculating whether she wanted a child in her household, whether we could work out the finances, and so on. The worst of it was that she had stolen my role. I had always been the pragmatic type, and now, when I had finally fallen totally in love, the other person went practical on me. She decided, rationally, that it couldn't work in the long run, so she cut it off. Whack, like a malformed branch on a fruit tree."

She paused, then added, "That's when the rain finally got to me."

"The rain?"

"Yes, the rain. The interminable wetness and greenness. Vegetation crawling over the landscape, dripping with moisture, growing and spreading right in front of your eyes. I thought I would suffocate on the lushness. I was crying out for the sight of bare rock and clear air, and the smell of grass burned dry by the sun. I wanted to be in a place where you see the bones of the land, and not just the fur and flesh of vegetation. That's when I wrote to my folks. It was all mixed up in my head, this country, my family and the town, but I missed all of it. When they wrote back and said to come for Christmas, I felt it would be worth braving my mother's visions of hellfire to be back here."

"Has it been?"

"By now, it is," she said. "When Jordy and I got on the plane to come back for the first time, I started pouring sweat. My heart was jumping around in my chest, and I thought I was going to pass out. Fred and my parents met us at the airport in Seco Springs, and none of us knew what to say or do. We'd never been much for hugging and kissing, and my folks have never talked much, so we all stood there, shuffling our feet. When they started unloading the baggage, my dad asked which was mine and practically leapt to grab it, as if it were a life jacket, because it gave him something to do.

"We all got in the car and started off, and still no one had said anything after the first hellos. I asked how things were on the ranch, my dad said, 'Fine,' and that ended that. Then I asked Fred how the kids were doing, and Fred said, 'Fine,' and that ended that. So I gave up and we drove about twenty miles without anyone saying anything. The roads were hardpack and slick, so my dad was concentrating on driving. Jordy was busy staring out the window at all that open space and snow.

"And then, all of a sudden, my mom asked, 'Have you stopped going to mass?' We all jumped about six inches and my dad jerked the wheel by mistake and the car skidded and did a two-seventy degree turn and slid into the snowbank on the wrong side of the road. We were shook up, but no harm had been done, so we pushed the car back onto the road and drove off. We were feeling shaky, the way you do after a near miss, and Fred started to laugh and said, 'I guess we'd better not talk about religion,' and my dad laughed, too, and said, 'Not in the car, anyhow.' All of a sudden they were full of news, about how my nieces and nephews were dying of curiosity about me, about how my mom had been baking all week and worrying about what things Jordy might like, about the new calving shed they had built, and on and on."

"Did your mom ask about mass again?"

"Not in the car," Donna said. "She waited until she had me alone. She was afraid that Fred and my dad might not be sufficiently adamant in their support of her."

"I suppose when you're fighting about religion, a half-hearted ally is worse than none," I said. "He might admit the possibility of doubt."

"Or a second point of view."

She looked at Jordy, who was still sprawled on the couch, within easy arm's reach of the plate of Oreos. In that moment, his indolent posture was a reminder that he was almost in his teens.

"My mom and I worked out a compromise in the end," Donna said. "I agreed to go to Christmas mass, and I told her she could take Jordy whenever he was willing, so long as she didn't badger him about it. I figured it wouldn't hurt him to hear some other ideas besides mine."

"Had he ever been baptised?"

She nodded her head, a little ruefully. "Yes. It's funny how the things you grow up with take hold of you sometimes. I didn't believe in the kind of damnation Catholicism teaches and I was willing to take my chances about going to hell, but I wasn't so sure I was right that I was willing to take the same chance for Jordy. I rationalized it by saying I should keep the church as one option for him when he came to make his own choices. The truth was, those beliefs still lurked in me somewhere and I couldn't cast them aside so completely that I dared risk his soul as well as my own."

"Do you go to mass now?" I asked Jordy.

He shook his head. "I went for a while with Grandma, to see what it was like. It never made any sense to me. What kind of God would punish a person forever and ever because he did one bad thing here on earth? The priest made God sound like those dictators that torture the people that don't obey, only worse, because the dictators have to stop once the person dies, but God could keep the person alive forever to be tortured. I couldn't see any point in praying to a God like that."

"Did you say that to Grandma?" Donna asked.

"No. She would have been upset."

Donna smiled. "Yes, she would."

We all fell silent. I was thinking about Jordy's vision of God, and perhaps the others were, too. Around us the hills were green and the air scented with young growth. In such surroundings, it was easy to believe there was a god, and a benevolent one, not the omnipotently vindictive creature that the priest had conjured up in Jordy's mind. In Jordy's vision of Christianity, God and the devil must look like two equally cruel prison wardens. The only difference between them was that God could be bought off with flattery, pleading and self-abasement, while the devil was implacable. I thought it must have been a long-suffering race of slaves who could come to see their god in such a light.

36

WHETHER HE LIKED IT OR NOT,
Clay had an audience for the final stage of blasting. It was early June, school was out, and the rumor of his arrival needed no subterranean channels for its propagation. The blasts could be heard for miles.

He went to work on a Wednesday and by Thursday morning the kids began to appear, some on their bikes, some having begged a ride from an older brother or sister with a car. They gathered in clusters along the road, waiting with surprising patience while Clay drilled holes and placed the charges. When the explosions finally came, they were greeted with shouts and hurrahs.

It became my job to stop anyone from coming closer than the road.

"I can't have kids running loose on your land," said Clay. "They might come too close when I'm not looking. It's bad enough to have them all watching. It gives me the jitters."

I patrolled the road, invoking the only threat I had, a call to their parents, should any of them come closer than my cattleguard. At noon, I called Pops and asked him to work the first part of my shift.

"I've got twenty kids here," I said. "I know if I turn my back, some of them will try to sneak closer. They wouldn't be normal if they didn't."

I stayed home Friday afternoon, also. The numbers had thinned, but there were still enough that I couldn't leave them unsupervised. On Saturday, Donna came with Jordy, and some other parents came, so I was able to leave the afternoon patrol in their hands.

Before I left for work, I climbed up to talk to Clay. He would be finished that afternoon and I wouldn't see him again, only the final bill for his work.

"I'm sorry to be done," he said. "This is the most fun I've ever had with explosives. If you ever want to do another one, I'll be ready."

"I couldn't face another one, even if I had the rock," I said.

"I hear you're in a little hot water about it," he said.

"So the news has traveled beyond Kilgore, then."

"Sure. Towns aren't much different from people. A piece of news like that is too good to keep to yourself. People say to me, 'I hear you're the one helping that crazy lady sculptor over in Kilgore. From what I hear, you ought to blow the whole thing to smithereens.'"

"What do you say in answer?"

He shrugged. "I don't pay much attention. The world has so many people in it nowadays, you can't do much of anything without making somebody mad. If you start worrying what every single person thinks, you had just as well be a soccer ball that everybody is trying to kick in a different direction."

"How would you like to talk to Peggy Treadwell for me?" I asked, joking.

"Who is Peggy Treadwell?"

"She is the commander-in-chief of the forces of outrage."

He smiled. "Not me. I'm not much good in a fight. The only thing I'm good with is dynamite, and I wouldn't be allowed to use that."

I shook hands with Clay and said goodbye with regret. I barely knew him. I knew nothing at all about his personal life. Yet he, more than anyone, had looked at my sculpture with the same eyes that I did. He had been able to see something that wasn't there and calculate how to bring it into being. He had many of the same hopes and imaginings, as well as labor, invested in the outcome.

I picked my way down the slope, past his van, while he returned to his methodical work with drill and explosives. At the bottom, I turned for a moment to look back up.

The sculpture looked almost complete. Only the bent elbow and knee, and the bed beneath her, remained to be carved. She had not turned out quite as I had originally intended. I had set out to reproduce in stone what my pencil had sketched on paper, a true-to-life human figure. But stone was not a blank sheet of whiteness, receptive to whatever design I wanted to impose. Perhaps the perfect white marble used by the Greeks took shape exactly according to the skill of the carver. This stone of mine did not.

It had colors and textures and shapes of its own that refused to yield entirely to the chisel. It held layer upon layer of brown, red, tan and cream, bent and sheared and pressed into rock by millions of years of time. Lines of color ended abruptly, crossed by other lines. Perhaps a stream had dried up or changed course. Perhaps the earth's crust had buckled upward, and a hill that had been washing away became a hollow collecting silt.

Even from a distance the layers of color and the fracture lines could not be erased. Nor did I want to erase them. They were almost a camouflage, drawing the sculpture back into the layers of red and brown that surrounded it. At times, when the light was soft and subtle, the carving almost seemed a trick of the eye, a momentary play of shadows across the painted rock. At other times, when the sun blazed down and the colors were washed away by the glare, the shape of the carving stood forth stark and human.

The next day, Clay's task was finished and I set to work clearing away the rubble. By now, there was no trace of inspiration left to push me forward, only a settled resignation to the task I had set myself. Though this last section was the least and simplest, I thought it might well take me years to finish.

My hands were strong. I knew exactly what I was doing. I could sharpen my chisels with the speed and skill of a master craftsman. Yet, as I set to work, I felt lassitude spreading through me with the chill of embalming fluid. I knew that, for all my skill, I would progress only by inches. I could no longer muster any feeling of urgency. The last few details did not seem important. They were something to be finished for the sake of completeness, and that was ceasing to be a motivation.

That Sunday, Donna and Jordy did not come for their visit. It was the senior McNeils' fortieth wedding anniversary, and several relatives had come for the day. Missing that diversion, I worked mechanically, and the days of the coming week stretched out ahead of me like the hills repeating themselves all the way to the horizon. But then, on the following Saturday when I did not expect it, Donna's car appeared in my yard. She had come by herself.

"Jordy's staying over with a friend," she explained briefly. "I thought I'd come help with your rocks."

She was untalkative, and I thought she seemed almost tense. We each picked a stretch of rubble and went to work heaving stones. She moved with the rapidity and steadiness of someone who is accustomed to routine physical labor and does not let daydreams slacken her pace. As we worked, the tension that had been in her seemed to dissipate and we settled into a comfortable side by side motion, bending and tossing.

I was grateful for her help. The task, which had been dividing itself into an infinite series of smaller halves, now moved forward at double speed. For a moment, I could feel a hope of completion.

Even more than her help, her company cheered me. It did not matter that she was silent, and the only sound between us was the clatter of bouncing rocks. Her presence occupied my mind, and gave me relief from my own thoughts, which by now were threadbare from too much use. I did not mind that she was not inclined to talk. Since Chuck left, I had not had a friend with whom I could be quiet in this way.

I barely noticed the passing of time, until Donna asked,

"Don't you have to go to work this afternoon?"

I looked at my watch and found that it was after twelve.

"I suppose I should stop, so that I have time for lunch," I said. "Do you want something?"

"I'm not hungry. I think I'll stay and keep working."

"You don't have to do that," I protested.

"I want you to get done with this darned thing," she said. "I have this notion that we might go for a ride on the ranch one day, or go for a weekend to the mountains, but you can't ever tear yourself away."

"I don't dare stop," I said. "I might lose momentum and never finish."

"And when you do finish, what will you do then?" she asked. Her tone was one of challenge.

"I don't know."

"Doesn't that worry you?"

Did it worry me? It would worry Donna, I was sure. She was the most purposeful person I'd ever met. She would never wander into making a barn-size sculpture without a clear idea of why she was doing it.

"I wasn't doing anything in particular before I started carving," I said. "It didn't worry me then."

"Ah." She didn't look convinced. "So you'll go back to where you were before, as if nothing had happened."

Darn her, anyway. Why were people so determined to make me discontented? First Alma Rose, now her. Obviously I wouldn't be back where I was before. I could equally well try and unscramble an egg.

"I've got a lot of reading to catch up on," I said.

Donna did not answer. She just looked at me steadily, ignoring my facetiousness.

"I'll figure out what comes next once I do finish the sculpture," I said. "At the rate I'm progressing, that may be when I'm old enough to retire to a warm climate."

She smiled, then, and it felt like rain after too much unrelenting sunlight.

"Probably you'll just launch yourself into something else without thinking," she said. "You'll wake up one morning and discover you've gotten married or founded a new political organization."

"More likely I'll become one of those people who buys a telescope and spends six hours every night searching for an undiscovered comet. That would keep me busy."

"Busy, yes," she said, and then murmured, almost to herself, "It's always safer to be busy."

"I can't leave this unfinished," I said. "There may be no point now, but I have to finish her. I'm so afraid I won't, because . . . "

I paused, trying to figure out just what the barrier was.

"Because what?" Donna asked.

"Because she's the past. The sculpture seems like an irrelevance now. She's long gone, but I'm not ready to think about what's ahead. You say, what do I do next and it sounds so simple, but to me 'What next?' looks like a big void. Because I can't be content with what I had before. I'm not the person I was before. It took me about fifteen years to figure out how to make that person happy, and I hope to God it doesn't take me fifteen years to find out how to make this new one happy. All I know right now is that I have to finish this crazy sculpture."

I paused and then I started to laugh. "To spite Peggy Treadwell, if nothing else."

"That's a noble purpose," said Donna.

"I never claimed to be noble."

"You'd be unbearable if you were," she said. "Spite is a much stronger motivator than virtue anyway. Pick the right enemies and spite will drive you to greatness."

I laughed. She was grinning, too, and it occurred to me that if she had not come back to Kilgore, if she had not kept me company through this last year of tedious labor, my brain might well have detached from reality entirely.

On an impulse, I decided to say what I was thinking, though she might shy away. "You're the first true friend I've had since school," I said. "My best friend, really. I hope you don't mind my saying that."

"Best friends, are we?" She had a curious expression on her face, a guarded look, and I felt I must have trespassed.

"Maybe that was presumptuous," I said quickly. "I was speaking for myself."

"No, it wasn't presumptuous. It's quite all right. We are best friends. That's exactly what we are."

Something in her tone sounded dismissive. I thought she must consider the idea of best friends a childish one, two little girls making a private clubhouse out of an upstairs closet, and inventing secret languages and passwords, and giggling together about boys. I was startled by the pain I felt at her dismissal.

I didn't say anything for a while. I could feel myself pulling inward, curling around the soft underbelly I had ventured to expose. She didn't say anything, either. Finally, she looked at her watch and said, "You're going to be late."

At that moment, I didn't care if I was late, but I couldn't say that without digging my hole of awkwardness even deeper than it already was. So I said, "I guess I'd better go." I thanked her for coming to help, then set off down the slope and left her there, working on my rock pile.

37

JUST BEFORE THE FOURTH OF
July weekend, the last of the rubble was cleared away and I
began work on the final tier of the sculpture. Donna had
resumed her regular Sunday visits with Jordy, and there did
not seem to be any residue of strain between us.

The holiday weekend was the kickoff to our tourist season, such as it was. All the National Parks were open by
then, and we began to see the occasional out-of-state plate
downtown, someone in search of a supermarket or a diner
with local flavor. The Fourth itself fell on Tuesday, so everyone was muddled about what was the real holiday, Monday or Tuesday. Pops decided not to close the store for the
holiday at all, since different people had different ideas about
when the holiday was. We closed on Sunday, as usual, but
no other time.

It was a sign of my inertia that I chose not to work on

Alma Rose that Sunday, even though I had barely begun the last stage. Instead of working, I invited Donna and Jordy to come for a lazy picnic. Donna agreed, on condition that she provided the food. At first, I had suggested going to the reservoir, but she had protested that it would be too crowded with people on the holiday weekend. Jordy wanted to try out the cave under Alma Rose's belly, now that Clay had blasted a bigger hollow there.

I invited Pops and Marge to join us, but Pops declined. He said he was busy with something else. He spoke with such an air of mystery, and with so much smiling and wagging of eyebrows, I knew that the "something else" must have to do with me and that he did not want me to know what it was.

Donna brought roast beef sandwiches, potato salad, fruit, wine and cinnamon rolls, all packed in a cooler which we lugged up the slope to Jordy's cave. I brought some cushions and a retired bedspread on which to lay out the feast.

It was a very hot day. June had been dryer than usual, and the grass had already turned its summer shade of tan. It stood in bunches, brittle and fragrant, like dried herbs still rooted in the ground. Grasshoppers leapt out from underfoot as we walked. At intervals, their winged relatives, hidden in the grass, gave forth a long rising buzz, first from one direction, then another. The sound, echoed back and forth among its invisible sources, seemed as hot and dry and brittle as the grass and air.

The cave felt comfortably shaded by comparison. The rock, sheltered from the sun, still held some of the night coolness. We spread out the picnic and sat down on the cushions with our back against the rock. Seen from our shadowy hollow, the landscape looked glaringly bright, all color faded by the blazing light.

Donna poured the wine, and handed Jordy a can of pop. We sat for a while, sipping slowly.

"You've got your bare rock and dry grass, anyhow," I said.

She smiled. "When we first arrived, Jordy thought it looked as if it had been burned clean by a nuclear bomb. He couldn't see anything that looked alive, except the cattle, and he couldn't figure out how the cattle stayed alive."

"Do you still think it looks that way?" I asked Jordy.

"It sure isn't anything like Oregon," he said. "I'm not sure I like it. I know there are things living here, but it doesn't feel like there are. There aren't even any squirrels."

"There are prairie dogs," I said.

"I know there are. Uncle Fred is teaching me how to shoot them with a twenty-two. He's a good shot."

"Do you have a lot of prairie dogs?" I asked Donna.

"We have one town that must cover two hundred acres. It's completely ruined for grazing. Fred is so fed up, he's been considering getting a lot of rattlesnakes and releasing them there. But he's not sure whether we might end up with a worse problem than the one we have now. Once you start tinkering with those balances, you can't ever stop."

She stood up and went over to the cooler to serve up the salad and sandwiches. Then she poured more wine. I was starting to feel a pleasant fuzziness in my brain. It was like silence after an irritating noise, to have the company of friends without my tools close at hand, reminding me of work I should be doing.

I ate slowly. Sometimes I paused to lean my head back against the cool stone. I closed my eyes and felt the tingling numbness of wine spreading toward my toes. I thought, I could stay like this for any amount of time and be content.

Donna was talking, in slow rambling fashion, about her family's ranch. One thought came, then another, idly, with indefinite pauses between.

Jordy finished eating long before Donna and I did. He grew restless with sitting and left the cave, taking the now half-grown Skipper with him. They walked over to the elbow, still raw and rough from the blasting. Jordy studied the topography for a moment. Then he hoisted the puppy up into the crook of the elbow and scrambled up himself. The two of them disappeared, heading toward the summit of the sculpture.

Donna watched them until they were out of sight.

"He's crazy about Fred," she said. "That might be reason enough to stay here. Besides me, you and Fred are his two favorite people in the world."

"Me?" I was startled.

"Sure. He decided almost immediately that you were OK." She hesitated, then added, "He has been doing his best to play the procurer ever since."

"What do you mean, play the procurer?" I asked.

"I mean, he wants us to fall in love. He wants you to move in with us. He's been using every method he could think of to make us spend time together. And then he goes off and leaves us alone. Haven't you noticed that?"

"I assumed he was bored with being around grown-ups."

"He likes grown-ups better than he likes kids," she said. "No, he is trying to get us alone together, as if being alone together is what makes people fall in love."

For a moment, I couldn't think what to say. "I thought

kids were supposed to be jealous when their parents remarried," I said finally.

Donna shrugged. "Maybe most of them are, but not Jordy. Maybe he has figured out that I'm a lot less crabby when I'm sleeping with someone. Though he might not think of it in those terms. Or maybe he likes having two parents. He liked Cindy a lot. He was very upset when she moved away, more upset than I was. He didn't like Rachel, though. She was too talkative and highstrung. Maybe he is afraid I will choose someone he doesn't like again, so he is trying to set me up with someone he does like before I can."

I was still too dumbfounded to have any coherent response. The wine had evaporated from my system, but its departure had not left behind any clarity of thinking. "Does he really think you can put two people together like that, like putting together flour and shortening and milk and coming out with biscuits?"

She laughed. "He has always been the hopeful type. And he knows you definitely won't get any biscuits if you don't put the flour and milk and shortening together."

I sat still for a full minute, trying to figure out what I thought. My insides were in turmoil, but I couldn't tell if the turmoil came from delight, or dismay, or just plain confusion. Nor could I tell what Donna thought. She had related it all as if it were just an amusing story.

"Do you think he has any chance of success?" I asked.

She didn't answer immediately. She seemed to be gathering her thoughts, or maybe bracing herself.

"That depends on you," she said finally.

"On me?"

"On whether you ever come around."

"Why just me?" I asked. "Is the decision all up to me?"

"You're the one who's holding out."

"Holding out against what?"

"Against my irresistible charms, of course. I'm a patient person, but I can't wait around forever."

"I wasn't aware that you were waiting around."

"Surely it's been obvious that I'm in love with you."

"It has not been in the least obvious," I said. "You haven't given the slightest hint."

"Why do you think I froze my tail off sitting out on this ledge with you all winter? Do you think I'm plain crazy? I'd forgotten how goddamned cold it gets in this country. I almost gave up, back in February."

"Then why didn't you say something, instead of just waiting around?"

"Because you were totally absorbed in Alma Rose. I wasn't going to try to compete with someone you said yourself was beautiful and funny and devastatingly charming, and a hundred feet tall in the bargain."

I knew now what was in her mind, but the muddle in my own had not grown any less muddled. I turned and looked at her, the way I had when she announced she was a lesbian, as if she had suddenly become a different person and must look different. I saw the face I was used to, thin, with brown eyes and freckles, and long, light brown hair pulled back and tied. She looked ordinary, much the way I did. I could see how she might pause in the face of Alma Rose.

She did not meet my gaze. She had declared her affection with cheery bravado, but now, as she awaited my reaction, the bravado had deserted her. I thought she was holding her breath.

I was trying to sort out an answer, but the only feeling I

could identify clearly was a wonder that she had been looking at me as a possible lover all this time. How was it that the
possibility had not occurred to me?

"Why were you attracted to me?" I asked, buying time.
"What on earth do you see in me?"

"Maybe you're the only game in town," she said. She was
trying to sound teasing, but she still wasn't looking at me. "I
mean, I couldn't believe my luck, to move back out to the
middle of nowhere and discover I was living right next door
to a notorious lesbian. And then, when you turned out to be
a decent person, too, it seemed too good to be true. I felt like
a cow who finds the the grain room door open. I was planning to wait until you were done with Alma Rose before I
said anything. But then it was starting to look like you might
not ever be finished, and I couldn't wait any longer."

She had her wine glass in her hand and she was twirling it
round and round between her fingers. I watched her in silence. I was looking at her hands. The fingers moved with
restless energy, playing with the stem of the wine glass, which
looked slender and easily broken. They were broad, capable
hands. I could see them handling machinery at a paper mill,
pushing a cow into the squeeze chute, folding laundry.

Could I see them also, traveling over my body? Could I
feel their warmth against my skin, their touch moving lightly
across my face? Could I see my own hand, tracing a slow path
from the hollow at the base of her throat down to the breast-
bone, and across the roundness of belly?

I felt my insides turn to liquid current, sap pulled upward
by evaporation, tides pulled landward by the moon. My body
had answered in a moment, yes and yes and yes.

I told myself to slow down. I was more than a body. What

about the rest of me? The body might decide in one moment, but the mind was more complicated. This time I would consider the whole picture. This time I would wait until I had heard an answer from every part of myself. The current pulled, but I held back.

I tried to focus my thoughts on the wider realities—daily habits and dinner table conversation, family background and places to live, finances, hobbies, moral values.

"Are you ever going to say anything, or are you going to leave me here dangling in the breeze?" Donna burst out.

"I'm going to say something, but I'm trying to be clear before I do."

As I spoke, she turned to look at me. Facing her, with gaze meeting gaze, I felt my resolve to be balanced, careful and reasonable begin to crumble away.

"I'm just too amazed . . . " I began.

"Halloo, Pat!" The deep-voiced bellow came from somewhere on the slope below us.

We both leapt to our feet, startled. Donna dropped the glass from her hand. By chance, it landed on the cinnamon rolls and didn't shatter.

"Who's that?" she asked.

I squinted down at the figure that was slowly climbing the hill. I knew who it was, not by the face, but by the huge linebacker's body and the sandy hair, still scalped into a crewcut.

"It's Chuck Eiseley, my pal from school. I haven't seen him in years."

Chuck saw me looking and waved. I waved in return, distractedly, and turned back toward Donna. Her face still looked tense.

"I do want . . . " I began and then stopped. How could I explain all I felt in the next half minute? It was hopeless. Maybe Greta Garbo could say everything with one look, but I was not Garbo. I had no idea what my face might be telling her. I gave a half shrug of helplessness and apology.

"I don't know what to do," I said. "I suppose I should go say hello."

"Probably you should." She smiled then, the smile with which she always greeted obstacles.

"Yes."

Still I hesitated, and she gestured down the hill.

As I stepped past her to leave the ledge, I paused for an instant and touched her hand with my fingertips. Then I started down the slope, scrambling over the shifty piles of rubble from the sculpture.

Up close, Chuck no longer looked like a high school football player. I was momentarily startled to be confronted by a solid middle-aged man, until I remembered that I was on the edge of middle age myself. The crewcut was now a fringe of stubble surrounding a large bald patch, and his belt had begun to recede under an overhang of belly. He still had freckles, though.

For the first moment, we stood a few feet apart, awkwardly. We had never hugged in the past, and we couldn't start now, but a handshake would have felt too formal. So we stood and did nothing.

"Good to see you," he said. "You haven't changed much."

"I haven't? You have," I said.

"I guess I've lost a little hair," he said.

"No, it's that you look so responsible. You look like somebody's father, instead of somebody's kid."

He grinned, then. "The sheriff doesn't keep an eye on me anymore, that's true."

"I'm glad you decided to visit," I said.

"I've been meaning to all along, but you know how it is. The time goes by. If it weren't for my wife, I'd probably give my kids their birthday presents at Christmas because a few months had got away from me. I don't know how you found the time to make this sculpture."

"I don't have kids," I said. "And I've hardly done anything else for over two years."

"You always were single-minded. If you set your mind to doing something, a person could as good as call it done. You still have my pups?"

"I have Lulu. I had to put Tess down." My conscience awoke, painfully. On this topic, Chuck's disapproval was more terrifying than any judgment by God or public opinion. "I had to put another dog down, too, because of my neglect," I said. "Lulu's daughter Lucy." I told him briefly what had happened.

He listened silently, scowling more and more. When I had finished, I waited for his censure, but he didn't say what I had expected. He shook his head slowly. "It's a shame. Life is just a damned shame. There are so many things a person knows he ought to be doing, and no matter how he tries he can't get all of them done. I don't know why it is that way. We haven't visited my wife's folks for weeks. If they died tomorrow, we wouldn't have seen them since Easter. I've been meaning to write the governor about that new severance tax and I haven't done it. I'm working twenty hours of overtime most weeks. I start expecting my kids to say 'Who are you?' when I do get home in time for dinner."

"It still doesn't excuse it," I said. "About Lucy, I mean."

"I know it doesn't. Not in your mind. But then you made this thing." He gestured toward the sculpture. "She's really a sight."

I turned and looked. Instead of scrutinizing the sculpture, which I already knew by heart, I looked at Donna. She was sitting perched on the ledge below the torso, waiting while Chuck and I had our reunion.

"Can I come see it up close?" Chuck asked.

"Of course."

We started up the remainder of the slope. Chuck was soon puffing hard. "They've got me sitting at a desk, now," he said, when he stopped to catch his breath. He took out a hand-kerchief to wipe his face. "It's too darned hot."

He folded the handkerchief neatly and put it back in his pocket. Was it age and responsibility, or his wife, that had trained him? As a boy he'd carried his handkerchief in a crumpled wad, if he carried one at all.

"When you called me up to ask about dynamite, you didn't tell me you were going to carve a naked lady," he said.

"I wanted to see how she came out," I said. "Besides, there was too much to explain, to do it over the phone."

"Is it true, what people say about you and her?"

"It depends what people say. Probably some of it is true." I took a deep breath. "It's true we were lovers," I said.

For a minute, Chuck didn't say anything. He was look-ing up at Alma Rose, with a little smile. "That explains it, anyhow," he said. "Why you were so unenthusiastic when I kissed you. Now I don't feel so bad. For years I hardly dared go near a girl. I thought, if Pat doesn't want to kiss me then for sure no other girl is going to want to. When Beth wanted to, I figured I better marry her quick."

"She couldn't have been the first girl you kissed after me," I said.

"No, there were a couple of others. But they were the ones who would go out to the gravel pit with just about anybody."

I knew exactly which girls he must mean. Did every school in every town come supplied with its handful of public-spirited girls?

"I can breathe again," he said, and we resumed the climb.

Just as we reached the ledge, he asked, "How come your signs don't say anything about her being naked?"

"Signs? What signs?" I asked.

Donna had stood up to greet us, so he didn't answer. He was waiting to be introduced.

"This is Donna McNeil. You remember the McNeils?"

"Sure do," he said, and stuck out his hand.

As they exchanged politenesses, he was looking at her with speculation. Obviously he wanted to know 'who she was' but couldn't figure out how to ask.

"Have you two known each other long?" he asked instead.

"Only since last fall," I said. "We've become good friends."

I knew he wanted to ask, "Only friends?" He was daunted by Donna's presence, and the question stayed confined to his scrutiny of her.

I smiled to myself. He couldn't know that the answer to his unasked question was at that moment in the midst of a metamorphosis. Until its new shape was clear between the two of us, I could hardly try to describe it to Chuck.

Instead, I asked the question that had been lodged in the back of my mind all through the formality of introductions.

"What signs were you talking about?" I said.

He turned and gestured toward the Interstate. "The ones on the highway." I turned and looked, too, as if the signs might be visible through the gap.

What I saw instead, as I gazed off the ledge, was another figure starting the long hike up from my house. This figure I recognized instantly. It was Peggy Treadwell. Her stout, cinched-in figure was marching up the hill with the demeanor of a cavalry officer leading the charge. Except that in place of a horse and upraised sword, she was equipped only with her pocketbook. She clutched it in one hand, probably from habit and not because she thought it would be of any use in the upcoming battle. A few paces behind her came her husband Marv. His steps did not appear to be propelled by the same fury of determination.

The one advantage I had was that she was completely out of breath by the time she reached the ledge. For a moment or two, she could only look her fury. Except for saying 'Hello,' I remained silent and waited for her to speak. She was the one who had something to say.

When Marv arrived, panting and reluctant, she took it as a signal to open fire.

"Just what do you think you're doing, putting up those billboards?" Her tone would have cut through steel, if that had been what was wanted.

"I don't know what you are talking about," I said. "What billboards?"

"The ones on the Interstate. What other ones could I possibly mean? It's bad enough that you went and made this filthy object, but to go broadcasting it to the whole world is beyond anything. The Lady Giant indeed. You have no shame at all. We had just come from church, too. We drove all the way to Ungerton to visit Marv's sister for the night, and we all went to church together, and then what should we meet driving home but those signs, proclaiming to all the world that Kilgore is a town of sin."

"I haven't put up any billboards," I said. "I still don't know what you are talking about."

In fact I was beginning to have a suspicion. I saw a cloud of dust, whirling up my road, moving so fast it could only be a local driver in a very great hurry. The dust resolved itself into a familiar green Chevy pickup, and my suspicion became a certainty.

"You know very well what I'm talking about," Peggy was saying. "No one else has any reason to put up those billboards. It was bad enough when you tried to claim that this disgusting object was art, but now you're trying to make it into a commercial enterprise. You sold your own soul, and now you're trying to sell the soul of the town. The town has put up with you because you were on your own property. Well, you're not on your own property now, and we won't stand for it. People are not going to back you up when you label Kilgore as a city of sin and invite the general public to come look."

While Peggy was talking, the green pickup had careened across my cattleguard and up my driveway. It barely slowed down as it passed the house. It kept right on going into the pasture, bouncing wildly over the rocks and sagebrush and humpy ground. Halfway up the hill, it finally stopped. Pops leapt out and started up the rest of the way on foot, running until the steepness forced him to a walk.

When Peggy paused for breath, I turned to Chuck and asked, "Do the billboards really call Kilgore a city of sin?"

I didn't want to argue with Peggy directly until I knew exactly how far Pops had gone.

"Not that I saw," Chuck said slowly. "They talked about the world famous Lady Giant, but . . . "

Peggy interrupted him. "You don't have to put it in black and white for people to know what you mean. If you put up a billboard advertising naked women, you don't have to tell people you're talking about sin. People's imaginations can figure it out, even if it's not spelled out."

"Sounds like the sin is in the people's imaginations, then," Donna murmured.

Peggy was too swept up in her own argument to hear what Donna had said. She paused for an instant at the sound of a new voice but then continued with her thought. "I think the things that aren't completely spelled out are the most obscene of all. They leave people room to imagine all the very worst sorts of details. Heaven only knows what kind of things people are going to think about Kilgore."

Peggy turned abruptly and fixed her glare on Donna. "I suppose you're one of that sort, too," she said.

"What sort is that?" Donna asked. She looked toward me with a slow smile that was like an offer of a steadying hand when the footing is uncertain. I smiled in return.

Peggy saw our look and scowled. She shoved her pocketbook more firmly into place under her arm, mustering her fury, and drew in her breath to speak. Whatever she meant to say was cut short by the sudden appearance of Skipper, scrabbling with his claws for a foothold on Alma Rose's elbow. Just behind him came Jordy, slithering down the upper arm as if it were a playground slide. He landed in the crook of the elbow and stayed there, sitting with his legs dangling off the unfinished rock. The person he saw first was Marv Treadwell, his school principal.

"Hi, Mr. Treadwell," he said. "Don't you think it's a great view from up here?"

In a reflex response of friendliness, Marv glanced across the valley and said, "It is nice. It's . . . " He caught a withering glare from his wife, and stopped abruptly.

Peggy lowered her voice and hissed at Donna, "I can't even imagine what sort of a mother you must be, exposing a boy of that age to such close contact with this sort of thing. It's a very sensitive age." She looked over her shoulder and gave a shudder at the sight of an almost-pubescent boy perched within twenty feet of the massive stone breast.

Donna followed the direction of Peggy's gaze and said, "Jordy has yet to discover the sex appeal in a roundish piece of rock that's as big as our living room."

"He'll discover it soon enough," Peggy said ominously.

By now Jordy had realized there was more happening than social chat. He sat watching us all with silent curiosity. He had one arm around the neck of the dog.

"I've been meaning . . . to tell you . . . Pat." Pops speech was punctuated by gasps for breath as he clambered over the last heaps of loose rock and joined the party on the ledge. Far below him, I saw Marge, climbing at a slow walk.

"I wanted . . . to see . . . how they looked." He stopped and panted for a moment.

"You're the one who put up those billboards?" Peggy was incredulous.

"I knew Peggy was steamed about it," Pops said, still talking to me. "I tried to get out here and tell you, but she beat me to it." He looked around at the others for the first time.

"Is that Chuck Eiseley? Hello, Chuck, haven't seen you in a dog's age. Anyway, Marge said the signs were a bad idea, but I figure folks will get used to them after a while. Especially if they brought in some business."

"Business!" Peggy almost shrieked. "You're willing to sell off our moral principles just to bring in some business? What are people going to think about this town? You could just as well set up a . . . " She stumbled for a moment, searching for a decent word for something indecent. " . . . a house of ill-repute," she settled on finally. "That would bring in business, too."

Even Pops looked startled at her vehemence. Evidently he had not foreseen how strong a reaction his billboards might provoke.

"Now, Peggy, it's not quite the same as a house of ill-repute. It's just a statue, and what's the harm in bringing some tourists to look at it. Maybe some of them will buy gas and eat a meal. Maybe some of them will spend the night. Maybe after a while we'll have a few more businesses in town and the kids won't all have to leave Kilgore to find work."

"What good is it keeping the kids here, if we've turned the town into a haven of depravity?" Peggy said. "Before you know it, we'll have a whole town full of people like your daughter."

Pops didn't usually get angry at women, but he got angry now. "As far as I can tell, the only depravity in this town is what goes on inside your head," he said. "My daughter never has hurt anybody and she never will hurt anybody and her private life is her own business. It's just your own mind that turns her life into a peep show, and you could do the same thing with anybody's private life, if you set your mind to imagining all the lurid details."

"This statue is not private!" shouted Peggy. "It's right out where anyone can see it, and now you've gone and publicized it to the whole world."

"There's no harm in this statue."

"It's indecent."

"What's indecent about a person sleeping?"

"She's not wearing any clothes."

"How do you know she's not?" Pops demanded. "Maybe she's wearing one of those skintight nylon suits, like the skaters at the Olympics."

"She's not wearing anything and you know it."

"How would I know? You can't tell by looking."

"Pat said as much. She offered to put a bathing suit on her."

"Maybe she put one of those nylon suits on her instead."

Peggy turned to me. "Is she naked or not?".

I shrugged. "Hard to say. I couldn't decide. If I made it obvious that she has clothes on, it would only make people try to imagine what was underneath, and who knows what they might imagine?"

"You think you're so clever, twisting words around. I see now that the two of you are a pair. It's no wonder you don't have any morals since your father doesn't either." She turned back toward Pops. "We're going to stop this thing even if we have to take you to court. Marv knows a good lawyer in Seco Springs, don't you, Marv?"

Marv nodded. He did not look happy.

"We all know lawyers, if it comes to that," Pops said. "I hope it doesn't, because they can turn a squabble into a war faster than anyone."

"This isn't a squabble," said Peggy. "The whole reputation of the town is at stake. The sculpture was bad enough, but those billboards are beyond anything."

Before Pops could answer back, I interrupted. I had to raise my voice to divert their attention. "Would somebody here please tell me what those darned billboards say? I don't even know what I think of them yet, because I don't know what they say."

"All they say is come see the Lady Giant in . . . " Pops began, but Peggy immediately interrupted.

"They have a huge picture of a naked woman," Peggy said. "And they say, 'Come to Kilgore. Come see the world famous Giant Lady in the Hills.'"

"They do not show a naked woman!" Pops shouted. "All you see is an outline, like a silhouette."

"It was obvious to me she was naked."

"That's because you've got a dirty mind."

"How dare you say such a thing!"

"I'll say what I please."

"Would you two shut up!" I yelled.

There was silence, suddenly, Pops and Peggy and I all equally astonished that I had yelled. I recovered first and took advantage of the lull to ask, in normal tones, "You saw the billboards, Chuck. Could you please tell me what they look like?"

"They look like billboards for a tourist trap," Chuck said. "All splashy and razzle-dazzle. One of them says, 'Come to Kilgore, Home of the World Famous Lady Giant.' The other one says, 'Come see the Giant Lady Asleep in the Hills. Next Exit at Kilgore.' They both have a picture of the statue, but I couldn't tell she was naked. It was like your Pops said, kind of a silhouette. Maybe Mrs. Treadwell thought the picture looked naked because she's seen the statue and put the two together."

Peggy pounced on his last statement. "So you agree that the statue is naked. You saw it for the first time today and it looked naked to you?"

Chuck hesitated. "You don't see any part of her that shows she is, but I couldn't see any clothes, either, so I figured she must be. Besides, you wouldn't make a sculpture of someone sleeping in her pajamas. It would look silly."

"Of course she isn't wearing clothes," I said. "I've never claimed she was, not seriously. But that doesn't mean she's indecent."

"To my mind, it does," said Peggy. "Once people have seen the statue, it will be just the same as if you had put a naked woman on the billboards."

"Not quite the same," said Donna. "If the billboards don't use nudity to lure people here."

"The word will get around," said Peggy.

"Good thing if it does," said Pops. "Maybe it will bring some life back to this town."

"Not the kind of life we want," said Peggy.

"Why didn't you tell me about it, Pops?" I asked.

"I knew you wouldn't like it," Pops said. "Marge didn't like the idea, either, but I talked her around. You're so stubborn, I knew I'd never talk you around unless it was already done."

He was right. He would never have talked me around. It was a crazy idea. I couldn't say so now, though, not after he had leapt so immediately and fiercely to my defense.

As it happened, I didn't have to say anything, because Peggy hastened to say it for me.

"This is the craziest thing I ever heard of. How could you

go ahead when you knew half the town was against the statue?"

"I decided a good offense might be the best defense," said Pops. "Your side has done all the pushing up to now. I decided it was time to push back. A lot of people would be glad to see some new business in town."

"Not that kind of business."

"What other kind of business is there, way out here?" Pops said. "Would you rather have that five-state trash dump the governor is pushing for? If we get some tourists coming here, maybe they won't put the dump too close. I thought it was a darned good idea."

"What makes you think any tourists will come here? I don't know what devil ever planted the idea in your head, Smoky Lloyd."

"It was the Wall Drug," said Marge. She had arrived a while ago and had been listening quietly in the background.

"The Wall Drug?" said Peggy. "What made him think about the Wall Drug?"

"We went there on our honeymoon, on the way to the Badlands," Marge said. "He's had the Wall Drug buzzing in his brain ever since."

"Well, heck," Pops burst out. "If they can turn a curio shop into a big tourist attraction just by putting up a lot of billboards, we ought to be able to do it with Alma Rose. You should have seen that town. It was packed with cars and RV's, and all of those people were spending money. It occurred to me that maybe we could bring some of that money to Kilgore. So then, when that reporter was so interested in Alma Rose, I thought, 'Shoot, I ought to go ahead.'"

"What reporter?" Peggy and I asked simultaneously.

"Some reporter came through town a few weeks ago. She does stories on the American Scene or something like that, for a national news program on the radio. I forget the name of it, because we don't get it here. I figured you wouldn't want to talk to a reporter, Pat, so I took care of her for you."

"Just how did you take care of this reporter for me? What did you tell her?"

"Don't go getting all excited," said Pops. "I didn't tell her anything private. Or anything scandalous," he added, with a look in Peggy's direction. "I told her the sculptor was very reclusive and wouldn't ever talk to a reporter. I didn't tell her you worked at the Mercantile. I was afraid she would track you down. Instead I kind of hinted that you might be hiding out in the hills watching us while I showed her the sculpture."

"Where was I in fact?"

"You were at the Mercantile. I waited until you were at work to bring her out here. The whole time she was looking at the statue, she kept looking over her shoulder, too, as if she thought you might be behind a rock with a shotgun. Then she saw the name carved underneath the statue, and she wanted to know who Alma Rose was. I told her Alma Rose wasn't a real person. I said you made up the name because you thought it fit, and I threw in some stuff about Mother Earth and nature goddesses."

Pops grinned. "The lady got really excited then. She started going on and on about how the female is tied in with the earth, and how Alma means soul and the rose symbolizes passion, and so it all fit together perfectly. I couldn't see it, myself, but she was happy as a lark, so I went along with her. Then she got curious about you again, Pat, and she asked, was I sure the sculptor wouldn't talk to her. I said I was positive, because the sculptor barely talked to the people she had known her whole life. I made out that you were a very solitary, spiritual sort of person, and that a reporter would be a rude intrusion and very painful for you. When I said that, she started glancing all around again, as if she thought you were a disembodied thing floating around in the air."

Pops was launched on a good story and there was no stopping him. I thought about the unfortunate reporter, who had fallen into the clutches of someone who could spin a whole tapestry out of the barest threads of fact. Had she had the good sense to doublecheck?

Pops went on, "I could see that half of her was the typical reporter, ready to barge in anywhere to get the news. But the other half of her was trying hard to be respectful of your sensitive nature. She asked a whole bunch more questions, trying to angle her way toward finding you without pushing her way straight in. I told her all I could without giving you away. I thought it would only ruin her image of you if I told her that you were probably ringing up someone's basket of TV dinners and dish soap at that very moment. She ran out of time, finally. She had an appointment somewhere else first thing in the morning, so she packed up her tape recorder and left."

Except Marge, everyone was staring at him in astonishment. Pops was still grinning. At first I had been furious, but now I felt inclined to smile, too. Peggy did not see anything funny at all.

"So now we've been on nationwide radio, too. Where will you ever stop?"

"I didn't invite the lady here," Pops said. "Anyway, I'm not sure we actually made it onto the radio. The reporter said she tapes dozens of stories that never get broadcast. I sure would have liked to hear it, though."

"I certainly hope it didn't get broadcast," Peggy said. "Heaven only knows what a reporter might think up to say about us . . . "

She was winding herself up for another tirade, and she might have gone on indefinitely, if Jordy had not stopped her with a shout.

"Look at that!" He was pointing down the hill.

We turned to look.

While we had been absorbed in debate, a car and two Winnebagos had pulled up and parked along the road near my driveway. Half a dozen people were clustered near them, talking together and snapping pictures.

One of the men with a camera gestured, and the rest of the group gathered around my mailbox to pose for a picture. While the group was arranging itself, a car towing a camper pulled into line behind the Winnebagos. We all stared in silent fascination as another group of people got out, surveyed the statue, pointed up at us and snapped some pictures. Then, when the first group had moved away, they seized the opportunity to pose themselves for a photo with my mailbox.

Even as we watched, a pickup-camper and another car joined the line, and more people got out. They stared at us and we stared at them. One of the tourists balanced his video camera on his shoulder and began filming, although there was no action to record. None of us had moved an inch. We could almost have been part of the statue, the eight of us frozen into mute immobility by some combination of horror, amazement and glee.

Only Jordy remained untroubled by any consideration of

the larger implications of that caravan of tourists.

"It's just like it was when Mom and I went through Yellowstone last year," he said excitedly. "The line of cars, I mean. That's how you knew when there was a bear beside the road."

Epilogue

As it turned out, Pops was right. A good offense was the best defense. In one stroke, he shifted the battleground to a whole new front. People stopped arguing about the sculpture and started arguing about the billboards. The sculpture became a given. The issue became the billboards, and all of a sudden I was off the hook and Pops was on it. That was fine with both of us.

No one tried to argue that Pops had loose morals. They only argued that he had bad taste, cluttering up the landscape with garish billboards. Somehow, that argument never gathered the same force as had the earlier one.

In the end, Peggy and her allies were borne under, by passing time, by newer news, and by a lengthening train of Winnebagos and camper-trailers coming through town. Cattle prices hit a ten-year high, and then the elections brought accusations of embezzlement and fraud in the race for county treasurer. People just couldn't stay interested in a months-old issue. Even Peggy found it necessary to divert her energies toward proving the guilt of the incumbent county treasurer.

Kilgore never became another Wall Drug. The first trickle of out-of-state license plates did not swell to a flood. Traffic on Main Street did not slow to a crawl.

The billboards did multiply themselves, however. Within a year, half a dozen patrolled the Interstate to the west, and nearly a dozen flagged down the drivers from the east, the ones numbed by hundreds and hundreds of miles of American heartland. After two or three days of driving, only a farmer could still feel joy and wonder at the sight of another thousand or ten thousand acres of agricultural soil. For everyone else, the billboards held out a promise of relief, a chance to get bickering children out of the car, a chance to restore circulation to middle-aged buttocks. Enough travelers were weary enough and desperate enough that a small but steady stream of traffic began to divert itself through Kilgore to look at Alma Rose.

A large gift and curio shop opened in the building that was once the Kilgore Ranch Supply. A new gas station opened downtown. Someone bought one of the long-closed motels, refurbished it, planted wild rose bushes around the entrance, and opened for business as the Sleeping Beauty Motel. Two doors down from the Donut Hole, a young couple from New Jersey opened the Alma Rose Cafe, serving vegetarian food among ferns and art museum posters. When that failed, the young couple moved away, and another young couple from San Antonio came to town to take their place. They kept the name of the cafe, but replaced the ferns and posters with piñatas and sombreros, and served Mexican food and hamburgers. The business thrived.

We gained another bar, a drug store and an auto mechanic. There the expansion stopped. A few other businesses tried and failed. Some limit had been reached, the limit of how many people could be cajoled into a detour from their seventy-mile-an-hour rush toward the places the federal government had identified as scenic.

In truth, most people in Kilgore were relieved when the limit was reached. Even as it was, people sometimes had to park a block away when they came to the Mercantile to buy groceries in the summer, because of all the tourists parked to shop at the gift shop across the street.

In numbers, the town did not grow much at all. The school stayed just within the size limit to stay in Class C in basketball. For a while there were rumors that a McDonalds and another chain motel might be added to the cluster of logos beside the on-off ramp, but nothing ever came of it. Probably the town's growth failed to follow the projected curve, so the plans were abandoned.

The small flow of money and employment was enough to counter the drain of young people away from the town, but not enough to start a movement in the other direction. Some young people still moved away, because despite finding jobs, they were bored. For the first time, though, they began to be replaced by other young people, who came from larger, busier places and wanted to slow down. After living a while in Kilgore, most of the new people decided they had slowed down to the point of stupor and moved away again. A few of them, a handful, found they liked it and stayed.

Though the town did not get bigger, it was never quite

the same. In a small way, it took on a gloss of hucksterism, the high-pitched, overeager tone of a salesman trying to sell a customer something they both know the customer does not need. It caught a faint reflection of the bright-colored, fast moving fakery of resorts and carnivals, the distracting light show that is designed to convince people they must be having fun.

The presence of strangers intruded on the casual gossip at the Donut Hole, and the traffic made people near Main Street less inclined to sit out on their porches on summer evenings. It became a town where strangers had to pay for their welcome, because there were simply too many of them.

Other things came, too, besides the tinsel. With the strangers came unfamiliar ideas and habits and opinions. No longer was the satellite TV dish the town's only link to a more diverse existence. Occasionally, one might see skin of a different color than pink, or hear a language other than English. The kids could mimic urban hairstyles and fashions from living models, not just from magazines and TV. Customers came into the Donut Hole and asked for bagels or grits or camomile tea. They came into the Mercantile looking for sesame oil or the New York Times or a metric wrench to adjust the handlebars on their Japanese-made mountain bike.

Alma Rose herself never quite got finished. The time became too long, the audience too intrusive, and life moved on. From below, the incompletenesses are barely noticeable. Up close, the bed beneath her looks too lumpy for someone to be lying on it so peacefully, and the tip of her elbow still has a cauliflower growth of rough stone where there should be a pleasing triangle of bone.

About the Author

Edith Forbes is the author of *Exit to Reality* (Seal, 1997) and *Nowle's Passing* (Seal, 1996). She has worked as a computer programmer, carpenter and farmer. She grew up on a ranch in Wyoming and for the past ten years has lived on a farm in New England, where she raises cattle and writes.

SELECTED TITLES FROM SEAL PRESS

Nowle's Passing by Edith Forbes. $12.00, 1-878067-99-0. A beautifully crafted novel about a woman who faces her exacting family legacy to discover her own life.

Exit to Reality by Edith Forbes. $12.00, 1-58005-003-4. It is the 29th century and all social problems have been eliminated. Lydian and Merle meet online and ignite an unlikely love affair of the minds—and bodies—leading to a confrontation between civilization and technology.

The Dyke and the Dybbuk by Ellen Galford. $12.95, 1-58005-012-3. A highly unorthodox tale of one London lesbian and her Jewish ghost. Winner of the Lambda Literary Award for Best Lesbian Humor.

If You Had a Family by Barbara Wilson. $12.00, 1-878067-82-6. An unforgettable novel about a woman who struggles to come to terms with memories of her childhood and gains a greater understanding of what family is and can be.

Gaudi Afternoon by Barbara Wilson. $10.95, 0-931188-89-X. Amidst the dream-like architecture of Gaudi's city, this high-spirited comic thriller introduces amateur sleuth Cassandra Reilly as she chases people of all genders and motives.

Where the Oceans Meet by Bhargavi C. Mandava. $12.00, 1-58005-000-X. This incantatory debut novel explores the rich textures of Indian culture through the lives of four Indian and Indian-American women.

Nervous Conditions by Tsitsi Dangarembga. $12.00, 1-878067-77-X. A lyrical story of a Zimbabwean girl's coming-of-age and a compelling narrative of the devastating human loss involved in the colonization of one culture by another.

Working Parts by Lucy Jane Bledsoe. $12.00, 1-878067-94-X. An exceptional novel that taps the essence of friendship and the potential unleashed when we face our most intense fears. Winner of the American Library Association Gay, Lesbian & Bisexual Award for Literature.

Another America by Barbara Kingsolver. $12.00, 1-58005-004-2. A new edition of Barbara Kingsolver's luminous book of poetry, with six new poems and a new introduction. Also available in an unabridged audio edition read by the author, $12.95 1-58005-009-3.

If you are unable to obtain a Seal Press title from a bookstore, or would like a free catalog of our books, please order from us directly by calling 1-800-754-0271. Visit our website at www.sealpress.com.